AMBUSH!

In the roadway before the Ehleen troops three noblemen sat their horses, blocking the narrow track. The Ehleenee halted as one of the men spurred his mount forward.

"You come from the Lady Mehleena?" asked the troop commander.

The stranger merely nodded.

"You are of The Brotherhood, then, my lord?"

Again the stranger nodded.

"My lord must give a Sign," said the commander, tracing a complicated pattern in the air.

"Aye, I'll give you a sign," agreed the stranger. Still smiling, he raised his hand and sent something shiny spinning through the air. The commander grunted, then his horse screamed and reared and, in the split second before his body tumbled from the animal's back and a deadly sleet of arrows began to fall, everyone could see the polished bone hilt of a knife jutting out of the commander's left eye socket. . . .

ROBERT ADAMS lives in Seminole County, Florida. Like the characters in his books, he is partial to fencing and fancy swordplay, hunting and riding, good food and drink. At one time Robert could be found slaving over a hot forge, making a new sword or busily reconstructing a historically accurate military costume, but unfortunately, he no longer has time for this as he's far too busy writing.

Great Science Fiction by Robert Adams from SIGNET

THE PATRIMONY

A Horseclans Novel

by

Robert Adams

A SIGNET BOOK

NEW AMERICAN LIBRARY

COPYRIGHT © 1980 BY ROBERT ADAMS

SIGNET, SIGNET CLASSIC, MENTOR, PLUME, MERIDIAN AND NAL
BOOKS *are published by New American Library,
1633 Broadway, New York, New York 10019*

FIRST PRINTING, APRIL, 1980

6   7   8   9   10   11   12   13   14

PRINTED IN THE UNITED STATES OF AMERICA

This volume of Horseclans is
dedicated to Poul Anderson and
L. Sprague De Camp, two most
illustrious colleagues,
and to
two lovely and talented young
ladies, C. J. Cherryh and
Katherine Kurtz,
and to
Jerry Tishman and the VSR.

THE PATRIMONY

by

Robert Adams

See how our White Hawk flies
Free in the open skies,
Leading us on.
Forward, then, Sanderz men,
Forward, to bring again,
Glory to Vawn.
    —Warsong of the Clansmen of Vawn-Sanderz

Prologue

Sir Geros was ensconced in the privy behind his small, neat house when a scurrying servitor brought word that the tower watchers reported two armed riders approaching from the northeast. As the old warrior dropped worn baldric over his scarred, shaven head and fitted its links to those of his scabbard, he heard the first belling of the hall's pack of hounds.

By the time he reached the courtyard, the riders were through the open gates—which laxity was as a rasp drawn across a raw nerve to the old soldier. He and the old *thoheeks* had always seen eye to eye on tight security for both hall and hard-won duchy, even if their ideas had differed on other points, but now *Thoheeks* Hwahltuh was gone to wind and neither his widow (the fat, Ehleen bitch, thought Sir Geros) nor the regent followed very many of the practices of the old lord's lifetime.

The riders guided their big, northern horses at a slow walk through the broil of leaping, snapping dogflesh, the second, larger man pulling along as well a pack-laden sumpter mule. As they came closer, Sir Geros could see that, under the thick overlay of dust, the scarred faces of both men were lined with fatigue. Weary too were the beasts, their heads drooping low, but the riders sat straight, their plain half-armor dented and patched here and there but polished and oiled beneath the road dust.

Polished, also, were the unadorned hilts of their broadswords and the light axes dangling from their saddlebows. The heads of the two lances socketed on the mule's load sparkled like burnished silver in the first rays of Sacred Sun. Sir Geros did not need to examine the scabbarded swordblades to know that they too would surely be well honed and unblemished.

He knew—and respected and empathized with—this stripe of men from the days when he was a warrior and had ridden with and fought beside Middle Kingdoms freefighters. The

1

Sword was not only their life but their grim god—and they treated that god with respect.

As the hall servants kicked and cuffed the pack away from the mounting blocks, a groom reached for the reins of the lead rider's stallion and nearly lost a hand for his courtesy. Big, square yellow teeth clacked bare millimeters from the jerked back fingers.

Sir Geros detected a fleeting glimmer of soundless command—his mindspeak, for all his strivings, had never been very good—and the warhorse stood stockstill while, jackboots creaking, the wiry rider dismounted and, after hitching his sword around for easier walking, strode toward the old castellan.

A swordlength away, he halted. "Don't you recognize me, then, old friend? Have these years of soldiering changed me that much?"

Sir Geros looked hard then. He took in the gray-blue eyes, their corners crinkled from much squinting against sunglare and the elements, the high forehead, permanently dented by the heavy helm which probably was now part of the mule's cargo. He could see that the skin must once have been fair, but now it was weathered to the hue of polished maple, with the fine, high-bridged nose canted slightly to one side and with two large and innumerable small scars scoring the reddish-bristled cheeks.

A short, red-blond spade beard spiked forward from the man's chin, and a thick, luxuriant mustache must once have flared, though now it was plastered to his face with sweat and dust.

The stranger had stripped the leather gauntlets from hands which were square, with a dusting of blondish hairs on their backs; the fingers were long and the nails clean and well kept. A small ruby set in carven gold adorned the least finger of the right hand—which digit, Sir Geros noticed, was missing its last joint—and the next finger bore the steel-and-silver band of a noble Sword Brother. This last proved the old warrior's first estimation correct; this man was a sworn member of the Sword Cult.

But Sir Geros' black eyes strayed at length back to those gray-blue ones, so like to . . . to *hers*, to those of the Lady. The Lady Mahrnee, she who had been the beloved first wife of *Thoheeks* Hwahltuh, and whom Sir Geros had worshiped at a distance for all the years he had served her husband.

And he *knew* then that, at long last, their eldest son was come to claim his patrimony.

Roaring, heedless of the dust and filth of travel, Sir Geros flung both arms about the younger, slighter man, pounding the armored shoulders and trying to speak his heartfelt welcome through tightened throat.

The riderless stallion reared, nostrils flaring. Men and dogs scattered as the big horse pirouetted on his hind hooves, the front ones lashing out, while he arched his thick-thewed neck, showed his fearsome teeth and screamed a challenge.

"Let me go, Geros!" laughed the younger man. "Steelsheen thinks you're attacking me. Let me go before he hurts someone."

Chuckling, the warrior strode over to the big gray, took the scarred head in his arms and gentled the beast for a few moments. Then he turned and walked back to Sir Geros, the stallion sedately trailing him.

"Has your mindspeak improved any these last years, old friend?"

The rays of Sacred Sun glinted on the shaven pate as the castellan shook his head ruefully. "No, my lord, I still can receive well enough, but . . ."

The younger shrugged. "Very well. Hold out your hand to Steelsheen, rub his nose, let him get your scent. I'll tell him you're a friend."

When the stallion had grudgingly accepted the fact that his brother would be most wroth were he to flesh his teeth in this particular two-legs, the younger man turned about and walked back to where his companion still sat his horse.

"Dismount, Rai, I want you to meet my oldest friend." His ready smile returned. "You know of him, even though this will be your first meeting."

"At the captain's command," was the crisp reply.

The big-boned, broad-shouldered, long-armed man hiked a leg over the high, flaring pommel of his warkak, slid easily to the flagstones and walked to meet them with the slightly rolling gait of a veteran cavalryman. His bushy, chestnut brows met over a thick, slightly flattened nose. Across the front of his corselet was painted the device which signified his rank, that of troop sergeant. And Sir Geros noted that the left gauntlet had been altered to encase a hand lacking two fingers.

When the sergeant came to a halt, the captain said, "Rai,

this is Sir Geros Lahvoheetos, *vahrohneeskos*—that's 'baronet,' as we would say it—of Ahdrahnpolis."

The sergeant swept off his broad-brimmed travel hat of soft felt and grinned widely, bowing easily for all his binding armor and clumsy boots. "Now this be a true pleasure, my lord baronet. It's right many a long, weary mile I've rode a-singing the songs of yer noble deeds."

Sir Geros' fleshy face encrimsoned, whereupon the young officer laughed merrily and clapped a hand on the shoulder of each of the men. "Rai, you embarrass Sir Geros; he's a very modest man, for all.

"Geros, know you that Rai here is not only my sergeant but my friend, as well. Had he not taken me under his shield when first I went . . . was sent . . . a-warring, I'd have long since fed the crows on some battlefield. Captain Sir Bahrt of Butzburk assigned Rai to me when I was but a pink-cheeked ensign, and we've soldiered together ever since.

"Since you both are my friends, it is meet you should be friends to each other."

Wordlessly, Sir Geros extended his hand and, after a brief hesitation, the sergeant shucked a gauntlet to take it.

As hand clasped hand, Sir Geros spoke from the heart. "Sun and Wind witness that ever shall I be true to our friendship, sergeant. And may Sacred Sun shine blessing upon you for bearing Lord Tim safely back to us. He is the hope and salvation of this duchy, and there are those here who do love him."

He moved closer and dropped his voice to a hushed whisper. "But there are also those here who hate our lord, who would see him dead, so we must guard him well, you and I."

Stepping back, Sir Geros clapped his hands and bespoke the throng of servitors. "Master Tahmahs, see to the horses and the mule. Majordomo, the *thoheeks* suite must be opened, aired and prepared by the time Lord Tim has done with his bath. Oh, and see to our lord's gear, as well. Send a lad to the bath to pick up our lord's armor, clean it and take it to his suite."

More orders were snapped to other servants, and shortly, like a well-oiled machine, the hall staff were immersed in their various functions.

Chapter I

The Lady Mehleena, widow of the six-months-dead Hwahltuh—who had been *Thonheeks* of Vawn, chief of Sanderz and stepfather, through his first wife, of his overlord, the still-living and much respected *Ahrkeethoheeks* Bili, chief of Morguhn—was breaking fast. Beside her at high table sat her personal priest, Skahbros, and her eldest son, hulking, black-haired Myron. Beyond the seventeen-year-old man her other three children sat, while her companion—some servants whispered "tongue-sister," some others muttered "witch" and speculated privately that the old lord's death might have been less than natural—Neeka flanked the priest.

The Lady Mehleena more than filled her chair. Although the massive piece of furniture had been constructed to seat a full-grown and armored man, it was all she could do to wedge her monstrously fat rump and meaty thighs betwixt the arms; nonetheless, she would have no other chair, for this one had been her late husband's and, to her, it symbolized the power and privilege of the greatest noble in the duchy. Not that she deluded herself into the thought that she ever could lawfully occupy that position—for, though the stray Middle Kingdoms burklet or distant Kindred holding or tribe of mountain barbarians might be ruled by a woman, Mehleena was Ehleeneekos through and through, and the positions of women in civilized society were distinctly inferior to those of Ehleenee men.

On the silver plate before her was a two-liter bowl which formerly had been brimful with maize porridge topped with butter, cream and honey, her usual morning meal. Within the short time they had been at table, Lady Mehleena had reduced the bowl's contents to something less than half, washing it down with long drafts of sweet, potent honey wine, the servitor behind her refilling her cup whenever it neared emptiness. But not quite all the sticky mess had gone to maintain her overample girth. Her lips and chin were gooey with it, and so was the fine silk of her clothing over the mountainous swell of her breasts.

Poking an elbow into her eldest son's ribs, she snarled, "Sit up, you oaf! Sit straight. As a soon-to-be, *must* be, *thoheeks*, you must learn to make an appearance. And keep your hand off Gaios' legs. You must learn to confine your loveplay to the privacy of your chambers. Your peers are still half-barbarian at heart. They neither can nor will understand or tolerate such; they'll think less of you and make sport of you for your sophisticated tastes."

Absently wiping at the bits of porridge which had sprayed over him along with his mother's harsh-voiced words, the young man grumbled, "Mother, for all you say, you know that damned *ahrkeethoheeks* will never allow me to be *Thoheeks* of Vawn, any more than my oafish cousins will ever confirm me chief of Sanderz. They hate us one and all, you, me, or any person of the Old Race, and you know it."

Dropping her golden spoon with a clatter, Mehleena's fat, beringed hand lashed a backhanded slap which caught Myron full in the mouth.

"*Shut up!* How *dare* you gainsay your mother? You *will* be, *must* be, *thoheeks*. This land must be returned to civilized control and its people to the worship of God.

"Besides," she smirked her satisfaction, "we have the barbarians hoist on their own hooks this time. Your brother Ahl can never be chief; the barbarians' own laws forbid confirmation of any man who cannot lead in war. And how can a blind man do such, eh? So, since Behrl died last year you are the eldest living, uncrippled son of Hwahltuh." Waving the line of servitors back, she lowered her voice to a harsh whisper. "As I have said before, Myron, all that is needful is that you make the proper appearance at the *ahrkeethoheeks*' court and play-act a little. He'll be bound to confirm you *thoheeks*—which is where the power and wealth lie. Let your cousins name whomever they wish their chief. It's just an empty title, anyway.

"Once you're confirmed and secure back here in Vawn, we can see to setting the land and people to rights and forget the *ahrkeethoheeks*, the black-hearted pig. He never comes this far west, and—"

"But . . . but, Mother, they . . . they say he has eyes and ears *everywhere!*" Myron looked about him, squirming uneasily in his chair. "And . . . and for all we know, Tim could come riding in any day."

With a scream of rage, the corpulent woman sprang up, overturning the heavy chair and, with a sweep of her arm, sending porridge bowl, plate and brimming cup smashing down the length of the table. The priest gasped a gurgling cry as a sudden lapful of hot porridge burned through the fabric of his robe to highly sensitive portions of his anatomy. Maddened with pain, he dumped an ewer of cool buttermilk atop the discomfort.

Fearing the onset of one of her cousin's fearsome and ever more frequent rages, Neeka, too, arose and moved toward Mehleena. Behind the high-table serving area, the servitors huddled in a knot, trembling, for their lady had, on occasion when thwarted, near killed servants.

But this time their fears proved groundless, as did Neeka's solicitude. After taking several deep breaths, Mehleena signed for the chair to be righted and the floor and table cleaned, reseated herself and resumed her conversation in an almost normal tone.

"Myron, my son, I can but thank God that womenfolk of my house are long-lived, for I can see that, for all my efforts to improve you, you are going to need someone to think for you for the rest of your life.

"Of course the *ahrkeethoheeks* has spies and informants in the halls of his liegemen, but Neeka knows who all of them are—every one, Myron. And we await only your confirmation to see to suitable 'accidents' to rid ourselves of them.

"As to the Lord of Incest, your half brother, let me assure you that as surely as we sit here at table, we are rid of him. There's been not one word from him since we heard of that battle wherein his captain was slain and most of the officers and common sorts slaughtered. That was over five years ago, Myron. Both Neeka and I feel certain that the young swine is dead. And—"

The door at the end of the dining chamber swung open and a tall, spare man and a tiny, brown-haired woman entered. At sight of the newcomers, Myron started to rise in habitual deference, but his mother shoved him back into his chair, snarling wordlessly.

The tall man smiled wryly. "Good morning, dear stepmother. For all your preachments, I see that sweet Myron still knows his place and, except for you, would defer to his betters."

Rage darkening her puffy face, Mehleena made to rise, but the man languidly waved one well-kept hand, "No, no, my dearest stepmother, keep to that place . . . for all that it should be mine. I doubt me there's another dining chair that is massive enough to hold the hundred *kaiee* you must weigh without splintering 'neath you." He chuckled, and his diminutive companion pealed a silvery laugh.

"Were your poor father alive," Mehleena hissed in cold rage, "you'd not bespeak me so, you eyeless spawn of a barbarian bitch!"

But another, maddening chuckle was her only answer.

In a slow, stately advance, the couple came up the length of the room and took seats at one end of the wide table. While servitors set the places and brought food, the blind man rubbed absently at inkstains on his fingers, ran a hand over his neck-length ash-blond hair and then steepled his long fingers before remarking, "Ah, the good Father Skahbros is setting a new fashion in clerical garb, a robe bedecked with food stains rather than crusted with jewels. Most original, I must say, holy sir." His dry chuckle came again, while the embarrassed priest hung his head.

"If all you've come for is to insult me and bedevil my priest, you are to quit this board!" Mehleena snapped, her voice quivering with the intensity of her hate. "I'm the lady of this hall and I'll not have—"

The blind man's palm smote the table with a sound like a thunderclap. All mirth had departed from his handsome face, and, when he spoke, ice shards crackled in his words.

"*You* will mind *your* words, my lady . . . and your manners! You forget yourself and overestimate your station. While still my father lived, you *were* lady of Sanderz Hall, and the years of pain and misery you brought us all were many indeed.

"But the *thoheeks* is gone to Wind now, his body ashes for half a year. *Ahrkeethoheeks* Bili of Morguhn has appointed *me* regent over clan and *thoheeksee* until it is known for certain if Tim Sanderz will return to claim his patrimony—that office and rank to which he was born.

"For the sakes of those of your children who are more like our father than like you, I have allowed—understand me, madam!—*allowed* you to retain the outward trappings and authority of chatelaine. But, as all save you and your creatures seem to know, you rule within your sphere *only by my sufferance*!

"Were my sweet sister, the Dowager Princess of Kuhm-buhluhn, amenable, she would be in your place. But for all the evil you wrought and tried to wreak against her and Tim, she would not see you debased and humbled within this hall, nor will she allow me to send you, your cousin, your pervert of a son and your priest of an illegal cult packing.

"But mind your flapping tongue, madam, and your manners around me. I have neither love nor even bare respect for you. I . . ."

But Sir Geros—whose hatred and contempt for the second wife of the old *thoheeks* was matched only by her hatred of him—had entered the room and, ignoring its other occupants, made his way rapidly to Lord Ahl. Bending, he whispered a short message into the blind man's ear, then, at a curt wave of the regent's hand, departed as quickly and quietly as he had come.

Chapter II

Captain-of-Lances Tim Sanderz floated on his back in the gently steaming, herb-scented bathwater, his eyes closed, allowing the soothing warmth to sink into tired muscles. From shaven pate to stubby toes, there was hardly an inch of visible skin that was not crossed by scars, and torso and limbs alike were ridged and callused at the weight-bearing points of armor. As he slowly moved his arms and legs to and fro to keep himself afloat, the muscles rippled under his skin.

Opening his eyes, he allowed his gaze to wander across whitewashed ceiling, down the painted stucco walls. How familiar it all was; it almost seemed that the past ten years had never been, that he was still the eldest boy growing up in his father's hall.

"Father . . ." he mused, conjuring up the image of that aged and stooped, but gnarled and powerful little man, always smelling of the milk and curds and cheese that had made up so much of his diet. "The long years I hated you and cursed you. And now I have returned, and you are gone to Wind and Brother Bili says that none of it was really your fault."

Closing his eyes again, the captain thought back to that last conference with his half brother and overlord, the *ahrkeethoheeks*, Sir Bili of Morguhn.

For all his exalted rank, Sir Bili's private office was spartan in its simplicity. A refectory table, a few chairs and stools in a windowless and lamplit room, the thick, stone walls lined with cabinets and the floorspace cluttered with chests, the double-thick door fitted with iron bolts as thick as a warrior's wrist.

Glancing about while the nobleman poured wine for them both, Tim felt certain that he sat in a second hall armory, was sure that the many chests would yield up plate and swords, dirks and axes and warhammers, that the cabinets held resting hornbows, bales of arrows, stands of pikes and bundles of darts.

For it was common knowledge that Bili of Morguhn had never gotten over the Ehleen-spawned rebellion that had burst forth in Morguhn and Vawn long before Tim was born. Bili remembered well the ruthless butchery of his kin, the besieging of this very hall. He recalled how he and his uncles, cousins and one of his brothers had had to hack their way out of his own capital, Morguhnpolis, and remembered also the death of that much-loved brother, Djef Morguhn, ere the siege of Morguhn Hall had been broken by the approach of Confederation troops.

All of Bili's personal servants were Middle Kingdoms men, as were his picked bodyguard. Not one servitor in Morguhn Hall was of Ehleen blood; moreover, all were, if not of the Middle Kingdoms, Kindred or Ahrmehnee from the western marches. He governed his own duchy harshly, as pitilessly as a northern burklord ruling a conquered province, trusting none but his brothers, his sons and Kindred of proven loyalty. Few men of any race liked him, but there was not one who did not fear and respect Bili.

Sliding a cup of wine across to Tim, Bili said bluntly, "To me. Tim, you're already *thoheeks*, and that's a load off my mind, young kinsman. I've been worried sick these past months with no word from or of you, afraid I'd wind up having to confirm a thrice-damned Ehleen pervert to the Duchy of Vawn, your stepmother's eldest, Myron. Not that he'd have ruled, of course; *she* would've, and she's far worse than even such as he will ever be. Why, my informants tell me, that, since your father's death, she's brought in a priest of that damned, baby-butchering, blood-drinking Old Church of the Ehleenee; that she flaunts the outlawed bastard before all at the hall, clothes him in silks and supports him in indolent luxury."

Tim shrugged. "Well, my father's been dead half a year. Perhaps this so-called priest is her lover."

Bili smiled coldly. "That thought came to my mind when first I heard of this priest, but my folk tell me such is not the case. For one thing, Mehleena is as perverted as her son. Her lover is reported to be her cousin, the witch, Neeka; for another, this priest is what the Ehleenee call 'one of God's Holy Geldings'—before they'll ordain a man into that order, they take his ballocks off, and most of his yard, too."

Tim shuddered. "Sun and Wind! What kind of people are these Ehleenee of the Old Cult?"

"Fanatics, snapped Bili, adding, "to be born and bred Ehleen is to be inculcated with fanaticism and treason with your mother's very milk. My peers speak most unkindly of me, claiming that I blindly hate and unreasonably mistrust such few Ehleenee as remain in Morguhn. But their duchies did not—a bare generation ago—suffer civil war and ruin because of an Ehleen holy war. Yes, many of them did lose kith in the Vawnpolis campaign and in the mountain fighting that followed, but those dead are only memories to them now, and dim memories at that. Every time I ride over my lands, I am confronted by stark reminders of what evil deeds were committed here."

The passion faded from his pale blue eyes. "But, to your case, young kinsman. Could we do this the way I feel to be proper, we'd ride into Vawn at the head of your lances and my dragoons, put every Ehleen who looked at us sideways to the sword, impale that outlaw priest side by side with your stepmother, burn Neeka alive and cleanse your duchy of any taint of the Old Cult or like treasons.

"But alas, we are not honest burklords, you and I, and if we did such, we'd have Prince Zenos and his army at our throats in a twinkling. We'd be flagrant lawbreakers, y'see, and—for all his pro-Kindred sentiments—the prince could not allow us to get away with it.

"However, man, I think you should take at least a couple of files of lancers with you. Only a few of the hall folk are Sir Geros' people or mine. And as old Hwahltuh became more and more senile, that damned Mehleena persuaded him to let go almost all his Freefighters. I know, for I hired most of them onto my own force. I doubt there're now a half-dozen overaged blades left."

Tim just smiled. "I'm taking Rai with me, Brother Bili—he's a weaponsmaster. And I'm no mean swordsman, myself."

"Of course you're a good fighter," Bili snorted. "Else you'd not be here, after ten years of Freefighter life. But many a good blade has fallen to the poisoned cup, the strangler's cord, the knifethrust in the dark. You can't wear armor all the time, kinsman, can't go abroad everywhere full-armed. Nor can one or two men guard your back twenty-four hours a day.

"I am sure that these Ehleen swine have killed before, Tim. Ahl's blinding was said to be an accident. I think that even

Ahl believes it was, but not I. And there is and was much to be questioned in the matter of Behrl's death, so much so that the prince almost sent a committee to investigate it—would that he had! And, for all his great age, your father's passing was most strange. None of my informants had ever before seen a man die as he did. You are the last male Sanderz of untainted blood, Tim, and I fear for your safety if you take risks among such folk."

But Tim had ridden off with only Sergeant Rai, a single packmule and an assortment of his oldest clothes, leaving his lances camped in Morguhn and his two wagonloads of loot from the intaking of Getzburk locked in the cellars of Morguhn Hall.

The water had begun to cool, and Tim momentarily debated jerking the bellrope to summon the servants with more heated water, but ended by rolling over and pulling himself out of the bath and, after making certain his heavy blade was near to hand, stretching out on the tiles to await the arrival of Rai with clean clothing. But Sir Geros came in first, bearing a brace of cups, and a small bottle of brandy and wearing a self-satisfied smile.

Wrapped in a length of thick cloth, Tim sniffed, sampled then drained the small cup. "Where'd you liberate this, you old bummer? It tastes to be twenty years old."

Sir Geros odded. "Twenty-five, my lord. It—"

"Enough of that," said the younger man, shortly. "Appearances are well kept, in public, but, man, you jounced me on your knee and paddled my arse, when I needed it—which as I recollect was right often. In privacy, let's be on a first-name basis, eh? Geros?"

"I . . . I'll try . . . Tim." The old knight stammered. "But, my lord—but you must know, Tim, I was born a nobleman's servant, as were both my parents and all their folk before them. My father was a majordomo to a *komees*, which was higher than any of my folk had risen . . . until me."

"And you raised yourself on the strength of your arm, on the richness of the blood you shed for the Confederation and on your matchless valor, Geros," nodded Tim. "If ever any man deserved a cat, it was you." He gently tapped the silver likeness of a prairiecat which rested on the old warrior's breast. "I've never understood why you, a nobleman in your own right, entitled to rich lands in Morguhn, forsook those lands to serve as castellan here, at Sanderz Hall."

Geros sighed. "My . . . Tim, I could never have been happy as a lord. I was born to serve, and service is my pleasure. I . . . but let us talk of these matters on another day. There are things you must know, and I know not how long my folk can keep others out of earshot of us here."

"How many in the hall are you sure of, Geros?" asked Tim.

The elder set down the bottle to tick off names on his fingers. "Old Tahmahs, the head groom, is loyal; then there's Mahrtun, the dragoon sergeant, and the five troopers. The majordomo, Tonos, blows first hot then cold; I can't say he's our man, but he doesn't seem Lady Mehleena's either."

Tim frowned. Tonos' name was not one of those given him by Archduke Bili, and it could bode ill to have so powerful a servant leagued against one.

Geros continued, graying brows knitted in concentration. "Our only reliable people in the kitchens are Hahros, the meat cook, and his eldest apprentice, Tchahrlee. Hahros is a retired Confederation Army cook and far better qualified to be head cook than that mincing effeminate, Gaios, but naturally Gaios has simpered his way into Lady Mehleena's good graces. Anyway, I've taken the liberty of promising Gaios' position upon my l—" At a warning frown from Tim, he hurriedly corrected to, "*your* assumption of your patrimony."

Tim nodded. "You know these folk better than I; speak in my name when it seems wise or needful. I'll back you up."

Geros smiled thanks and went on. "The keeper of the cellars, Hyk, is an Ahrmehnee and another of the ones I can't figure."

"In that case," said Tim, grimly, "I think we should start bringing arms up out of the armory a few at the time and secreting them somewhere where we can get to them easily, when and if we need them." Then, noticing the return of Geros' smile, he inquired, "Or have you already commenced such, old friend?"

Quickly, the castellan told of the stocks of arms hidden in various parts of the hall and outbuildings—enough to equip forty men, if somewhat sketchily. Adding, "But Tim, even if we do see troubles, they'll be nothing like the risings here and in Morghun years ago. For one thing, there be precious few Ehleenee in Vawn, save those servants hired since your lady mother's time. Almost all the farmers in the duchy are Ahrmehnee, so too are the mechanics and tradesmen hereabouts. The nobles all are first- and second-generation Horseclansmen . . . and you know well what sort of shrift *they'd* give Ehleen rebels or religious fanatics.

"No, Tim, the only danger lies in the fact that Mehleena is set on her spawn, Myron, sitting in your father's place. There were some very peculiar aspects to the death of your brother, Behrl, last year."

"Yes," Tim answered. "So Bili informed me. Something to do with a mock fight, wasn't it?"

Geros grimaced. "Closer to an out-and-out duel, my . . . Tim. It was during that last, long illness of Lord Hwahltuh. Young Behrl was at the sword posts, one morn. Myron and the boy who then was his lover sauntered out and began to make crude and disparaging remarks. Finally, Behrl—who never could stomach Myron for any length of time, any-how—suggested that his tormentor get a sword and see if he could do better.

"Now, Tim, Myron is no mean swordsman. He is long in the arm and strong. But, in all my years, seldom have I seen a man handle steel as did Behrl; the lad was an artist with the sword.

"Anyway, Myron sent his bumboy running and soon was at the posts himself. I'm told that Behrl, in his turn, twitted Myron's showing—at least, this was overheard by Gaib, the farrier, who happened to be passing by. I was in my house when I heard the first ringing of the blades and the fighting shouts. I headed for the practice yard as fast as these legs would carry me, but halfway there I heard a terrible cry and, when finally I panted up, Behrl lay dead in his blood, his chest hacked half through, just below the shoulderblade.

"Tim, Myron is a good swordsman, as I said, but Behrl was his master—and mine own. Without outside help, inter-ference, there be no way that Myron could have even nicked Behrl, much less slain him!"

Tim pursed lips and squinted. "There were no witnesses?"

Geros shook his head. "Only the bumboy. What I got out of him on the spot was little—he was verging on hysteria—and seemed to back up Myron's lies. And when I wanted to question him the next morning, he was nowhere to be found. It was nearly two weeks before Mouruhd, the hall hunter, hauled what was left of the corpse out of the north forest. A hot summer that was and the body was ripe, and animals had been at it till there was no way to tell just what had killed him. We only knew it was the runaway by a silver torque Myron had given him."

"Very convenient . . . for somebody," grunted Tim. "So now, the only way we can get at the truth is to put dear half brother Myron to the question. And if the man he is be as stubborn as the child he was it would have to be rather severe questioning. Hmmm."

A grin split Geros' face almost from ear to ear. "Ah, Tim, it will do these ears good to hear that strutting, buggering popinjay howl! Of course, your father's Room of Truth has not been used in some years, but I doubt not it can be put to rights quickly enough, and . . ."

Tim grimaced. "And we'd have the archduke, possibly even the prince as well, down around our ears before the echoes had died. We must never forget that this isn't a northern burk but a duchy of the Confederation, wherein, what we have here contemplated is illegal; not even the High Lords, up in Kehnooryos Atheenahs, can put a Confederation nobleman to the torture without ironbound proof of wrongdoing."

The young captain smashed scarred knuckles into horny palm. "*Why*? Why could there not have been *one* living witness? The deed must've been planned long and carefully to have been carried off so cleanly."

Then he fell silent. A dim, almost imperceptible farspeak was nibbling within his mind: "But there was another witness, Brother Tim, and Sir Geros is right, it *was* murder—pure and simple. No, brother, do not try to range me, please—there are other secret mindspeakers in your hall. And do not expect me to make myself known or to reveal what I saw until you have made it safe for me to do so."

And the fleeting contact was gone, like a wisp of morning mist.

"Who are the mindspeakers, here, Geros?" asked Tim. "How many of them are ours?"

Geros frowned. "Beyond any doubt, the best is your brother, Lord Ahl. You must recall that he always was far above average in that faculty, and it has been improved by a couple of years of training at the Institute in Kehnooryos Atheenahs and the year he lived at the duke's court. But my daughter, Mairee, is almost his peer in mindspeak . . . and the two are seldom parted; he even took her to the capital with him, and the duke seems to think highly of her."

"And," grinned Tim, shamelessly picking thoughts from the older man's mind, "you know how she feels toward my brother and are thinking that Ahl would not prove a bad son-in-law, eh?"

Though red with embarrassment, Geros nodded vigorously. "Lord Ahl could do worse, Tim. Blind as he is the Kindred will never accept him *tahneestos*. But he has the wisdom to make a fine townlord, and my baronetcy in Morguhn boasts a fine little town, and, since my stepson and both my natural sons died, Mairee is my only heir."

Tim nodded emphatically. "No need to convince me, old friend. I think it a marvelous idea, not to mention a stroke of pure luck for Ahl. I agree he'd be a better townlord than perhaps anything else; neither custom nor law requires a townlord to be sound of body himself, just to maintain a few Freefighters and a ready levy under a loyal and efficient captain.

"But back to this question of mindspeakers, Geros . . ."

"Master Tahmahs and most of his grooms are good to fair, of course, Tim."

Tim nodded. "Yes, good horse handlers have to be."

Geros went on, "There are many with middling mindspeak, like mine own, among the servants and the soldiers, though definite eye contact is necessary to range most of them."

"How of Mehleena and her litter?"

Geros looked the disgust he so strongly felt. "If she herself has any at all, she'll not ever own to it, since her damned priest says that any who can use that ability are witches and damned of his crucified god."

Tim snorted a short, harsh laugh. "That any of that accursed, traitorous pack should accuse normal Kindred of 'witchcraft' surely surpasses sane understanding. But, pray continue."

"Well, Tim, as to the piglets: Whenever the bitch has the chance to talk to Vawn or Morguhn Kindred, she's always prating about the mindspeak ability of Myron, but he's got no more than have I. Treena, the eldest girl, has none, and neither does Speeros, her year-younger brother. As for the two youngest, Maia and little Behti, it's possible they're more of Vawn than the rest—at least they *look* like they are, and, when the bitch or the others aren't about, they *act* more like they are, too.

"Sun and Wind alone know just what talents that damned Neeka owns, and . . ."

Suddenly there was a quick, measured series of knocks against the outer door and Geros opened it a crack, then closed it and turned back. "There's no more time for talk, Tim. The majordomo is hotfooting it out here, and Lord Ahl has come down to break his fast. I'd best let him know you've arrived."

Chapter III

The edifice known as Vawn Hall was new, as structures went in this ancient land; its construction had been started at the close of the great Ehleen rebellion and finished only a few years before the death of Hwahltuh Sanderz, first *thoheeks* of the new line, all the original Vawns having fallen under the dripping blades of the rebels.

Like all the older halls, it faced east—toward the rising point of Sacred Sun—the main building rising three stories aboveground and descending four levels of cellars below. A wide, spacious, flag-paved courtyard fronted the broad stone stairway leading up to the entry. The courtyard was bounded on either side by lines of small, low-ceilinged cubicles built against the twelve-foot granite walls. Opposite the hall stood the squat, two-story stable-cum-barrack-cum-gatehouse. To the west of the main structure was a smaller court, likewise walled, with the castellan's neat home snugged into one corner and the kitchen—with its huge hearths and cavernous ovens and soaring chimneys—in the other.

Just beyond the postern gate lay a well-appointed yard for the exercise of arms skills, with the summer smithy on one side of it and the hall privies facing. Around and about the hall stretched the rolling, grassy leas, across which ambled the hall horses and a herd of milch cows with sheep and goats in the near distance. In the fringes of the oak woods, a half mile distant—for *Thoheeks Hwahltuh*, ever mindful of the fate that befell his predecessor, had cleared all woods and brush within four arrow flights of his hall—rooted and foraged half-wild swine.

Having interbred countless times with the huge, indigenous boar tribe, these "domestic" hogs ran to lean strength and such fearsome ferocity that only starvling wolves or a ravenous bear or the occasional mountain cat would brave

19

their porcine rage. But they had learned to fear two-legs on horses, for this was how they were taken in the fall, by two-legs on horses, armed with lances and bows and ropes.

Farther into the forest ranged deer and elk, and, more rarely seen, wild cattle—called "shaggy-bulls" in the Middle Kingdoms, huge and fierce and dangerous if provoked; they were roan or dusty black, dark brown or sometimes whitish, but both sexes equipped with wide-flaring, needle-tipped horns and the strength and speed to use them to awesome effect. Rabbits scuttled through the underbrush, sometimes pursued by weasel or bobcat, wolf or fox, while squirrels chattered from the trees above.

Beyond the miles of forest lay the westernmost domain of the duchy, the lands of *Komees* Tahm, youngest uncle of the late *thoheeks*' children, known as Tahm of Lion Mountain because most of the mountain cats which plagued the duchy of hard winters seemed to come down through his desmesne.

Even farther west, the tracks became narrow, winding amongst weathered rock and trees clinging precariously to the steeps which were the eastern wall of the Marches, the *ahrkeethoheekatohn* of the Ahrmenee *Stahn*, staunch allies of the Confederation. Once the fiercest enemies of the Kindred and Ehleenee, these hawk-nosed, dark-visaged men had become in the generation since the first *ahrkeethoheeks*, Kohk Taishyuhn, had perceived the folly of continuing hostilities, the veritable cream of the Confederation Army, whilst producing within their own *stahn* works of artistry in metals eagerly sought throughout the Confederation and well beyond.

The *Stahn* buffered the middlewestern *thoheekatohnee* from inroads of the savage tribes of mountain barbarians, few of whom dared incur the wrath of the well-armed, determined, head-collecting Ahrmehnee. Nor were warfare and metalworking the only accomplishments of these people or their only value to the Confederation. Straddling shaggy mountain ponies from near-infancy and hunting cunning mountain beasts from pre-puberty, Ahrmehnee boys and men made excellent hunters and the increasing number of them gifted with mindspeak ability were the best and most highly paid of horsehandlers, farriers and equine leeches.

In the twelve generations since first their Undying God had led the Horseclans Kindred across the violent, blood-soaked two thousand miles from their former home on the limitless plains of the interior to the decadent coastal principality of Kehnooryos Ehlahs, the vital, virile Kindred had brought all

the Ehleenee south of the Middle Kingdoms into their Confederation—sometimes by conquest, sometimes by alliance—
as well as the Ahrmehnee *Stahn* and several non-Ehleen
northern states.

From the northernmost point—Nohtohpolisburk in the
Principate of Kuhmbuhluhn—twenty days of hard riding
would lead to the southern border, unmarked amidst the
treacherous salt fens beyond which lay the legendary evil
Witch Kingdom and, even with the matchless roads built and
maintained by the army, the remainder of a full month needs
must be ridden out before the southwesternmost principate,
on the eastern and northern shores of the brackish River-Sea,
was reached.

From their capital of Kehnoorvos Atheenahs, the four
Undying ruled over six principates, over a hundred
ahrkeethoheekatohnee and nearly six hundred *thoheekatohee*
Five major races—Kindred, Ehleen, Middle Kingdoms
Mehruhkuhn, Mountain Mehruhkuhn and Ahrmehnee—and
numerous smaller ones made up the heterogeneous population. Three principal languages—the various dialects of
Mehrikan, Ehleeneekos and Ahrmehnee—were spoken and
written, though it was traditional for official records to be
kept in Ehleeneekos.

The population was larger than ever it had been under the
old Ehleen sway and, moreover, was growing larger with
each passing year. Cities were replacing towns, becoming
larger and more congested, and even the land was becoming
crowded. The oceans encroached farther upon the verdant
coastal croplands with each succeeding year and Middle
Kingdoms states were no whit less populous, so the only via-
ble direction for expansion lay to the west.

Compared to the east—from which their ancestors had
been driven by the Ehleenee nearly a thousand years before—the peaks and glens, plateaus and vales, were thinly
settled, but every tribe or clan or family group felt a fierce
pride of ownership in its stony acreage and expressed that
pride in bitter, unremitting warfare against the lowland in-
vaders.

And so the huge Army of the Confederation had been en-
gaged in almost constant warfare for over a century, fighting
scores of battles and skirmishes for each mile of near-wilder-
ness brought under Confederation control, every inch of ara-
ble land bought with the lifeblood of Confederation regulars

and Middle Kingdoms Freefighters. Precious few liked the enduring situation of endless war to the west, but most recognized the necessity and inevitability of the advance of civilization against barbarism.

The Undying would have preferred to gain the use of western lands through treaties of alliance, as they had done a generation back with the Ahrmehnee; but, unlike the tightknit Ahrmehnee *Stahn*, the mountaineers were for the most part crude, brutish and highly fractious among themselves, though they displayed a modicum of twisted honor in their internecine feudings—and some of the clans and tribes seemed to hate other clans and tribes nearly as much as they all hated the lowlanders—they seemed to feel that treaties with non-mountaineers were made to be broken as quickly as suited them. Further, their chiefs thought nothing of claiming and selling lands not their own, so the Undying had long ago reconciled themselves to the fact that needful expansion of territory could only advance behind the point of a spear.

Within the Confederation itself, however, there had been no warfare since the crushing of the Ehleen revolts nearly thirty years before. Within cities and towns, crime was petty and small-scale, and in the countryside, brigandage was almost unheard of. The descendants of the Ehleenee pirates who once had been the scourge of the mainland coasts now were the officers and crews of the swift oarships and far-ranging sailing ships that made the coastal waters too dangerous for any but honest merchantmen and the most suicidally foolhardy raiders.

Save on the western frontiers, few towns or cities were still completely contained by walls. All the older, lowland urban areas had spread well beyond their walls and many had wholly or partially dismantled them. Even some of the conservative hereditary nobility had defortified their ancestral halls or even deserted the grim stone piles to live in the new-style manor houses.

But these nobles were not among those who had fought against the fanatic rebels of Gafnee, Morguhn and Vawn. Those nobles bided within their castellated halls, locked their gates each sundown, slept lightly and with a pillow-sword close to hand. And they distrusted all Ehleenee—for all that most of them had more than a trace of that blood in their own veins—especially the self-styled *kath-ahrohs* or Ehleenee of pure lineage.

Such a *kath-ahrohs* house had spawned her who had been Mehleena Lohgos, ere she was taken to wife by Hwahltuh, chief of Sanderz and *Thoheeks* of Vawn; and loud, long and fierce had been remonstrations of his Kindred at word of the projected match. But he was a stubborn man; moreover was he the son and grandson of chiefs and unaccustomed to tamely submitting to the bidding of his subchiefs. Also, he had the full support of his premier wife, the Lady Mahrnee— widow of the chief and *Thoheeks* of Morguhn, ere she wed her second husband—and against those two the combined Sanderz Kin stood no slightest chance, for all their ranting and raving of Ehleen plots, past, present and future.

But before her bridal year was spent, Mehleena was first and only wife, Lady Mahrnee being suddenly taken with a wasting sickness which claimed her life within two months of its onset. The servants had all loved and respected their dead mistress as cordially as they had quickly learned to hate and fear Lady Mehleena, and there were whisperings of witchcraft and poison. However, the unprovable charges remained but the mutterings of older servants.

However, the mutterings increased as ill fortune seemed to stalk the house of Sanderz. In his twelfth year, Gilbuht Sanderz, eldest son of the chief and heir presumptive, drowned in the lake, for all that he had been an excellent swimmer. And that same year, his twin, Ahl, was blinded and almost killed in a freak accident. The mutterings had it that neither "accident" had occurred until *after* Mehleena had been delivered of her firstborn son, dark little Myron.

With one older brother dead and another disqualified for any clan office due to his blindness, the aging chief and his male kin commenced crash-course schooling in the duties, privileges and responsibilities of a chief and a *tahneestos* with Tim and Behrl, the two remaining boy-children of Lady Mahrnee and Hwahltuh. More and more frequently, this training fell to the uncles and older cousins of the boys, for the health of the chief was failing. Nor was this failing remarkable to any, for Hwahltuh had counted more than threescore years when his first child was born.

But the old chief gradually fell more and more under the sway of Mehleena, for only the potions brewed by her and her cousin, Neeka, served to relieve the unbearable headaches which had taken to plaguing him. These potions cast him into a deep and lengthy slumber, and for days after his eventual wakening, he was meek and biddable as a child, seemingly incapable of formulating his own opinions or of making his own decisions, bowing to Mehleena's will in every particular.

And that weakness was Tim's downfall.

Chapter IV

"I saw them myself, Hwahltuh!" Mehleena's dark eyes were wide with horror and her voice strident with emotion; her soft, beringed hands were clasped tightly at her heaving bosom. "Tim and Giliahna, in her chamber, on her very bed! *Clipping*, they were, Hwahltuh, and . . ." Her voice sank to a horrified whisper. "And *kissing!*"

The bearded, white-haired man looked up from the arrows he had been fletching for his short, powerful bow. His bushy brows bunched and merriment shone from his light-blue eyes. "Well, Sacred Sun be praised for that much, wife. Or would it more please you to see them trading daggerthrusts or seeking to poison each other, as is the wont of siblings in some noble houses? I'd hate to go to Wind leaving the makings of a battle royal within my own house."

"But, Hwahltuh, *no*." She bent closer. "It . . . it was not as brother with sister, Hwahltuh, *it was as man with woman*, they were! Embraced, kissing, their hands . . . *their hands*, husband, moving under each other's clothing *in private places!*"

Mehleena moved back, expecting violent rage. But her husband just straightened a bit on his chair, shook his head slowly and chuckled.

"Sweet Jesus save us!" burst out the stupified Ehleen woman. "Don't you understand me, Hwahltuh? Your depraved son is about to have his incestuous way with his own blood sister, your daughter! You must do something to stop this nastiness or send him away until she be safely wed."

"Send my heir away? Nonsense," grunted the old chief, then voiced another throaty chuckle. "He's a Sanderz, right enough, shows good taste in womanflesh. Randy young colt, he is, as I was, and for all she's only thirteen, Giliahna is a handsome filly and no mistake."

25

Mehleena's earlier horror was magnified by his attitude. Hastily, she crossed herself to ward off evil and clutched her jeweled cross for comfort and strength.

"Hwahltuh, Hwahltuh, he will take her flower. Then how will you find a decent husband for her? And . . . and everyone knows that if a child be gotten in incest, it always is either born dead or born an idiot. Have you thought on that?"

"Hogwash!" the old man snorted derisively, casting down his arrow and split quills. "Ehleen hogwash, woman! Do *I* look like the spawn of idiots, *eh*? My great-grandfather married his sister and got my grandfather on her. If Tim wants Giliahna to wife, he'll have her with my blessing and that of the clan. What better bloodline could he choose for breeding chiefs and warriors? And if his dalliances quicken her, he'll have her to wife, like it or not. As for her maidenhead, *pah*, it's of no importance. She's a comely chit, wellborn and well-dowered, and there'll be no lack of noble suitors, wife, believe me."

He picked up the arrow again, adding, "Mehleena, love, this is not your father's hall. We are Kindred, here, not Ehleenee, and you must always remember that our ways, our customs, are not your people's. I have allowed you to cleave to your preferred religion since you wed me, for all that it's proscribed the length and breadth of our great Confederation, but don't try to force Kindred into that narrow mold, dear.

"We are free men, we Kindred. We reverence Sun and Wind as did our Sacred Ancestors back to our very beginnings on the Sea of Grass. We never have been priest-bound and saddled with those silly, childish rituals and taboos which your religion has foisted upon you Ehleenee.

"Now, please let me get back to these arrows, love. There's not much light left and I'd like to finish them today."

Mehleena left him. Pale and shuddering with frustrated rage and soul-sick of her—to her, justified—horror at the mortal sin her husband was countenancing under his very roof. But, heeding Cousin Neeka's advice, she did nothing more, said nothing further . . . until the chief's next headache.

By the time that Hwahltuh recovered his will, nearly a month later, Tim was beyond the borders of the Confederation . . . and Giliahna was on her way to be wed to the Prince of Kuhmbuhluhn, a man but ten years her father's junior and recently widower of his seventh wife.

The aging chief sent a letter north with the next Confederation rider to pass through his duchy. In it, he humbly asked his son to forgive his temporary weakness to Mehleena's importunings, begged him to return at once to his home, his father, and his family, but that letter was never answered. Nor were any others of the scores the repentant old man sent north. At length, his hurt pride surfacing, Hwahltuh stopped writing directly. Instead he entrusted weights of gold to Chief Bili, *Ahrkeethoheeks* Morguhn, that Tim might at least clothe himself well, own the protection of good weapons, decent armor and a well-trained destrier. Nor did the saddened *Thoheeks* of Vawn ever again hear directly from his heir. Only through Archduke Bili—who had been reared and wartrained in the Middle Kingdoms and who had kin and old comrades now in high places—did bits and pieces of Tim's career trickle south, of Tim's appointment as an ensign of dragoons in the Freefighter regiment of a well-known and renowned noble officer; of Tim's knighting into the Order of the Blue Bear of Harzburk by King Gy, himself, on the blood-soaked field of Krahkitburk; of his defeat and capture of a famous champion in another battle; and, later, of the lieutenancy Tim purchased with said champion's ransom.

It was on Hwahltuh's last visit to the *ahrkeethoheeks'* hall that he heard of the purchased promotion. In the few years of life he then had remaining, his infirmities precluded travel, and the yearly taxes were, perforce, delivered to the overlord by his brother, the *tahneestos*, and Tim's brother, Behrl.

"You know these strange northern ways, Chief Bili. What does it mean, this title my boy's bought himself? How many bows will draw for him? Is he still an underling to this Colonel What's-his-name?"

Bili nodded. "Yes, Colonel Sir Hehnri, Earl of Pahkuhzburk, is still his commander, but the title means that Tim now commands a contingent of fifty horse archers—they call them 'dragoons,' up there—with an ensign or two and a senior sergeant to assist him. Tim's now responsible for the training of his troop, for their welfare and provisioning in garrison or on the march and for recruiting replacements after battles. Their weapons and armor and their horses, however, are provided by Sir Hehnri, except for those men lucky enough to own their own."

Hwahltuh sighed his relief. He still meant to provide for his loved son, but he had suddenly realized as the archduke spoke that he could beggar his duchy if he had to buy trained warhorses and weapons and armor for fifty-odd men.

Bili went on, grinning, obviously inordinately proud of this younger half brother who had succeeded so well in the land of their mother's birth and Bili's own fond boyhood memories.

"Give Tim a couple more good ransoms, if his luck holds, and he'll be a captain in his own right. He'll be totally independent of his present regiment and able to negotiate contracts for his services."

"With only fifty horse archers, Bili?" the old *thoheeks* asked. "What sovran or lord would be willing to hire on so small a contingent?"

"Ask any one of the hundred I might name, Hwahltuh," attested Bili bluntly, adding, "You've never been in the Middle Kingdoms, good stepfather, so you're thinking in terms of the vast host of Lord Milo's army. But none of the states of the north is even a tenth the size of our Confederation, and even if the three largest could somehow be brought into alliance, even that alliance could not pay either the hire or the maintenance of a force the size of our Regular Army.

"Oh, yes, there've been the rare times in years agone when one kingdom or another briefly fielded fifteen or twenty thousand fighters, but not recently. They've been fighting among themselves for so long that warfare there is almost a game—a violent, bloody and sometimes fatal game, but a game, nonetheless. Quality of troops is of far more importance to the prospective employer than is numbers—quality of the troops and the fame of their commander.

"You can bet your last silver *thrahkmeh* that Sir Tim's exploits have by now spread far and wide. So if his luck holds and he can manage to put together a good, independent command, he'll soon be able to pick and choose among some very lucrative contracts. His fortune will be assured. You can be justly proud of him. Hwahltuh. Sun and Wind know that I am."

"I could burst of my pride in my son, Bili." The old man's voice was low but filled with feeling. "But his place is—should be—here. He should be in Vawn, Bili. I'm an old, old man, even for our race, and . . . and I'm not well. If . . . if something should happen to Tim, if he should be killed or badly crippled . . . well, I just don't know.

"You know how it is with Ahl—he'd never be confirmed chief. As for Behrl, well, he'll make a fine *tahneestos*, he'd be a first-class war chief, but he's just not the temper for the kind of chief a Confederation clan needs, and the Kindred know it as well as I do, too. And his mindspeak is a chancy, come-and-go thing, atop it all. So, I doubt me that the Clan Council would ever confirm him.

"And," his voice assumed grim overtones, "you and I both know who that leaves to succeed me. *She* is forever preening the lout in front of any Kinsman of Sanderz who'll hold still long enough to watch the act. And act it is, Bili. Myron is totally Ehleen, the worst kind of Ehleen. I cringe to think how my duchy and kin and our folk would fare under so unnatural a creature."

Bili squirmed uncomfortably in his high-backed armchair, then shrugged, "Well, if the act is really so apparent, the clansmen might not confirm him, and, even if they should, I can always refuse to recognize that confirmation, you know."

Hwahltuh sighed. "Be realistic, Bili. Admittedly, I was born in a hide tent on the Sea of Grass, but I've dwelt among your eastern Kindred for near a score and half of summers now. Men will be men, whatever their birth or race, and they have their pride.

"Prince Zenos is first cousin of Mehleena, and you know as well as I do that he'd never allow you to override a Clan Council confirmation of a man of his house. No, you wouldn't dare but recognize that pervert in my place."

Bili cracked one big knuckle, then another. "Hwahltuh, I am not without certain influence at Kehnooryos Atheenahs, the Undying . . ."

Hwahltuh slowly shook his head, raising a hand. "The High Lords are up to the eyebrows in the mountain business, and the last thing they want to see is any bare trace of internal discord. Neither the High Ladies nor God Milo could afford to countenance your barefaced insult and defiance of your overlord."

The two noblemen finished their honey mead in silence; there was nothing more to say. But as Hwahltuh was mounting his easy-gaited mule for the long ride back to Vawn, he leaned close to the archduke and said, "I have a strange feeling, Bili, that I'll never see you again. Please, promise me one thing. By the love my dear Mahrnee so freely gave to the three of us, swear that immediately I seem about to go to Wind you will see Tim in Vawn to take his lawful place."

Chapter V

It was not often that *Thoheeks* Bahrt, chief of Skaht, forked a horse and rode a dusty road on so hot and humid a morning. But neither was it often that a simple country nobleman of these hinterlands of the Confederation was granted the opportunity to accompany so high and important a personage, nor to do so in proximity to such expensive splendor.

But, all other considerations aside, his escort was no less than his bounden duty, for the personage now riding a fine-bred, richly caparisoned gelding at his side had been his guest for three days and was both Kindred and blood kin. And, for all his fifty-three years, Bahrt was still virile and appreciative of his companion's beauty.

Not that that beauty was readily apparent this morning, for the costly gowns which had had the ladies of Skahtpolis fairly squirming with envy were all packed away in the trunks strapped into the boot of the ponderous coach and in the two wagons which followed it. She rode in Horseclans garb of the ancient cut—baggy trousers tucked into soft, felt boots, wide dagger belt mounting a silver-hilted dirk, tight-sleeved pullover shirt which for all its bagginess still could not conceal the proud upthrust of her mature breasts, drooping velvet cap; the only outré touch was a thick veil to protect her nose and mouth from the choking dust.

"Duke Bahrt . . ."

Bahrt turned in his high saddle, feeling afresh the stimulation of that throaty voice. "My lady?"

"Archduke Bili knows not that I near his desmesne. Think you I should send a galloper," she half-waved at the handsomely equipped squad of dragoons who followed the two nobles at a discreet distance, the slow trot of their mounts setting their armor and weapons to jingling and clashing, "or two, that he might be prepared to receive guests?"

Bahrt shook his head. "No need, my lady, no need at all. Bili the Axe is ever ready to receive and entertain Kindred. Besides, when you told me of your intention to return home by way of Morguhn, I took the liberty of dispatching a messenger. We should be meeting the lad, shortly."

The pale-blue eyes above the veil softened perceptibly, and, reining her gelding closer, the woman laid a gloved hand upon her host's bridle arm, saying, "You have been more than kind, Duke Bahrt. I had not expected such tender consideration from one who had not seen me in . . . how many years?"

The slight mistiness he detected in her eyes added unaccustomed gruffness to his voice. "You are my *kin*, my lady, if naught else—your dear mother's blood sister was my dear first wife and the dam of my firstborn son, Mylz. Too, there be right many who are and will be overjoyed to see you again where you belong, here with the kin who love you.

"You must know, my lady . . ." He paused and glanced about, the very picture of a man who customarily must seek out eavesdroppers before he speaks his mind, then went on in a rush of words, "For all the respect we bore him, most of the Kindred hereabouts thought ill of your father for what was so quickly and rashly done, and your return gladdens my heart. It will gladden Bili's, too, and those of all true Kindred. I feel free to say— Now by my steel, what's this?"

Fifty yards ahead, the Freefighter who had ridden the point all morning rounded a turn at full gallop. But the duke was not the only man to see the oncoming rider or to be alarmed at his precipitate haste; from behind the two nobles came a ripple of metallic sounds as targets were unslung and the various points and fastenings of armor checked. Without a word, the lieutenant kneed his mount forward until he was abreast of his mistress.

When he had halted his steed, the point rider saluted. "My lady, a column approaches; their van be less than half a mile from this place. I counted a score of dragoons and at least two noblemen, no baggage."

"Is there a banner, man?" put in Duke Bahrt. "I'd like to know what scapegrace leads armed men across my land without a by-your-leave."

The Freefighter nodded. "Aye, my lord, it looked to be a bird of some kind. Red, I think."

Bahrt slapped his thigh. "The Red Eagle of Morguhn, by

Sun! Bili's come to meet you himself, my lady. I should've expected that of him."

The lady turned to the lieutenant. "No cause for alarm, Leeahn, it's the archduke, Bili of Morguhn, my half brother."

Had the pointman watched a bit longer, he would have seen that the column from the south was assuredly no war party. It moved at an ambling walk, and the only man erect in his saddle was the pennon bearer, and he was kept alert only by the occasional gust of wind from off the distant mountains that unexpectedly bellied out the heavy, silken banner and made fair to tear the ashwood shaft from his grasp. The twenty troopers behind him slouched in restful postures, feet loose from stirrups and many with a leg hooked up around saddle pommel. They chatted and joked and cackled, blew at the sweat coursing down their faces and now and then sucked at the sun-warmed water in their journey-bottles.

But the short, powerful hornbows protruding from their cases were strung, the quivers were all full, and a heavy saber depended from every man's belt. The armor which peeked from under the light cotton surcoats had been polished to the sheen of fine silver, and, indeed, every scrap of their equipment mirrored the devotion and hard work of upkeep. One familiar with warriors would not have needed to see the hard-eyed, scarred faces to ascertain that these men were professionals or to guess how quickly, for all their present relaxation, they could become two tens of mounted, steel-swinging death to any rash enough to oppose them.

A few paces ahead of the pennonman, astride identical black stallions, rode two noblemen. The elder—thick of body, wide at hip and shoulder, big, square hands thickly dusted with fine blond hairs, lined, scarred face cleanly shaven—rode in silence, listening to the younger, his favorite son.

" . . . so there we sat, Father, through the whole damned night, all twelve thousand of us. Had we attacked immediately we arrived, at dusk, before all the barbarian host had assembled, we could have slaughtered them piecemeal. But no, we must perforce hunker down until dawn, then assault the works they'd been preparing all night. The upshot of that idiocy was near two thousand casualties. And, after the fact, when it was far too late to save those good men we'd lost, Senior *Strahteegos Vahrohnos* Gaib of Hweelahk and his entourage rode into camp."

"I've not seen Gaib in twenty years, I guess." The elder showed strong, yellow teeth in a broad grin.

"He's inspector of cavalry, Father. But when he saw and heard all, he relieved *Strahteegos Vahrohnos* Hwyt on the spot, sent the craven bastard back to Kehnooryos Atheenahs under guard, and took over command himself. Then he called all commanders of field grade to his pavilion and had each of us tell all we knew of the Djahrehtee opposing us, of Skuhltuhn, the approaches to which they were defending and of the lay of the country thereabouts. He pored over the maps for a bit, then called us all back from the wine tun and issued his orders.

"As soon as it was dark, he sent out the cats to sweep any barbarian scouts from the area. Then, ceding command of the camp and the infantry to Sub-strahteegos *Vahrohnos* Djak Sanderz of Kahrtuh, he took all of the cavalry on a forced march.

"Father, we kept at it all through that night—first east, then south, then southwest, then, finally, due west. Sacred Sun and our columns both struck Skuhltuhn as one. Few of the tuhns are even stockaded, and none are truly walled. The cats had taken out the sentries, so the first warning the Djahrehtee had were three volleys of the *kahtahfrahktoee's* arrows, every fifth a firearrow. Then we rode in from all four sides.

"When we had sabered or lanced or axed everything that moved, we fired every structure not already burning and," he winked, his dark eyes twinkling mischievously, "my Ahrmehnee boys got in a bit of fast looting. Then *Strahteegos* Gaib positioned us and the *kahtahfrahktoee* behind thick cover on either side of the eastern road, whilst the lancers and barbarian light horse rode, whooping and cavorting, around and about the blazing tuhn."

The elder nobleman drew out a pipe and pouch of tobacco and commenced to stuff the former with the contents of the latter, as his son continued the tale.

"Well, as *Strahteegos* Gaib had foreseen they would, the Djahrehtee came boiling up the east road, some of them riding mountain ponies, but most afoot, and in no kind of formation."

"No, western barbarians aren't known for their discipline," his father remarked drily, speaking around the stem of his pipe between puffs.

"When their vanguard saw the corpse-littered streets and

the burning houses and only about a squadron strength of
cavalry opposing them, I think they went a little mad. Anyhow, they forgot their normal guile and threw caution away.
It was a textbook example of a successful ambuscade. When
all the arrows and darts were sped, the *strahteegos* led the
charge.

"And then it was all over, all but the butchery. They were
thoroughly broken on that road, Father, routed; the only ones
that got away were those who took to the wooded slopes—the
strahteegos refused to allow pursuit of those."

The older man nodded. "As one who has fought barbarians
in their mountains, I'll say that Gaib showed good judgment
in that, my boy."

"The bulk of the survivors, though, clove to the road,
fleeing back the way they'd come, so that they—and we,
naturally—ran head on into the barbarians retreating from
their works which had fallen to the assault of Sub-*strahteegos*
Vahrohnos Djak and the infantry.

"A largish number of them took to the hills then, caught as
they were between the pursuing infantry and us, and with all
our missiles spent there was damn-all we could do about it.
But at least a couple of thousand stayed on that road and
fought. And they fought well, Father. Sun and Wind, they'd
make firstwater soldiers, if only they could be disciplined!"

Removing his smelly pipe from between his teeth, the older
man smiled. "Oh, they will be disciplined, and they will be
soldiers, son, Confederation Army soliders. Well, maybe their
sons will anyway, their grandsons, certainly. The western
frontier's moved near a hundred miles within my lifetime; it'll
do as much or more in yours. And this is how it's done. It's
the High Lord's plan, you see. Do you remember living in
Kehnooryos Atheenahs as a child?"

The younger man shook his head slowly. "No, Father,
when was that?"

"For two years after your dear mother died, I couldn't
bear to bide in Morguhn, so I took you and your brother and
sister with me to the capital. We lived in the palace while I
further developed my farspeak at the academy. I was much
the favorite of all four Undying, in those days, and the High
Lord spoke long and often with me of his plans for the Confederation and its expansion.

"Ah, those were exciting days." The older man's blue eyes
clouded over with memory. "In the wake of the Great Rebellion, the High Lord had dissolved the Ehleen Old Religion

throughout the realm—lest it spawn or be the spawning ground for other insurrections. The clergy had been proscribed and all their lands and treasures had been seized in the name of the Confederation, so there was much wealth at the disposal of the Undying, and this was quite evident at the court in those days.

"That was when the New Palace was begun, and the Western Palace at Theesispolis, as well. Old roads were improved and new ones laid. There were official feasts four or five times each week and colorful processions, horseraces, warcart races, galley races on the river from the capital to Ehlai and back, parties and music and dancing somewhere every night—and it was at one such that I first met your stepmother, Mahlee. I— What is it, Flopears?"

The prairiecat who had been scouting ahead of the column mindspoke, "Chief Bili, I think that those you seek are just ahead of you. One male rides ahead, and well back of him two more males and a female ride. Just behind them more males, fighters by the look of them. Then wagons with both males and females."

"Little sister." *Ahrkeethoheeks* Bili toed his stallion close, opened his arms wide and warmly embraced the Lady Giliahna, Dowager Princess of Kuhmbuhluhn. Releasing her, he reigned about and took the hand of *Thoheeks* Bahrt in a firm grasp, smiling cordially. "Thanks for the rider, Bahrt, it gave me a good excuse for this outing. I trow, desk work gets more wearisome from one day to the next, and this is a fine day to fork a horse. But where've you been keeping yourself, cousin? You've not set foot in Morguhn since you brought in last year's taxes."

The *thoheeks* rumbled a laugh. "Behind my desk, Bili, where else? Trying to make sure I'll be able to pay this year's bite."

"Well," chuckled the *ahrkeethoheeks*, "guest with me at Morguhn Hall, this night, and I'll feed you back a little of your money's worth. Besides, that mustachioed and thoroughly distinguished looking gentleman yonder is my eldest son, Djef, just down from Goohm, taking his accrued leavetime after three years of campaigning in the west. Mayhap he'll spin us a few tales if," he chuckled again and raised his voice a few notches, "he can take his eyes off his Aunt Giliahna for longer than two heartbeats at a time."

Chapter VI

Giliahna was awakened by one of her servitors as the woman laid and lit a morning fire on the bedchamber hearth. It grew cold at night, even in summer, this close to the mountains, so she snuggled back under the down-filled coverlet and waited for the new-lit blaze to warm the room a bit, thinking that after the enervating, sultry nights which had marked her travel through the lowlands, this brisk and healthful coolness was almost like home.

"Now, dammit!" she snapped aloud. "This *is* home, for all that that Ehleen and her piglets are rooting and squatting here. I'm rightful chatelaine of Vawn Hall, not Mehleena!"

Eyes closed, hands pressed together between her cheek and the pillow, the snap and crackle of the resinous kindling her only distraction, she thought on the past. She thought of the last time that Giliahna Sanderz had slept in her father's hall. She had wept herself to sleep that long-ago night, wept for poor, exiled Tim, wept for her dead mother, wept for her father whose age and infirmity had made him the tool of her scheming and thoroughly hateful stepmother, and wept for herself.

But she had steeled herself the next morning, denied her enemy, her father's wife, the satisfaction of seeing a Sanderz woman's tears. And though she had wept often during the long journey north, it had been in private, and when once her party had crossed the border into the Principate of Kuhmbuhluhn, her pride had refused her the luxury of more tears. Recalling the bardsongs of all her ancestors who had ridden bravely to confront danger and death, that fourteen-year-old Giliahna had squared her jaw and raised her head and, drawing the invisible blade of her inborn courage, toed her mount forward to her encounter with destiny.

Mehleena and her women had made much of the great disparity between Giliahna's youth and the rather advanced years of her groom-to-be, Prince Djylz of Kuhmbuhluhn. They had whispered horrible anecdotes of the brutal deflowering of brides by drunken or callous husbands, spoken often of the stark cruelty of the semibarbaric northerners and of the everyday, commonplace lack of culture and general discomfort of life in the primitive land to which she would so soon be borne. And the harpies had dwelt at length on the fact that Prince Djylz had already buried seven wives and offered gory speculations on the causes behind the deaths of her predecessors. They had deliberately done everything within their power to terrify Giliahna—and, though she strove to keep them unaware of the fact, they had succeeded. She had entered Kuhmbuhluhnburk in mortal terror, hardly even able to hear the cheers of the townsfolk impressed alike by her beauty and her proud, noble bearing.

The wedding had been just a kaleidoscope of shifting colors and textures—the gilded and lacquered coaches which had borne her and other noble notables to the marble and granite House of the Sword, the brilliant uniforms and silvery armor of the horsemen who led and flanked the procession, the hides of carefully groomed horses flashing like gems, flashing in the rays of Sacred Sun as brightly as the gold and the silver, the polished steel and the jewels had flashed back the light of the seeming thousands of candles which had illumined the soaring, cavernous interior of the Sword Temple. She did not even feel the first kiss of her new husband, but her legs bore her down the long, long aisle and down the marble stairs and into the coach. And all the endless-seeming journey back to the palace, she had managed a smile for the joyous populace.

The hours-long nuptial feast had seemed over in bare moments, and then, to a hearty chorus of deep-voiced masculine jests and laughter, a tide of smiling, giggling ladies and maidens had swept her out of the feast hall, through a succession of corridors and up the stairs, then through other corridors and finally into the suite of her new husband.

Giliahna never knew if she slept or just fainted after the luck-wishing bevy of noblewomen had disrobed her, bathed and scented her and tucked her into the huge bed, but when she again became aware, *he* was in the chamber.

Through slitted eyes, the girl studied him as the hunted deer studies the stalking panther. The prince was still damp from his bath, and as he apparently thought her sleeping, he was completely relaxed in manner and movements.

She saw a man of average height, his body deep-chested and muscular, but not very hairy, so that the pink and white puckers and cicatrices of scars which seemed to cover every inch of him were clearly visible. The dark-brown hair that fell in soft waves almost to his thick shoulders was streaked with white, as too were his short beard and heavy mustache. His teeth were big and yellow and a little crooked, his lips full and dark-red, his nose slightly flattened and canted. As he slipped his hair into a cotton nightcap and tied its draw-strings about his head, she could see that the top half of his left ear was missing, as was the lobe of the right one, while his high forehead bore that dent which was one of the marks of a veteran soldier.

When the cap was firmly in place, the naked man padded over to both doors and shot the bolts solidly home, then made for a large chest, lifted the lid and removed a short, heavy-bladed sword and placed the unsheathed weapon in a rack attached to the bedhead. He snuffed all but one thick taper and slid into the other side of the huge bed.

His settling weight brought a creak from the leather supports and, for all her iron self-control, a shudder and a gasp from Giliahna.

"Are you awake, then, wife?"

Giliahna tried to frame an answer, but the whirling of her mind precluded such, nor could she have spoken through her chattering teeth.

"My lady?" He slid close enough to place a hand on her shoulder, rigid from the tight-clenching of her icy hands. She gasped again, starting as if touched by a hot iron.

"Why . . . you're scared to death, child. There's no need to fear *me*. I'm your husband."

His deep voice was infinitely gentle, Giliahna could hear that. But she could only lie there stiffly, quivering like a spent horse, the sweat of terror oozing from her every pore and tears creeping from under her closed eyelids.

"Giliahna, I mean you no ill . . . ever. But it's true, you do not know me, I'm a full stranger to you in most ways. If you'd prefer, I'll bide this night upon the couch yonder. I'm an old campaigner and I've slept many a night alone."

At last, she got out a few stuttering words. "No . . . your bed . . . hall . . . do my duty . . . honor of my clan . . . my house . . ."

"Nonsense!" He cast off his coverings and, crossing his legs, sat facing her. "You talk as if you're giving an excuse for leading a suicide charge. Honor was fulfilled this noon, before the Sword Altar. What takes place—or doesn't—here in our bedchamber is between you and me, between Giliahna and Djylz. The conjugal affairs of the prince and princess of this Principate of Kuhmbuhluhn are their very private business, not open to meddling, peeking, or the proddings of ministers and high nobles; the succession of my house is assured whether you be quickened or no. Anyway, I didn't wed you simply to get a noble broodmare."

He shifted his legs, slowly so as not to startle her, straightened his right one and, grimacing, massaged the flesh and muscles under a jagged-edged, deeply indented scar running from midthigh to knee.

"No, little Giliahna, I first became interested in you when I saw the sketch of you made by Duke Rahn of Hwahlburk during the months he was guesting with his cousin, your half brother, the Archduke Bili of Morguhn. My dear Karohlyn was deathly ill even then and all knew it, including her."

He gritted his teeth, spoke through them. "I've had bad luck with wives. Had to bury seven, but I'm hoping you'll be the wife who outlives me. Anyhow," he smiled once again, "Karohlyn and I both studied the duke's sketch and had him to her chamber, where we both questioned him.

"His answers fleshed out that sketch. He told us of your faultless courtesy, of your grace, your vigor, of your soul-deep beauty. Your mother was a Zunburker, daughter of the hereditary duke of that house, so both Karohlyn and I knew that your maternal stock was good, and discreet inquiries established the facts that your father, though a duke for only a score or so of years, was a chief and the son and grandson of chiefs.

"Karohlyn and I then decided that, after a suitable period of mourning, I should wed you. Almost a year passed after that mutual decision, Giliahna, then her pain became too much for flesh to bear, so that not even huge doses of the physician's—Master Ahkbahr's—drugs could long ease her.

"One night she sent for me, told me that she loved me with all her heart, but that she no longer could abide a life of increasing torment. She asked for my dagger and I gave it to her. In return, she gave me one last kiss and a letter for you. Here."

He slid his fingers along one of the woodcarvings decorating the bedhead and a small drawer slid silently open. From it he withdrew a slender roll of vellum sheets, tied with a faded bit of ribbon. He extended his hand, proffering to her the dead woman's last message.

"I know you can read, Giliahna, and the contents are for you, not for me. Besides, your young eyes should be better than my aging ones. Here. Draw some pillows behind your shoulders and sit you up whilst I get you more light."

Her fears lulled to some degree by the prince's lack of lust and obviously sincere solicitude for her, and her curiosity piqued, Giliahna did as she was bade, propping herself and spreading the letter on her lap. The writing was thin, spidery and filled with blotches from an ill-controlled quill so that she found it at first all but indecipherable. But with the lighting of additional candles, she could painfully make out the words—Mehrikan, of course, as Ehleeneekos was little spoken, this far north.

> My dear Giliahna,
> Although we never will meet, I feel a warm friendship—nay, a real kinship—to you and there is so very much I would like to tell you, but my agony is great, unbearable, and I am anxious to end it. Therefore, I will be brief, speaking only of the most important thing: my—our—husband.
> When first I came to wed Djylz, I was but a few months older than are you and I was terribly frightened. But I soon knew him to be the dearest, gentlest and most kind of men. I am much grieved to leave him, but for near three years now I have been unable to be the lover and companion and helpmate to him that I should and that he so deserves. I beg you to take my place fully, be all the things to him that I can never again be.
> Djylz needs love, Giliahna, much love, but if he receives it, he will return it tenfold. You will have heard much ill of him, of course, for, to his enemies, he is stark ferocity personified. But to those who love him—as do I, as do his children, as do his people, as you will and *must*—he is only warm generosity. And last, but very important, please find a little spare love to lavish on my little son, Gy. You

will not be sorry, for there is much of his dear father in him.

Oh, my dear sister, how I envy you that happiness which has been mine and now is yours.

Your true and everloving friend,
Karohlyn

Chapter VII

"And," Giliahna reflected, burrowed under the coverlets embroidered with the White Hawk of Vawn by the skillful hands of her long-dead mother, "every word that that poor, suffering woman wrote was nothing less than pure, simple truth."

The prince's wish had been fulfilled—his eighth wife had outlived him. And her love for him had early become complete and soul-deep, nor could young Gy's natural mother have shown him any more affection during the two years before he left for his war training at the court of King Sehbastyuhn of Pitzburk.

His first letters to her had expressed bitter homesickness, and Giliahna had wept for a little boy far from his home and lonely amongst strangers. But time had worked its curative powers, and soon the letters were abrim with exciting events of this richest court in all the Middle Kingdoms, as well as with pride of new skills mastered.

As boy grew into young man, the letters told of forays and of raids, of single combats and of great, crashing battles, and Sacred Sun never rose or set but that Giliahna importuned that Gy's life be spared—for all three of Djylz's sons by earlier marriages had been slain during their own war years, and she knew in her heart that she would not produce a son to replace Gy, for she could not seem to conceive of the prince.

But, as if possessed of arcane foreknowledge of what was to be, Prince Djylz never worried, seeming sublimely confident that this last son would live to succeed to the Principate of Kuhmbuhluhn.

Come of Horseclans stock, of ancestors who had thought nothing of arming and mounting and riding off to hunt or battle when they had seen more than fourscore summers, Giliahna never fretted that her husband, at a little less than seventy years, regularly took to horse with spear and bow and boarsword to hunt the nearby forest preserves with his foresters and his gentlemen. Sometimes she chose to ride with him, for, adhering to ancient Horseclans Law, Hwahltuh Sanderz had seen to his daughter's war training from her twelfth year, and she early proved more proficient with the horseman's hornbow than her husband or his gentlemen.

But though Prince Djylz's gentlemen were as proud and prickly and pugnacious as any similar aggregation of Middle Kingdoms nobles, no one ever begrudged the young princess her skill at archery. Any other woman might have found herself the butt of rough humor if not biting jibes, but not Giliahna; for the gentlemen truly loved their grizzled liege lord and so—young and old, one and all—they worshiped the merry, smiling new wife who was obviously making the prince so happy.

One brilliant morning, three days after the ninth anniversary of their wedding, the royal pair rode forth, trailed by a score of noble retainers. They rode west at a slow trot, with none of the usual racings from bend to bend, for this hunt was serious business and the horses wore pounds of quilted padding, while the riders were partially armored and bore more than the ordinary quantity and variety of weapons.

Djylz had done his damnedest to dissuade Giliahna, but she was as stubborn as her husband and he had at last relented—as always he did with her. But in the manner of personal protection, he had proved adamant, and so Giliahna rode sweltering in three-quarter armor, extra-heavy tournament plate borrowed for the occasion from one of the smaller noble fosterings of the court.

Giliahna edged her big hunter closer to the duke's side and hissed, "Damn it all, husband, you'd best halt the column, for I swear I'll not ride another ten yards in this infernal steel torture chamber! I can't remember when I've sweated so much. My smallclothes are sodden and they're chafing me raw in . . . in some very personal places. Besides, this damned cuirass doesn't fit properly and it's pinching me. Why couldn't I have just worn a scale jazeran, like you and the others?"

Prince Djylz chuckled, then grinned sympathetically. "Now, wife, you know why warriors call their suits of plate 'Pitzburk steamers,' and you can now truly appreciate why I'm in no condition for a love bout the first few days after a tourney."

Giliahna had leaned her spear against her shoulder and commenced to fumble at the cuirass buckles under her arm with the freed hand, but the prince leaned sidewise in his saddle and laid a hand on hers, his smile erased and his demeanor as serious as his tone.

"No, love, let be . . . let be, I say. You may need that plate ere this day be done. As I said this morning, killing shaggy bulls is less sport than warfare, and it's every bit as dangerous. Steel be praised," he touched fingertips to his lips, then to the polished ball-pommel of his broadsword, "that the hairy monsters usually stay in the west and the north and out of my domain. I'd be as happy if every shaggy bull alive were somewhere west of the Sea of Grass. But a small herd has chosen to come down out of the mountains, and, as protector of my lands and people, it's my job to see that they're killed before they do any more damage.

"I still wish you'd go back, Giliahna." She opened her mouth, but he raised his hand for silence. "You won't, however, love, I know that. Therefore, you are going to *stay* in that armor . . . and you had better know *that!*"

By noon, the party had left the western fringes of the flat country and ascended into the foothills. The farms here had smaller fields, most of them on hillsides; there were few cattle, but many goats and a few small herds of blatting sheep. Far west, Giliahna could see the hazy bluish rounded humps of the range that separated Kuhmbuhluhn from the Mahrk of Tuhsee—years agone, a bitter enemy of Kuhmbuhluhn, but now a fellow member of the Confederation.

A little after the noon, keener-eyed members of the party could see a host of black dots moving in slow, lazy circles in the clear sky some distance ahead. Shortly thereafter, they rounded a bend in the road to find three hunters squatting under a roadside tree and munching on cold bacon and cornbread.

The three were clad almost identically in sweat-stained green shirts, soft leather breeches and low-topped boots. All three were bowmen—as attested by the leather sleeve each wore laced to his left arm from wrist to elbow and by the big horn ring on each man's right thumb—and they all also bore an assortment of knives of various sizes, as well as slings and pouches of stones.

The trio of hunters were tall and slender, two of them with reddish-tinged brown hair, the third almost bald, but with a thick, dark-red mustache. There was distinct similarity in the casts of all three weather-browned faces and in the crinkle-cornered hazel eyes, big, jutting noses and high cheekbones.

The mustachioed hunter arose as the mounted party came into view, slapped a cloud of dust from his trousers, pulled off a billed leather cap, on the forepeak of which was emblazoned the princely arms, and trotted over to stand beside Prince Djylz's sorrel stallion, his coordination, speed and ease of movement belying his thin, graying hair and host of wrinkles.

Smiling warmly, Djylz shucked a mailed gauntlet and leaned to clasp the hunter's hand. "Roy, old friend, it's good to clap eyes on you again; I trow, you look younger every time I see you. Are you sure you're not an Undying?"

The hunter pumped the prince's hand enthusiastically twice, then bore it to his lips and kissed it, before replying, "Not as I knows, Lord Djylz. Thet be a fine, tall horse y' be a-forkin'; he has more the stamp o' a warhorse than a hunter though. Wher be yer good ol' piebald hunter, Stagfleet?"

The prince sighed. "Aye, Stagfleet is good, but he is getting old, too, and I thought this day's work might be better done with a younger, faster horse." He absently patted the quilt-armored neck of his sorrel. "Man-lover, here, I bought from the Duke of York-Getzburk, last year at the Harzburk Fair; he was bred for a destrier and has had a good bit of war training, too, but while he'll savage another horse or any other animal quick enough, he shies from attacking men, so Duke Randee had him retrained for a hunter.

"Now, to business, Roy. How many of the beasts have you seen? How far away are they?"

"The herd bull, o'course." The hunter ticked off his bow-thumb. "An' he be the bigges' I ever seed, too—eighteen han's at the withers, mebbe more. One young bull he ain't drove off, yet, but he's got his full horns. Three old cows, two of em with calves follerin' an' a couple of heifers. One o' them calfs is a bull calf, an' he be pure white, my lord Djylz."

The prince grunted in appreciation. Not only would a white shaggy-bull be a rare specimen for his menagerie, but if taken young enough, shaggy-bulls could often be gentled to the tractability of domestic cattle and, when bred to beef breeds, invariably sired or threw bigger, meatier animals with thicker, stronger, more long-wearing hides.

He turned in the saddle and addressed his nobles and the

retainers. "Roy, here, says there're a brace of nursing calves and one of the little buggers is even a white. You, Persee," he spoke directly to Count Parkzburk, whose wealth lay principally in his fine herds of cattle, "know what that means. I want both those calves alive and unharmed."

At length, the party came to a narrow track, leading off to the right between fields of thigh-high cornstalks. As the van entered a small, dusty farmyard, the old hunter kneed his big-headed pony forward and banged scarred knuckles on the thick, plank door of the small, log-walled house.

"Djaimos!" he yelled. "Djaimos Poorahbos! It be me, Roy Danyulz. C'mon out, heah. His lordship done come fer to kill them critters."

Following scraping noises that told of the removal of at least two bars, the door of the windowless house swung open and a short, squat, thick-limbed man strode forth with a noticeable limp. His close-cropped black hair was shot through with white, but his black eyes were clear and alert; his forehead bore the permanent dent which told of years of bearing a helmet, all his front teeth were missing, his nose was mashed and canted far left, one ear was missing entirely and the other lacked a lobe, his olive-skinned face was a mass of old scars and so was every inch of visible body skin.

At sight of the prince, the oldster drew himself up into military posture and marched to within an accurately gauged five paces of the nobleman, then rendered a military salute, snapping, "Poorahbos, Djaimos, my lord. Retired *epeelokeeas* of heavy infantry of the Army of the Confederation. Would it please my lord that Poorahbos and his sons accompany the hunt?"

Prince Djylz smiled. "Aye, sergeant, get your spear and your lads, you look to have the strength to push a pike clear through a shaggy-bull, lengthwise. But first, tell me, have you seen them?"

The former senior sergeant had not, but reported that he had heard much bellowing and what had sounded like screams from the direction of a neighboring farmstead. So, as soon as he and his sons were laced into homemade cuirasses of boiled leather and he had donned his old helmet and buckled on his shortsword and dirk, he and his twin sons took the lead. There were no mounts for them but they proved to need none, moving easily and as fast as the duke cared to extend the horses in the mile-eating jog-trot of Confederation infantrymen, spears properly sloped over right shoulders.

"That old bastard's trained his lads well," remarked Djylz to Giliahna. "They'll be first-class recruits, given another year of growth."

Up one grassy hillock and down another, then through a low saddle between two more hills the party wound along a trail through a small bit of forest, then debouched into another stretch of cornfields, with another cabin in sight ahead.

But this farmyard was not deserted as had been Djaimos Poorahbos', it was alive with movement and sound—the flopping and flapping and pecking and raucous noises of crow and raven and buzzard. That on which they gorged had not been pretty when they arrived and their razor beaks and tearing talons had done nought to improve appearances, but once the carrion birds had been driven off, a tale could still be read in the hoof-trampled, blood-soaked dust of the yard and the gory, horn-mangled and stamped lifeless bodies—six of them, five human and one big hound.

What was left of a man still clenched a hand around the shaft of a wolfspear, the weapon sticky brown to the crossbar with blood; near the body of a youth was a horseman's saber, gory for half its length. Another lad, younger, looked to have fought his last battle with a hewing axe. There was a burned-out torch near one hand of the dead woman. The corpse of what looked to have once been a slender, pretty girl was sprawled atop the roof of the cabin, dark-tressed head at an impossible angle and guts trailing from the belly torn open by the hooking horn which probably had thrown her there.

The shaggy-bulls had not been content to merely kill, however, they had obviously continued to savage their victims long after life had fled, and the results were hideous. Giliahna could only lean weakly against the high cantle of her saddle when she had retched up her stomach's contents—nor was she the only one. The prince himself, though he was no stranger to the sight of death and mutilation, was pale of face and grim.

"Sergeant Poorahbos," the prince called to the old spearman, who stood staring down at what the beasts had left of the man, "should these folk be buried or burned? What would they have preferred?"

Djaimos Poorahbos whirled and trotted over to snap to before the mounted noble, his stance proper and his spearbutt grounded. Tears streamed down his clean-shaven cheeks, but his voice was firm. "My lord, these folk were pawns to no priests. They should go to Wind."

Prince Djylz's voice softened. "Stand easy, Djaimos. You knew this man well, didn't you? He was a friend, and an old soldier, like you?"

Poorahbos' left foot moved forward and sidewise a precise eight inches and his two big callused hands clamped about the spearshaft, which he had allowed to cant at a thirty-degree angle from his body. "My lord prince, Imit Dyuh were senior sergeant-major of the Fourteenth Confederation Lancers, and the finest man as ever forked a horse for all the twenny-four years he served, till he took a poison arrer in his lef' arm and the flesh-tailors had to lop half the arm oft. An' t'won't be another like to him for a High Lord's lifetime, I trow!"

After having the bodies placed within the empty cabin to protect them from further ravages of the birds and other scavengers, the prince ordered the party on, following the clear trail of the murderous monsters, but more slowly and as silently as possible. The hunters and farmers were fanned out well in advance of the mounted men. Nor did they have far to go.

Less than a mile from the scene of slaughter, one of the younger hunters came sprinting back. "We have found them, my lord."

From a laurel thicket on the crest of a hillock, the men could look down into a grassy vale, through which tinkled the clear waters of a spring-fed brook. In addition to the shaggy-bulls, the herd had been increased by two orange-and-white milch cows—looking diminutive beside the dark, hairy, wild behemoths.

The old sergeant wormed closer to the prince. "My lord, those be poor Imit's cows. Most likely thet's why he tried to drive off them damned critters."

Prince Djylz just nodded, eyeing not the harmless domestic animals but their savage and deadly kidnappers. The big bull was an awesome sight—more than six feet high at the withers, his flaring horns black as crow's wings and at least two yards from tip to bloodstained tip. An attempt had been made sometime recently to hamstring him, but the blow had been delivered too far back on the ham and without sufficient force to cleave to the tendon. Nonetheless, the massive bovine had sustained a gaping wound; his tail whisked continually at the flies buzzing about it. The pain of the injury certainly had

done nothing to improve the bull's temper, but the conse-
quent loss of blood just might serve to slow him a bit.

The younger bull lay halfway down the slope and appeared
to be either dead or very near to death. The face and head
looked badly burned, and blood was still seeping from at
least two places on the deep chest. Even as they watched, the
stricken beast raised its head and tried to rise, then a great
gush of blood spouted from gaping mouth and distended nostrils, the head fell with a thump onto the bloody grass, the
legs jerked and twitched a few times, and dung and urine
gushed from the relaxed sphincters.

The two wild cows and the heifers grazed contentedly on
the tender grass. The calves apparently had been twins, since
both were nursing from the same cow. She was two-thirds the
size of the big bull, though her horns were neither as thick
nor as long, even allowing for her smaller size. The barren
cow might have been her twin, so close was the armament
and overall resemblance. One of the heifers was much like
the cows, but the other had no horns at all, only bulbous
knots where they should have been.

Back again with the main party, the prince described what
he had seen. Some of the younger nobles requested leave to
ride down and slay the bull with lances and spearwork, but
Prince Djylz curtly denied them.

"Yonder's no mere boar or stag to be stuck, gentlemen.
They've already wiped out an entire family of decent, loyal
farmers, and they'll add none of my noblemen to their tally,
if I can prevent it. No, our good hunters and my lady will
slay or cripple as many as they can with arrows fired from
the top of the hill. Then, and only then, will the rest of us
descend to dispatch or pursue if the animals flee. Persee, I
leave the capture of the calves to you; Sir Hyruhm, Sir
Djahn, you and your lads assist the count."

Giliahna's first shaft drove into an eye of the horned heifer
and pierced to the brain; the beast dropped like a leaden
weight and the remainder of the herd continued to graze
peacefully . . . but not for long. In courtesy, the trio of
hunters and the two other archers had waited for the princess
to loose first. Their own shots, when loose they did, were not
so fortunate.

One shaft went completely through the sagging udder of
the nursing cow, narrowly missing the white calf beyond—
whereupon the prince, sitting his horse a bit behind the line
of archers, swore sulfurously. Another went into the nose of

the hornless heifer, which then commenced to run about, bawling piteously. One, apparently aimed at the throat of the grazing bull, missed entirely when the beast raised his head; two sank to the feathers into the flank of the great beast, just behind the right shoulder, and bellowing, he slowly sank to his knees and began to exhale bloody froth.

At that point, knowing that his nobles would take ill being denied at least a modicum of dangerous sport, and with the largest and deadliest of the animals down and seemingly lung-shot, Prince Djylz kneed his mount between two of the archers and started down the slope at a slow, careful walk. Not caring to risk the goring of the horse, he dismounted a few yards from the stricken bull, drew his heavy broadsword and limped over to stand beside the creature. Gripping the pommel in his left hand, the old prince brought the battle-blade whistling down with all his strength to *thunk* into the thick neck and sever the spine.

When he had cleansed and sheathed his steel, he remounted and rode over to watch the younger men do battle with the two shaggy-cows. Count Parkzburk and his helpers had already roped the white bullcalf and were trying to maneuver a clear chance at the darker calf, while Sergeant Poorahbos and his sons had secured the two frightened, lowing domestic cows.

His spear set for stab or cast, young Baron Kairee of Balzburk set upon the biggest shaggy-cow, then standing broadside to him, her head lowered and her wickedly pointed horns aimed at the calf-roping party. He came at a fast trot, but the cow was faster. In a blur of motion, she pivoted her long, wide, thick body with the grace and ease of a deer. Frantically, at the last possible second, the baron reined aside, nearly losing his seat as the long horn tore through the brigandine protecting his horse from breast to where it clanged against the steel greave buckled onto his jackboot. At this point, he lost his spear and so prudently withdrew.

Prince Djylz allowed his nobles their fun until the second calf had been roped, then he ordered an end. It was a long ride back, and the slain beasts must be skinned, cleaned, and butchered and the hides and horns and meat packed onto the mules brought for the purpose, and he did not really feel well. He had been suffering from a peculiar ache in his left arm for a good part of the day and he could not recall having strained or bruised it recently.

With Poorahbos and his sons to help, the skinning and

butchering went far faster and more smoothly. The calves bawled incessantly and fought against the ropes; Giliahna suggested that full bellies might improve their mood and attempts were made to set them to nurse on the cows that had been stolen, but the milch cows refused to cooperate; they wanted nothing to do with the two shaggy-calves.

Tired horses and heavy-laden mules made the return slow. At Poorahbos' farm, the prince called the old sergeant to him, saying, "I thank you for your guidance and help. Take a quarter of meat and a hide."

The old soldier nodded, and his two sons trotted back to the packline. The prince continued, "You were the dead man's friend. Make a pyre and do the honors for him and his family and the cows are yours, along with anything else you want from his house and farm. If you and your sons will tend and harvest his crops, I accept a single basket of grain as my tax on it this year. Of course," the prince grinned, "the tax on your own fields remains the same."

Despite his iron self-discipline, Djaimos Poorahbos could not repress a grin, but he quickly recovered and thanked the prince formally.

Giliahna wished at that moment that she could kiss Djylz. It was just such acts as this that had so endeared him to his people, the lowly as well as the high. Another lord might have taken those fine milch cows as his own and sent men to watch over and harvest the growing crops, bringing him all, instead of his customary half. But not so her beloved husband. She raised the beaver of her helm, that the others might not see her small, pointed chin quiver with the intensity of her emotion.

That night, Giliahna shamelessly seduced the prince in his bath. And they did not appear for the night meal, remaining rather behind the closed and barred doors of their chamber until Sacred Sun streamed through the window. Each savored the other, knowing without knowing that this would be the last such night they would have together.

Chapter VIII

Lying snuggled under the White Hawk coverlet as the crackling fire slowly began to warm her bedchamber in her dead father's hall, Giliahna wept afresh and unashamedly for Djylz, for the loss—hers, the principate's and the world's—of the fine, strong, honorable, loving and much loved man that he had been.

At the very end, when the noble Sword Brothers had completed their secret and private rites and she was allowed back into the bedchamber, he had weakly signed her to sit beside him upon that big bed which had been theirs.

His voice was weak, but firm and precise as always. "Giliahna, love, promise me that you will remain in Kuhmbuhluhn long enough to set Gy on the proper path. A reign is molded, for good or for ill, at the ascension of a lord. And see him wedded to a good wife of good stock, not simply for land or wealth—Steel knows, I leave him a surfeit of both.

"Nor are you forgotten, my sweet, young love. All the jewels save only the heirloom treasures are yours. By our law, a dowager princess is Land-Lady of the Duchy of Vaizburk, which holdings remain exempt of principate taxes throughout her lifetime."

There had been more, much more. And then, suddenly, the old man had said, "My sword! Bring me my sword, quickly!"

Giliahna started to lift the pillow-sword from its place, but he shook his head. "No! My battlesword."

With the worn, wire-wound hilt in his weak grip and the polished steel ball-pommel under his forearm, he smiled fleetingly and sighed. "An affectation, mayhap, but no man of my house has ever died without his steel in hand. Now, my last love, please kiss me."

52

Giliahna's lips had but barely touched his, when she felt the life leave his body.

The state funeral was held only three days later, due to the unseasonable heat. Then Giliahna and the Principate Council ruled as regents until, a fortnight after his father's entombment, Gy of Kuhmbuhluhn rode in from the north to claim his patrimony.

Standing upon the steps of the palace to greet her returning stepson, Giliahna and the other councillors were all but deafened by the cheering of the folk who packed the narrow streets, hung out of windows and even clung to eaves and rooftops to catch a first glimpse of their new, young lord. Smiling, silver-scaled troopers of the principate horseguards and footguards gently pushed the crowds back to make way for the cavalcade with nudges of long, limber poles—Djylz had always forbidden the use of whips or polearms against his folk.

Giliahna felt a cold chill course over every inch of her body when first her eyes took in the lead rider of the procession. The armor, though highly burnished, was plain and the helm concealed most of the face from her viewpoint, but that figure could be none other but Djylz—dead Djylz, whom she had seen buried beside his father in the great crypt beneath the Sword Altar. How he sat his horse, erect but relaxed, that was Djylz; the movements of the gloved hands, saluting the crowds and handling his reins, that was Djylz . . . it could be none other.

But, at the foot of the steps, the illusion was dispelled. After dismounting from his tall destrier, the rider removed his helm to reveal a smooth-shaven face and head, both already scarred. Moving lightly in his heavy half armor, the warrior first rendered to Giliahna the homage due her—for until he was formally approved by the Council of Nobles and crowned in public ceremony, she was the reigning Princess of Kuhmbuhluhn.

Kneeling on the step below her, Gy brought to his lips and kissed first the embroidered hem of her skirt, then that small hand on which the massive Ring of Kuhmbuhluhn fitted so loosely. That done, he arose and gathered her into his strong arms.

Though his voice was not so deep as had been his father's, it was every bit as warm and gentle. "Mother mine. Little mother Giliahna. It has been so long and I have so missed you."

Prince Gy II of Kuhmbuhluhn proved to need little of the guidance which Giliahna had promised. He slipped into his place and duties as easily as sword into sheath. The polish he had gained at the court of Pitzburk stood him in good stead. He knew and automatically assumed the proper procedures whether granting audience to ambassadors or sitting at judgment in the city court on a case of two merchants accusing each other of unfair competition.

A truculent western noble, who had openly declared that what with the dry summer and the resultant damage to crops in the west he and his peers could not and would not render the usual taxes, was seen by Gy alone. Within an hour, he emerged, all smiles and praises of the young prince.

When asked by Giliahna how he had so quickly wrought such a change, Gy had grinned. "The western harvest was poor, but not so poor as he would have had me believe. Even so, I agreed to accept a sixth, rather than a third, this year; then I appointed him my official surrogate to accept and forward the grain and silver."

Giliahna wrinkled her brow. "But, Gy, how can you be certain that such a man will deal honestly?"

Gy's grin widened. "Little mother, I'm sending some of my own clerks—to save him the trouble and expense of hiring such, of course—and if he tries to steal from my revenues, I'll simply shorten him . . . by a head."

And Giliahna knew that the young man was perfectly capable of carrying out that threat, for when an especially predatory and ruthless band of cashiered Freefighters and assorted outlaws began to pray upon the trade road between Kuhmbuhluhnburk and Getzburk, the new prince mustered his horseguards and every resident or visiting nobleman and fostering who was not too old or too young, and sent gallopers to bear word to both the High Lords in Kehnooryos Atheenahs and to Duke Randee of Getzburk-York that he was campaigning to crush and extirpate the robbers and that he did not mean for borders to stop him.

Old Count Looiz of Kohlzburk, who had soldiered for nearly twenty years before succeeding to his own inheritance and titles and now was Duke Randee's marshal, met Gy just north of the border with an escort of heavily armed nobles.

After polite greetings, the grizzled veteran got down to business. "Lord prince, Duke Randee is every bit as anxious to do in these scum as are you and he regrets that he cannot join you himself since he much valued the friendship of your

late and much-lamented father. But the thrice-damned Iron
King has been foraying in force across the northern border,
and the duke is up there now with the bulk of our army.

"When your message reached him, however, he bade me
come and assist you as best I can. Lord prince, my gentlemen
and I are at your command."

Mounted foresters and hunters of both realms quickly
scouted out a large, sprawling forest camp, and after a long,
cold, wet, supperless night, the force struck at dawn. More
than twoscore bandits were slain or seriously wounded, which
meant death too. A dozen and a half were captured more or
less hale. A number of captives—mostly female and all
much-abused—were freed, along with fourscore horses and
mules and a fair quantity of assorted livestock. And there
was considerable inanimate loot "liberated."

For all their disparity in numbers—there had been only an
eighth as many Getzburkers as the southern force—Gy saw
to a precise halving of the booty between the principate and
the duchy. Even Count Looiz protested that his lord's allotted
share was too much, for all that he went about grinning like
an opossum. But Gy was adamant, pointing out that the action had been fought on the duke's land and that, as the
camp had been situated in Getzburk, the duke could—in
strict interpretation of law—claim it all, were he so minded.

"Though, if he did," Gy chuckled and clapped Count
Looiz on the shoulder, "he'd have a war on his southern border, too."

Back in Kuhmbuhluhn, the prince formally tried his nine
captives, found them all guilty of highway robbery, maiming,
stock-stealing, rape, kidnapping, extortion of illegal ransoms,
murder and numerous other offenses. After public torture and
mutilation, all nine were hanged in slow nooses.

But as to the other matter of which his father had bespo-
ken Giliahna, Gy simply shrugged. "My princedom is at
peace, I am not yet twenty and there is no urgency to assure
the succession. In good time, I'll wed and bed and sire."

When news of her father's death reached the Principate of
Kuhmbuhluhn and Giliahna broached her decision to journey
to the duchy of her birth, possibly to not return to
Kuhmbuhluhn, Gy and all the councillors tried mightily to
dissuade her, but she was adamant and spoke to them in
terms they could both comprehend and appreciate as the
Middle Kingdoms noblemen they basically were, for all their
principate's nominal Confederation allegiance.

"My Lord Gy, gentlemen, I must go back to Sanderz-Vawn on a matter of personal honor and of the honor of my house. A great injustice was done to me and my brother in years agone, and if he be unable or unwilling to go back, then it be my bounden duty to redress that wrong in the blood of those who perpetrated it. Your generous offers of lands and wealth make me feel truly humble in the light of the obvious love for me which impelled them, and please believe that the love I feel for Kuhmbuhluhn and for you all is no less in quantity or quality. But, noble gentlemen that you all are, you must recognize that satisfaction of this, my debt of honor, must come before other considerations."

The men grouped around the table nodded, one and all—in their minds blood debts took precedence over all else.

Old Archduke Rohluhn scratched at his skimpy white hair. "How many troops will my lady require? And can she estimate for how long the service?"

Before she could answer, Gy snapped, "Stop quibbling, uncle! Our lady is a Princess of Kuhmbuhluhn. She shall have at least one squadron of our horseguards—say, three hundred full-strength lances. And I'll command them; this business will be settled in short order, I trow!"

Giliahna repressed any trace of her mirth at his still-boyish enthusiasm, saying rather, "Lord prince, as you know, the High Lords permit organized bands of Freefighters to enter and leave the Confederation at will; but what do you think their reaction and that of the Prince of Karaleenos, in whose domains my home duchy lies, would be to an incursion of nearly one thousand household troops of Kuhmbuhluhn led by the reigning prince, himself?"

The aged archduke and several other veteran councillors nodded, and Duke Djaikuhb of Rahbzburk said, "My lady is right, my prince. Before you'd got five leagues south of the border, you'd find yourself boxed in by Confederation dragoons. They'd politely ask your business, then they'd politely point out the decrees of the High Lords forbidding the maintenance or the movements of private armies save on the frontiers, then they'd politely escort you and your lances back to Kuhmbuhluhn and, in a month or so, a messenger would arrive from Kehnooryos Atheenahs with a politely couched reprimand."

And so, Giliahna left Kuhmbuhluhnburk with only a dozen horseguards and her immediate retainers, conveyed in two coaches and three wagons. Upon hearing that there was a rumor that Duke Hwahltuh of Sanderz-Vawn had died of slow poisoning, Gy would not rest his entreaties until Giliahna agreed to include in her party a Zahrtohgah physician, one Master Fahreed, and his apprentice, Raheen.

The prince and a large cavalcade accompanied the dowager princess as far as the border, and, during their last, solitary conversation, Gy took both her hands and looked down into her eyes. "My lady, you asked weeks agone if I loved any woman and I answered nay, but that is not true. I do love a woman. I love *you* and, did our laws not forbid such, you would be *my* wife, *my* princess—after all, I am less than five years your junior. But such can never be and I know it. Therefore, I charge you this: Send to me a sweet, loving maid like yourself, one who can come to love and comfort me as you loved and so comforted my dear father, and I vow to cherish her as I would have cherished you."

Ahrkeethoheeks Bili of Morguhn had been as gracious and caring a host as she recalled from her childhood visits to the Hall of the Red Eagle, and such had been the attentions lavished upon her by his handsome eldest son, Djef Morguhn, that she had felt almost embarrassed, before her acutely perceptive half brother noted her discomfiture and found a convenient errand for his heir to ride forth upon. He then proved a veritable fount of information, all of which she found interesting, but it was not until they were closeted alone together within his grim little office at Morguhn Hall that he imparted the news which set her heart to pounding and raised tingling goose flesh on her body from head to toe.

"At our last meeting before his . . . shall we say, untimely death, I promised your late sire that, when he died, I would dispatch word to your brother, Tim. You should know that he and I have kept in touch over these last years and that, through me—though Tim doesn't know it—your late father's gold reached him.

"Please listen to what I say and believe it, Giliahna. Your father deeply regretted his hasty and ill-advised actions in sending you and Tim away, but by the time he recovered fully from whatever drugs those harpies—your stepmother and her damned tongue-sister—were dosing him with, the deed was irrevocably done. You were wedded and Tim, stubborn in his hurt and rage, refused to respond to what few letters Hwahltuh could sneak past those Ehleenee and out of his hall. For, understand you, Giliahna, your poor, ailing father was very close to a prisoner in his own duchy in his last years, spied upon when he was not actively guarded by his wife and her slut, his half-Ehleen brood and their adherents.

"Giliahna, your father was born in a Horseclans yurt and was past middle age when he led his clan from the Sea of Grass. Your Horseclansman, fresh from the west, has an inordinate love for children, any children, but especially his own. You'd have to fully comprehend that fact to be aware of just how deeply your father hurt himself ten years ago. He was a proud man and strong, with more real guts than a whole tribe of mountain barbarians, yet many's the time he has sat in that same chair and wept like a whipped child in his regret over banishing you and Tim.

"Had he chosen to cleave to that thrice-damned perversion of a religion upon which Mehleena so dotes, he might have at least had the idiotic precepts of that faithless faith to console himself with. But Horseclansmen do not harbor this idiotic fear of interbreeding that the Ehleenee do; indeed, there is no such word as *ahimomikseeah* in all the Mehrikan dialects, though the High Lord Milo tells me that there was once such a word, centuries ago.

"But, be that as it may, your father is gone to Wind, along with his sorrow. You are returned, and Tim soon will be."

Giliahna clasped her hands tightly to keep them from trembling. In a painfully tight voice, she asked, "When, brother, oh when?"

The archduke smiled at what his uncommonly powerful mind could read in hers. "Two weeks, little sister, possibly three, depending upon road conditions. He'll be bringing the Ruby Company, his condotta, down here with him. One of my men will make contact with him ere he crosses into Kehnooryos Ehlahs, delivering to him a pass from High Lord Milo countersigned by our own Prince Zenos. Once he's here, of course, there'll be no question about private troops, since Vawn is still considered a frontier duchy in some senses."

He paused to drain his cup and refill both his and hers. "But I tell you all this in strictest confidence, sister. Be damned careful which if any of your retainers you tell, and be certain that you breathe not a word of it once you are at Vawn, to *anyone*, mind you. Your brother, Ahl, already knows, but don't even discuss it with him, either aloud or by mindspeak, for Tim has plans for Mehleena, her litter and her folk and t'were better that they not be forewarned."

Giliahna sipped her wine, "What sort of plans, Brother Bili?"

Bili cracked his big knuckles all at once. "I'm sure he'll confide them to you when arrive he does. But I don't know any details, nor do I wish to know them, lest I forget my duty to my overlord, Prince Zenos, who *is* Mehleena's cousin."

Geros had told him where to find her. In the wide corridor outside that room which, long ago, had so often been their place of love, he enjoined Sergeant Rai. "Draw you up that chair, old friend. Allow no one to pass into these chambers without my leave."

In the sitting room, he surprised a small, delicate-looking Zahrtohgan girl brewing a spicy tea, the exciting fragrance of which filled the chamber. "My lord," she began, "my lady is not yet arisen and she . . ." Then a tiny, brown-skinned hand flew to her dark lips and her soft brown eyes widened perceptibly. Smiling secretively, she shyly inquired, "You, then . . . my lord is my lady's brother? The Duke Tim?"

At his nod, the girl's smile widened, despite the tears coursing copiously down her dusky cheeks. "Oh . . . oh, my lord, oh, oh, my lady . . . so very happy she will be . . ."

Giliahna half-heard the chamber door open and half-knew that she should at least sit up and greet the sweet, faithful Widahd, but the other half of her was lost in erotically pleasant reveries of lying here, upon this very bed with Tim . . . so very long ago. Almost could she still feel his sweet lips pressing upon her own, almost feel his hands upon her shoulders, almost . . . The lips had withdrawn, but there *was* still a warm hand upon her shoulder, and so reluctantly, she opened her eyes.

Chapter IX

"Mother, dear?" Ahl's voice contained a larger than usual note of mockery and he fixed his blind eyes directly upon his stepmother.

Mehleena squirmed inwardly and her rage rose in proportion. She could not bear it when Ahl skewered her with those sightless eyes that seemed to be staring directly into her very soul. But before her rage could burst out in words, he had continued.

"Mother, dear, it were best that you have one of the carpenters reinforce another chair if you intend to dine with the rest of the family in future. In their present condition, I fear, any one of the less massive chairs would splinter under your lard-sow weight." The blind man smiled broadly and Lady Mairee chuckled throatily, adding unneeded fuel to stoke the fires of Mehleena's boiling anger.

But such was the fat woman's ire that no words would come, only screams, hisses and stuttering. Ahl and Lady Mairee observed her briefly, then the tall man arose, extending his arm to the tiny young woman. "My lady, it is time we departed. This will be a very full day, I feel it."

To his sorrow, Myron, too, arose at that moment. With all the force of her rage, Mehleena spun on her broad rump and sank her fist into his midsection, the pointy little knuckles penetrating the vee below the ribs, driving the air from his lungs and his just-eaten breakfast up into his throat.

While the unhappy young man gasped and choked, dribbling gobbets of chewed food and turning purple, Ahl never lost his sardonic smile. Shaking his head slowly, he said, "My, such fierce maternal affection. Wind be thanked that our dear mother does not treat *me* to her love taps. Little bumboy, you had best whack your lover on the back a few times, he appears to be strangling." Then, both of them chuckling, he and

his lady made their slow, stately way down the length of the
dining chamber and out of sight, leaving Ahl's stepbrother in
his suffering and Ahl's stepmother still hissing and spluttering
in her impotent rage.

The White Hawk coverlet had long since been kicked off
the foot of the bed onto the floor, but not because of the fire
on the hearth. The heat of two long-suppressed passions, finally commingled, had rendered the room hot as a smithy for
a while. Now the evaporation of their love sweat was cooling
them and Giliahna had straightened a wadded linen sheet
enough to cover their wet bodies.

Raising herself on one elbow, she looked down upon the
face of Tim, her brother, her first lover, now once more returned to her. "I never stopped loving him," she thought.
"Yes, I loved Djylz, too, but . . . but it was a different kind
of love; Djylz was my husband, my dearest friend, my companion, but he was never"—her brow wrinkled in concentration—"was never *part of me*, was never and could never have
been what Tim is to me. It is as if all those long years something was gone, something was missing, I was but a shell of
myself. And now, Tim has refilled that shell, has made me
again complete. Oh, Tim, Tim, my dear dear brother; Sun
and Wind, how I love you!"

"And I you, my sister." Thinking him sleeping, her thought
had been unshielded and then, suddenly, Tim's mind was
there within hers, but not as intruder . . . never as intruder.

"You have changed, Giliahna. The body I cherished in my
memory those ten long years was that of a slender, tender,
nubile young girl."

"Oh, Tim, Tim . . ." She pictured herself as she was reflected in the long mirror of her robing room—the flat
muscles of shoulders, arms and legs well developed from
years of riding, hunting, archery and, more recently, from
fierce bouts of mock swordplay with her princely stepson,
Gy; the flare of her hips beneath the narrowness of her waist,
the waist, itself, made to seem smaller than truth by the
flared hips and by the breasts above; no, her breasts were
most certainly no longer those of a young girl, being full and
firm and proudly out-thrusting, the dark-blue lines of veins
meandering under the fair skin, the nipples small but prominent in their shade of fiery red-pink. "Do I? Does this body
of mine, then, so displease you?"

His warm, sweet mind embraced her more fully than mere

arms ever could. "Displease me, my sister? How ever could you displease me, you, who are a part of me? Ten years have passed and I am a man; for nine of those years—until word reached me of the death of the prince, your husband—I thought you lost to me forever, thought that I must then live out the rest of my years in the knowledge that the most important part of me was missing. Yes, I took other maids and women, even kept and maintained several for varying lengths of time, for I am a man with hungers that mere soul-sickness cannot erase."

Her mindspeak was gentle, hesitant. "Did you . . . love any of these, your women, Tim?"

"I suppose that I did . . . in a way. At least, I felt some emotion for a few, some attachment that I thought was love. But I never did, nor could I ever, feel for another as for you. As mere children, we forged together a truly singular relationship. It has passed through fires of hate and fires of war and been bathed in oceans of tears—yours, mine, and poor, used, victimized father's—but still its temper rings true."

A day's ride to the east, in Morguhn Hall, *Ahrkeethoheeks* Bili lay, fully clothed, upon his big, wide bed. His eyes were closed, but his unusual, highly trained and disciplined mental faculties were fully awake . . . and in contact with another of the few minds similar to his.

"It is only suspicion, Aldora. No, less than that, say, intuition. I have received a few unconfirmed rumors from the north, but then, you and I both know that warfare is always abrim with rumors, warriors being as gossipy as old women. I knew them both, of course, as children and they both seemed possessed of the uncommonly good mindspeak that runs in the bloodline, but Ahl's talents eclipsed theirs, especially after he lost his eyes. Then, too, they both were gone for ten years."

There was intense excitement boiling, bubbling in the faraway mind. "Bili, there are latent abilities, powers, in your mind that none of us was ever able to even recognize or categorize, much less probe and hone. So don't call your feeling about these minds 'only' anything—no doubt a sense of perception you don't even know you have is alerting you.

"I'll be in Morguhn as fast as horseflesh can bring me. But first I must contact Milo. Damn his short-range farspeak, anyway! I'll have to send a galloper . . . no, I'll go as far as Theesispolis myself, and send a galloper from there. He's on campaign, as usual, leaving me and Mara and Drehkos to rule the Confederation. Oh, Sun and Wind, if only you are right, Bili."

"Steel grant that I am," beamed the *ahrkeethoheeks*, with fervor. "For I fear me that they both bide in deadly danger at Vawn Hall, Aldora. That Ehleen sow that Zenos' uncle persuaded poor old Hwahltuh to marry is intent on her dung-wallowing son, Myron, being confirmed *thoheeks* and chief. I've always been dead certain that she was responsible for Ahl's blinding and for the death of my youngest half brother, Behrl, as well.

"Hwahltuh himself suspected that much of his progressive illness was due to some machination of Mehleena and her tongue-sister, the witchwoman. Since his death, she's discharged most of the Freefighters, along with many of the Kindred and Ahrmehnee retainers, replacing them with a carefully chosen pack of crafty, sneaking Ehleenee. Another thing you and the High Lord should know is that she has brought in one of those fanatic hedge priests, one of the gelded ones. He lives in the hall as a noble and honored guest, I'm told."

"And so?" she demanded. "Are you going soft, Bili? You know those black-robed troublemakers are proscribed throughout the Confederation. Why haven't you and your *kahtahfrahktvee* just ridden over to Vawn and introduced that priest's unwashed arse to a sharp stake? Such is your right, nay, your duty as *ahrkeethoheeks*. Milo would say the same, and you know it."

"The idea has crossed my mind more than once, Aldora. You know how I feel about Ehleen priests . . . and most Ehleenee, for that matter; I'd dearly love to impale the fat bastard, Mehleena and all her crew, as well, but that damned, chuckleheaded Zenos stands in the way."

"Prince Zenos of Karaleenos, sixteenth of that name," Aldora beamed. "I warned Milo and Mara and Drehkos not to confirm him prince. He is the diseased and decaying branch of a once-great tree. The last true king of Karaleenos, dear, old Zenos XII, would never have owned him as his, and Zenos XI would likely have had so poor a specimen drowned shortly after birth. He has then forbidden you to deal simple justice to this illegal cleric?"

"No," answered Bili. "Not in so many words, not directly. But when I took up the matter of the priest with him last spring at the Year Council, he brought up the fact that

Mehleena is his first cousin and, as such, the descendant of kings, as is he."

"Hens' ballocks!" beamed Aldora. "So, too, am I, so is Mara. So, likely, are most of the non-Kindred folk in this Confederation, if the lines were traced back far enough. But a royal pedigree cannot be considered a license for lawbreaking. I'm going to communicate all this to the others before I take horse for the west. Either Mara or Drehkos can care for things here in the capital, and the other can ride down to Zenos' seat and remind him of a few facts. Before all be done, you may be Prince of Karaleenos, as I said you should have been when Zenos' sire died."

"Dammit, Aldora, I don't *want* to be a prince, any more than I wanted to be an archduke; I was very happy simply as *thoheeks* and chief of Morguhn, and you know it."

"Nor do I want to be a High Lady of the Confederation; could I, I'd ride far west, to the Sea of Grass, and find a clan of the Kindred. But I cannot, I have responsibilities which shape my life. So do you, lord *ahrkeethoheeks*. You have responsibilities—to your sovrans, to the Confederation, to all the law-abiding folk of that Confederation and to your Kindred. A prince who would not need to be reminded to rule by law rather than to allow himself and his judgments to be swayed by ties of house or kinship would be of great value to all. Zenos—Wind take his wormy guts!—has never been such a prince; you would be, it's that simple.

"But that matter aside. I charge you, in Milo's name, to take whatever actions you deem necessary until he and I can reach Vawn, and Zenos' likes and dislikes be damned."

Arising from his bed, Bili of Morguhn took his famous axe down from its wall hooks and commenced replacing the rawhide-and-wire grip on the steel shaft, absently humming through his wolf-grim smile a song that had been popular during his war years in the Middle Kingdoms.

"Death rides all in plate and His tall horse is black.
He leads every charge and His bowstring's never slack.
He stalks ev'ry camp and He rides ev'ry raid.
His steel harvests warrior and merchant and maid.
Death rides a coal-black horse, and we are sworn to His service.
A Freefighter rides for Blood and Death."

Myron had been assisted from the room, still gasping, gurgling and dry-retching in his misery, his fine clothing fouled with vomit, his flushed face streaked with sweat and tears and most of his weight borne by Gaios and a husky servingman. His mother proffered no word of apology for her sudden attack, rather she called for another big bowl of buttered-and-honeyed porridge and for another ewer of chilled wine. In ominous silence, she shoveled down porridge and swilled wine, her movements jerky with undischarged rage. The other children cowered at their end of the high table, silent and wide-eyed with fright. The priest sat petrified, the stains of her earlier outburst drying on his robes. Only Neeka continued to consume her food in a normal fashion—the "mistress" knew better than to attack her.

When she had finished the last of her vegetable broth, yogurt, boiled eggs and cucumbers, Neeka sank back in the chair, sipped slowly at the watered, resinous wine and thought about blind Ahl's sudden comment that Mehleena would henceforth be forbidden use of the Master's Chair; then she closed her eyes and sent her powerful, self-trained mind questing, seeking through the hall and every mind in it. What she found gave her such a start that she almost dropped her goblet. Her features suddenly drawn and pale as whey, she turned and touched Mehleena's blubbery arm.

"We must speak privately—and very soon. That which we least expected is come to pass, but if we move quickly enough, we still may win the day."

A wall panel near the head of Giliahna's bed swung silently open on well-greased hinges and Mairee Lahvoheetos stepped out, followed by Ahl Sanderz. There was but the barest scraping of Ahl's felt boot against the frame of the secret door, yet before the two had advanced more than two paces into the bedchamber, Tim had spun out of the bed in a whirl of motion and stood confronting them, nude, but armed with both bared sword and dirk. Giliahna still crouched upon the well-used bed, but from some hidden recess she had drawn and now grasped a wavy-bladed Zahrtohgahn dagger.

Teeth showing in a sardonic smile, Ahl clapped his hands softly, saying, "Very good, brother Tim, sister Giliahna, for all that I deliberately provided a bit of noise for warning, I think me that perhaps a murder-minded Ehleen or three would not have been so considerate. Before we do or say anything else, both of you raise your mindshields, and *keep* them up. The mind of Mehleena's pet witch is nearly as powerful as mine or Bili's, though in different ways. Too, there's another exceptionally powerful mind in this hall. It's been here for some years, but I've never been able to contact it directly. Not knowing for certain that it is for us, we had best consider it to be against us. So do not mindspeak anything of import until this affair be sorted out and this hall cleared of our enemies."

Tim sank onto the bed and, as he resheathed his broadsword and dirk, said, with a grin, "I think my heart almost stopped when you two came through that damned panel, brother. Who's out to do me in, anyhow—you or Mehleena?"

The blind man did not return the smile. "Were it me, Tim, you'd never have survived your bath. You've been exceedingly careless since you rode in this morning. Didn't Bili make it clear that your life hangs on a frayed thread in this hall?

"These foes have already slain two of our brothers and our father—I believe that as surely as nits make lice, they're immediately responsible for all three deaths, and for the loss of my sight, as well. They drugged Father and maneuvered the poor old man into banishing both of you, which we all know he never would have done in his right mind. Mehleena was certain you were dead, Tim. Now that you are returned and stand between her and her nefarious designs on this duchy, you can be damned sure that she'll not stick at one more murder."

Again, Tim showed his teeth. "Then the fat bitch had better do it within the next couple of hours, dear brother, for at the same time I left Morguhn Hall, so did gallopers from brother Bili. They bore archducal orders that the Kindred electors of Vawn-Sanderz arrive at this hall no later than the second hour after the nooning. Yes, the Ehleen sow would gleefully slay me, but would she dare do in most of the nobility of this duchy? I think not, for she'd have Bili down on her in a trice and her kinship with Prince Zenos would be of no help to her—and she knows this.

"No, brother, I'll be duke by this time tomorrow. You'll so notify Bili by farspeak and he, in turn, will inform Kehnooryos Atheenahs by the same method, while sending word to the prince via galloper.

"But, by Steel and Blood," his face looked as if he had bitten into a piece of rotten fruit, "to have a Myron for tanist sets my teeth edge to edge."

Ahl said, "There's no need to fret about that, Tim. Even if we're unable to eliminate the pervert in any other way, the mere mention by the chief-elect that he does or does not want a certain man as tanist or subchief will usually change the minds of the electors. The tanist need not be a member of the chief's immediate family, you know—that's only custom not law; the Couplets of Horseclans Law only insist that tanist, chief and subchiefs of a clan be of blood relationship. All the electors are our blood relations, Tim, and any one of them would be happy, honored and even flattered to be selected the new tanist."

Tim sighed in relief. "You know them better than do I, Ahl. Whom would you say is my best choice?"

With no hesitation, the sightless man answered, "Young *Vahrohneeskos* Tahm Adaimian of Lion Mountain."

Tim snorted and shook his head. "Young is right; he must be a good six or seven years my junior, Ahl. Besides, he's half barbarian, isn't he?"

Mairee frowned and Ahl snapped, "Ahrmehnee! Barbarian is a relative term, dear brother. To be cursed Ehleenee, everyone who is not a *kath-ahrohs* is a barbarian, to a greater or lesser degree—Kindred, Ahrmehnee, burkers, everybody. Tahm is kin and Kindred through the maternal line, and lest you forget, Tim, that is how Horseclans kinship is reckoned, not by the silly and imprecise manner of the northern barbar . . ." He stopped in midword and grinned sheepishly, then both couples joined in laughter. The laugher erased the tension which had been present from the moment of Ahl's and Mairee's entrance; the atmosphere in the wake of those gales of merriment was considerably more relaxed and familial.

Ahl's right arm hugged his younger brother's scarred and muscular shoulders fiercely. "It's good to have you back, Tim. So damned good. Even so, I think you and Gil were wise to cover your hides. This gives promise of being a full day of settling old scores, and anything could happen at any moment, now. The Ehleen sow has schemed and slain for nigh on twenty years and she'll not give up easily or soon."

While Tim pulled on smallclothes, Giliahna summoned Widahd, donned a loose gown and felt slippers, then began to select clothing items as the tiny brown maid gathered the numerous necessities for her lady's bath. Tim was stamping into his second boot by the time the two were ready to descend to the bath wing. He had just placed his baldric over his head when his sister came hurrying back, horror reflecting from her eyes.

"Tim. Come quickly. It's . . . your sergeant. In a chair by the outer door, and he's dead."

Chapter X

The young captain insisted that Giliahna continue on to the bath, but he also insisted that Ahl and Mairee accompany her, then he and the apprentice of Master Fahreed carried the chair and its lifeless contents around to the master physician's suite in the north wing. While the brown-skinned apprentice cleared a long table of books and writing materials, Tim held the cooling body cradled in his arms, unashamed tears of rage and sorrow streaming down his scarred cheeks.

The master was a tall, slender man, topping Tim's own height by a head. Where the skin of the apprentice was the soft brown of Tim's boots, the master's was so black that it looked bluish. His scalp was as clean-shaven as his face, and both bore sufficient scars to attest to the fact that Master Fahreed was no stranger to the practice of arms, physician or no. There was an aura of concern and thoroughgoing competence about the man, and Tim liked him on sight.

"Lord Tim," said the master, speaking Mehrikan of the Middle Kingdoms, but with a peculiar lilt and accent the like of which Tim had never heard in a Zahrtohgahn's speech. "If this poor man was your friend, perhaps you had best leave the room whilst I inquire into the cause of his demise. Some of the procedures I may find needful might seem to you a discourtesy to the body."

Tim shook his head curtly. "Thank you, Master Fahreed, but I'll stay. The deaths of friends are nothing new to me. As for Rai's body, he would have been the first to tell you that a corpse is dead meat and can no more be offended than can a side of beef. It is imperative that I know, and know quickly, how he was slain, however."

With a nod, the master strode over to a washstand and scrubbed his hands and tapering fingers vigorously with strong soap and a small brush in a bowl of steaming water,

69

then shrugged off his outer robe, replacing it with another of bleached linen.

Waving a hand at the contorted features of the dead sergeant, the master said, "We already can safely assume that we know the immediate cause of death, Lord Tim. And what is that, Raheen?"

"Poison, master," replied the shorter, lighter-skinned man, unhesitatingly. Then he leaned close and examined the bulging, glassy eyes and, after a moment, parted the lips and sniffed at the mouth. Straightening, he added, "Most likely, arrow poison, master, since none of the characteristic odors of poisons are in the mouth and the lips show no burns nor the teeth any discolorations."

Tim shook his head. "Arrow poison? There's no wound on Rai's body, Master Fahreed."

"That remains to be determined, Lord Tim," replied the master in his softly booming voice.

When the sergeant's boots and trousers of waxed linen canvas were removed a great stench suddenly filled the room—evidence that the contortions of the facial muscles had been matched by contortions in other parts of the body. The apprentice, Raheen, examined the dung intently before consigning it to a chamberpot, squeezed a measure of urine from the sodden smallclothes and studied this sample too.

But the master all at once stepped close to the body, lightly resting two spread fingers at either side of what looked to Tim like a small, roundish bruise high on the frontal quadrant of the right thigh. Striding over to the heap of fouled, smelly clothes, the tall man squatted and carefully scrutinized the upper right leg of the breeches. Grunting and nodding, he arose and said something in the guttural Zahrtohgahn language. The apprentice cleaned his hands, then opened a chest and brought a small case over to the table. When he had selected the instrument he wanted, the master beckoned Tim closer.

Holding a silver-rimmed glass lens a bit above the bruise, he said, "Lord Tim, here is your man's death wound. The hole of entry in the trousers is so minute that one who was not searching specifically for such would ever see it."

With a small-bladed knife, the physician neatly bisected the small wound at the center of the bruised area, slowly cutting deeper and deeper and gradually lengthening the incision that he might better see into the depth. Finally, he dropped the knife into a shallow bowl, wiped his hands on his white robe and, after removing the robe, went over to the washstand and began to scrub his hands again.

While scrubbing, he spoke. "Lord Tim, a long and very slender blade—probably of less thickness than a wheat-straw—was suddenly thrust deeply into the man's thigh. Whether by design or by mere chance, it struck into one of the bigger blood tubes. Like many arrow poisons, the immediate result was almost total paralysis, though the body continued to live long enough for a bruise to form at the point of entry. He likely was generally conscious and in considerable agony almost to the end—probably about a quarter hour after the wound was inflicted."

Tim growled low in his throat. It was an ugly, feral sound, and Giliahna felt the hairs rise on the nape of her neck and goose flesh on her arms, despite the steamy heat of the bath in which her body was immersed.

"But where," mused Ahl, "would the bitch and her witch get arrow poison? I know of no place in the Confederation it's used, and I believe the Sword Cult has outlawed it in all the Middle Kingdoms. Of course, some of the western barbarians . . ."

Master Fahreed shook his shiny head. "No, Lord Ahl, the mountain folk of whom you speak do not use actual poisons, they rather steep the points in fermenting dung. But poisons are not so difficult to obtain. Anyone with access to certain plants or their extracts can compound such vile substances, and mere outlawry never deters those who have no modicum of respect for law."

Tim voiced agreement. "Aye, Ahl, what the master says be true enough, at least in the north. Sword Council decrees only cover the conduct of warfare, open and declared warfare; many bravos and assassins use poisons, though the unlucky lout who's caught with any in his possession is accorded a long-drawn-out and excruciatingly painful public death as a salutary lesson; so too are those few merchants whose greed led them to stock and peddle poisons."

Master Fahreed frowned. "Which facts—though they do not really apply to our present issue—are why all my Zahrtohgahn medicines are shipped by sea and brought to me by special couriers, since many of them could easily be considered or used as poisons."

When she was certain she was alone, Neeka Mahree-mahdees thrust the lethal brass pin deep into the glowing coals of a small brazier and then placed a couple of fresh briquets of charcoal atop it. Leaning back in her chair, she smiled to herself. It had gone better, easier, more smoothly than she'd hoped.

Following her directions to the very letter—which was more than the fat, slovenly, unpredictable bitch of a mother had ever been able or willing to do!—little Behti had skipped along the upstairs hall, her budding breasts tightly bound down to make her appear younger than her eleven years. She had entered into conversation with the ill-bred northern barbarian and finally sat upon his lap. After a few more minutes of conversation, the child had plunged the pin deeply into the man's thigh, then jerked it out and ran swiftly to Neeka's chambers. The girl showed definite promise.

But the dam . . . Neeka frowned. Mehleena had always been difficult to manage, very erratic, but she was gradually growing worse. That business at table, for instance. She could easily have slain Myron; he was lucky that his mother's choice in foods did not require the use of a table knife, else his guts would have been around his ankles. Mehleena had never been completely sane, but she was becoming more and more irrational, and the fits were lasting longer and longer. Any little thing could now trigger outbursts of violent rage in the gross woman; her servants and her children were alert as wild deer around her, and not even her priest dared to gainsay her.

That priest! Neeka ground her teeth at the thought of almost any priest. Her husband had been a priest in the land of her birth—Kehnooryos Mahkedohnya, far to the north, more northerly even than the Black Kingdoms. She had been but a girl then, but she had been happy with him. Until the blackhearted bastard had renounced her and his marriage to her so that he might advance to offices wherein marriage was not allowed.

It had not been enough for Demetrios to renounce her and simply cast her out. He had sold her to the slaver captain of a coastal trading ship, who had raped or otherwise molested her body at least twice each day all the way down the length of the coast to Esmithpolis, one of the Karaleenos ports. There he and his officers had been jailed and his ship and cargo impounded for his ill-starred attempt to bribe a newly appointed inspector of imports. Since slavery was illegal in the lands of the Confederation, Neeka had been turned out upon the beach with the crew of the ship, glad that she at least was in a land wherein Ehleeneekos was spoken, even if that land was all of twelve hundred *kaiee* from her own.

But she quickly discovered that there were no convents and monasteries, here, as in her northern homeland, nor even any churches of the Ehleen faith. In the wake of a great, bloody rebellion led by priests and higher clergy a few years before her arrival, the practice of any form of the ancient faith of the Ehleenee had been forbidden by decree of the High Lords, all church properties had been confiscated to the Confederation, all senior members of the hierarchy had been put to death and all the lesser sorts had been granted the choice of similar deaths or banishment for life.

So, since there was no organized group from which a stranger Ehleen might receive charity, and since she then owned no trade, Neeka, to avoid starvation, began to offer the only commodity she had. But after less than a week, she was confronted by uniformed town guardsmen as she left a waterfront tavern one midnight. Announcing loudly that she was under arrest for unlicensed whoring, the six guardsmen bound Neeka's arms and dragged her off to the port fortress. When they had thoroughly searched her, with many a crude and lascivious jest, robbed her of her few, hard-earned coppers and single, silver *thrahkmeh* piece, they stripped her and took turns raping her. Their sport finished, they loosed her arms and threw her and her tattered clothing into a narrow cell built into the wall of the fortress.

Neeka was never certain just how long she remained in that cell. It was damp and cold—so cold that she almost came to welcome the guardsmen who swaggered in in twos and threes to make use of her body, for at least then she was a bit warmer for a while. There were vermin, of course—fleas, lice, roaches and centipedes—but only once did she see a rat—and that was to prove a red letter day.

The big, gray wharf rat, large as a cat, scurried out from a hole in the wall, long, scaly tail dragging behind him. Neeka shrieked shrilly and took a precarious stance atop the rim of the straw-filled stone trough that served her for a bed, but the rodent gave her not even a glance, rather making a mighty effort to leap onto the sill of the high, barred window, through which the morning sun streamed. But it was too high and the rat fell back onto the floor with a meaty plop.

Before the rat could gather himself to try again, another animal followed him out of the wall. Neeka had never before seen such a beast. Long of body it was, at least two cubits,

but of no more thickness than the terrified rat; the tail was
thick and slightly flattened and furred like the body, with a
close-lying, glossy brown pelt; the legs seemed short and stout
and the paws were webbed and furnished with the retractable
claws of a feline; the head appeared to be a blending of feline and mustelid traits—cat and weasel—with a mouthful of
glittering white teeth, damp shiny black nose and slit-pupiled,
moss-green eyes. The newcomer gave the terrified Neeka no
more attention than had the survival-minded rat, heading
directly for its quarry in a brown blur of swift motion.

The rat tried to fight for its life, but both fight and life
were over in an eyeblink of time. While the rodent's dying
limbs still jerked and twitched, the strange beast lapped up
every droplet of spilled blood, then tore into the carcass, de-
vouring the tenderer portions of it.

Weak from suffering, abuse and privation—the guardsmen
only fed her at odd hours and then only scraps, and she
would long since have died of thirst had it not been that she
had taken to licking the ice off the windowsill and walls every
morning—Neeka could not stand on the stone rim long, then
she had sunk back into the verminous straw, hugging the
thin, filthy blanket around herself with numb, chapped hands.

Done with its grisly repast, the brown beast dragged the
ravaged rat remains over to the corner of the cell, used the
one paw to raise the wooden lid of the privy hole enough to
push the carcass in, then lowered the lid again. That done, it
sank upon its haunches and, catlike, began to cleanse its face
with well-licked paws.

Seeing those moss-green eyes upon her, Neeka began to
tremble, and a moan of terror bubbled up from her throat.
Then . . . then it seemed that the beast *spoke* to her!

"Why do you fear *me*, sister? The rat might well have
harmed you, but not me. Two-legs are my sisters and brothers; wherever two-legs build their dens, always are there
plenty of fat rats for my kind to kill and eat."

"Oh, my dear God," mumbled Neeka to herself, "I've finally lost my reason! I thought, really believed that that animal spoke to me in Ehleeneekos!"

So shaken was she that she did not even try to move when
the brown beast moved fluidly to the stone trough, leaped
easily upon it and snuggled close beside her in the straw, its
cold, wet nose pressed against her temple through her dull,
matted hair.

After a few minutes, it seemed that the beast spoke to her

again, but this time she came to the realization that the communication was silent and was not truly in words; she was "hearing" its thoughts in her mind.

"You have been ill used, sister. I have seen all that has befallen you in your memories. But I cannot comprehend why you allow these shiny-chest two-legs to mount you when you are not in season and do not wish to be mounted."

Neeka began to sob, thinking her answers since she now realized it was not necessary to speak aloud to the beast. "If I did not submit, they would just hold me down or hurt me and maybe not feed me or even take my blanket and clothes and this straw; then I should freeze to death."

The beast snarled without conscious thought, but Neeka no longer feared her furry companion. "I would like to see the male try to mount *me* out of my season, sister! I assure you, he would be a feast for birds and little fishes in short order. But your poor teeth are dull and your claws almost nothing, and you have not one of the long, steel claws such as two-legs often carry. But I think I know one who will make the males here stop this mounting of you."

After a long while, Neeka heard voices in the corridor, men's voices. They were none of them speaking Ehleeneekos, and so she had no idea what they were saying, but the presence of more than one man in the corridor had always led to but one thing for her. She began to whimper in helpless hopelessness, for she had so wanted to believe that brown beast . . . or had she only imagined it all? Was it a hallucination bred entirely in her mind, that mind now crumbling and disordered through starvation, cold and long abuse? She felt then that it must have been illusion, for weasel-like cats—catlike weasels?—did not talk to people, silently or otherwise.

The voices neared. There were at least two, perhaps three, and one was raised and choppy in rage. Nearer to the door to her cell, there was the sound of a blow—flesh and bone upon flesh and bone—and a cry of pain. Then the bolts were pulled back to disclose two of the men who had so often come to use her. But this time there was no lust in their eyes, rather was there fear, and one man's face was rapidly swelling and discoloring.

A third man stood between them, bigger than either and more richly dressed. He spoke to her in that strange tongue. When she shook her head, he suddenly bespoke her as she thought the beast had done.

"Ratbane tells me you can mindspeak, woman. Is this true?"

"Mindspeak?" Neeka thought. "What is mindspeak?"

The big man grinned. "Just what you're now doing, Ehleen. Never mind telling me what these degenerate scum have been up to. Ratbane imparted most of it to me, and I can guess the sorry rest of the tale."

He snapped something aloud, and both of the guardsmen suddenly stood rigid and unmoving, their faces devoid of emotion, but fear still dwelling in their eyes. Then, speaking for her benefit in pure, southern Ehleeneekos, he ordered, "Report back to your barrack, *on the double*! Inform the senior sergeant that you're under arrest and that he is to send two men to replace you here. Inform him that the initial charge is flagrant insubordination and that more charges will be added to that one as I think of them. *Dismiss*!"

The two guardsmen almost fell over themselves in turning about to run off up the corridor.

The big man did not come into Neeka's cell; instead he held out a hand. "Come out here. I have no doubt you'd enjoy a hot bath, and I, for one, would like to see what you look like in something besides dirt and rags and that old blanket. No doubt you could make good use of some food and strong wine too, eh?"

Captain Djordj Muhkawlee was as good as his word. When Neeka at long last emerged from the sunken tub, there were thick towels waiting to dry her body and hair, an impressive array of small flasks containing scents and fragrant oils, plus a pile of assorted items of female attire—few of the items were in her size, but all of them were wrought of far costlier fabrics than ever she had worn. Upon the top of the heap was a slender hair fillet that looked to be of pure gold.

When she had clothed herself as well as she might, Neeka was escorted by a manservant to a spacious, brazier-warmed room wherein the captain stood beside a low dining table filled with plate on heaping plate of meats, fish, vegetables, cheeses, breads and wine. At mere sight of so much food, Neeka's eyes overflowed and she gasped great, ragged sobs. Gently, the officer folded her into his strong arms and cradled her too-thin body against his red velvet brigandine, all stitched and embroidered with gold and silver threads. He stood immobile, silently patting her heaving shoulders, his mind broadbeaming soothing thoughts, until she had cried it all out. Then he led her over and sat her upon a dining couch.

"Eat your fill, Neeka. But be sure to eat before you take much of the wine—it's quite strong. I must go now. I've some matters to attend, but I shall return as soon as I may."

In her small workroom at Vawn-Sanderz Hall, Neeka used a pair of long-handled pincers to withdraw the glowing brass pin from its fiery bed, then dropped it into a flat pan of water with a hiss and a small puff of steam. The heat had discolored the brass, but any trace of poison-paste or blood had burned off in the brazier. She poured a half-cup of watered wine from an ewer and sipped at it until the pin had cooled enough for her fingers to lift it out and dry it, then she placed it in a box of similar pins. Master Lokos had always stressed the value of neatness to a practitioner of any of the arcane arts.

She sat back and stared into her winecup, staring as well into the dim past. Dear, dear, sweet, old Lokos. If only . . .

Neeka had remained Djordj Muhkawlee's mistress for the year and a half he stayed in Esmithpolis, until his tour as fortress commander was completed and his replacement brought down his new posting orders from Goohm, General Headquarters of the Armies of the Confederation, along with notice of his promotion to *mehyahlehltehros*, or major, of heavy infantry. The new commander, Lieutenant First Grade Eenzeeos Rahbuhtz, also brought with him his young wife.

Three days before his scheduled departure for the western frontier and the veteran battalion he was to command, Djordj had set before her a lengthy document.

"Neeka, as you are aware, I am not a wealthy man. As you also know, I had been expecting a posting to the command of another coastal fortress, not to a command on the frontier. Therefore, I've had to scrape together every stray *thrahkmeh* and sell many of my personal effects in order to buy a set of decent plate and other essentials for campaigning in those hellish mountains.

"I told you I would provide for you and I have. Although I can leave you no money, I've arranged an apprenticeship for you with Master Lokos Prahseenos, the *fahrmuhkohpios*. This is an agreement of indenture; he agrees in it to provide you food, lodging and clothing and, in return for eight years of work for him, to train you and impart to you sufficient of

his knowledge in his craft to enable you to earn a living anywhere as a craftsman of his calling. His mark is already af-
fixed and properly witnessed—you need only sign below and
I will witness your own mark. It is an honorable craft,
Neeka, and one of the few that will accept women as apprentices or masters.

"Now, Lokos is an old man and sometimes crotchety,
Neeka, but he is universally recognized a true master-of-mas-
ters and those whom he has trained are in great demand from
Kuhmbuhluhnburk to Ehlehfuhntpolis. That alone, that artistry at his craft and value as a teacher, has kept him out of
the fortress prison on more than one occasion, for he is one
of the most rabid of the Ehleen radicals. But learn his skills,
Neeka; you need not also imbibe of his politics."

She had signed, for, as Djordj had pointed out, few honorable professions or crafts were open to mere women, and apprenticeship under so renowned a master was a priceless
opportunity. That night, he had had her one last time in his
tender, gentle way. In the morning, he had set her off into the
city with a guardsman to guide her to Master Lokos' shop-
residence, his manservant having delivered her clothing and
effects there earlier.

In her eighteen months with Djordj, he had taught her
many things—to read and write in both the principal languages of the Confederation, Ehleeneekos and Mehrikan (in
her homeland, Kehnooryos Mahkedohnya, well-bred girls
learned household skills and nothing more; most could not
write their own names); how to ride astride a horse. He was
a mindspeaker and had encouraged and helped her to de-
velop and train her own powerful, but latent, mindspeak abilities; he had also, from time to time and in a spirit of fun,
taught her the essentials of good close-in knifework and the
accurate casting of knives, darts and light throwing axes.

She and Djordj had often ridden their horses through the
city, so she had a fair general knowledge of the various sections and streets. And she and her "guide" had not walked a
half mile from the fortress when she realized that this route
could not possibly lead to the area where the well-to-do
craftsmen's shops were situated. When she spoke of this to
the man, however, he smiled and nodded agreement.

"The captain sez to take you, lady, but he don' say how we
gotta go. It's a long walk, it is, but I got this friend, y'see, as
has this ass cart an' goes that way ever mornin'. Iff'n he ain'
lef' yet, we can save our pore feet a bit."

The tale sounded plausible, so Neeka nodded assent and continued to follow the scale-shirted guardsman. As they passed the mouth of a narrow alley between two stone warehouses, the guardsman stumbled and half-fell. Neeka bent to give him a hand up and, as she straightened, a thick sack was dropped over her head. Despite her struggles and her muffled cries, several pairs of strong, ungentle hands bound the mouth of the sack tightly about her, pinioning her arms firmly against her body. An unseen man lifted her clear off the ground, and another bound her at knees and at ankles with scratchy rope. A thrill of burning agony shot up her arm as the tight-fitting silver ring—given to her by Djordj, at the midwinter Sun-birth Feast—was jerked off her finger and she screamed.

But screams gained her nothing, nor did demands or entreaties. Rough hands lifted her, bore her up the alleyway, the stone walls scraping her. Then she was unceremoniously dropped into a fishy-smelling cart and, with the snap-crack of a whip and a shout and the shrill protest of a grease-starved axle, the conveyance began to move. Over the cobbled streets, the springless vehicle provided a swaying, bumping, jolting and thoroughly uncomfortable ride. Each time Neeka tried to sit up, a horny hand slammed her back down onto the slimy boards. The last time, her head struck the wood with enough force to fill it with flashing light before a total blackness descended.

Chapter XI

Djoy Skriffen had been miscast by nature. Only her genitalia and her huge breasts imparted a hint of female appearance; otherwise her physique was masculine—broad shoulders and muscular arms ending in big square hands, narrow hips and once-flat buttocks. Her jaw was square and her chin prominent; prominent too was her nose, and when she allowed them to grow out, her eyebrows were bushy. Nonetheless, twenty years before, she had been a highly successful camp whore, following condottas and armies on the march and to the rear of siegelines, ready and willing and able to take on a dozen or more men in a night.

Then, during the great rout at the Field of Hats, as she leaned forward on the seat of the cart she had hurriedly stolen to lash the mules to a full gallop, a war dart near the end of its cast had penetrated her hipbone after tearing through the flesh of her right buttock. Due to its angle, she had been unable to get either hand in position to remove it and so had, perforce, ridden the jolting cart on away from the lost battle, screaming with agony.

Eventually, the cart lost a wheel and she was thrown from the seat, to roll down a steep bank. This stress caused the ill-tempered dart point to snap, leaving only the few millimeters of steel that were imbedded in her bone, while the shaft and the rest of the head were jerked out of her flesh. Fortunately, she was shortly found by a small condotta of Freefighters from the victorious forces of the Count of Keelzburk. The men knew Djoy of old, and seeing her grievously hurt, they halted, kindled a fire and doctored her on the spot, laying a red-hot spearblade to her lacerated, blood-spouting buttock.

Even after her burned wound was become only puckered, purplish scar tissue, Djoy found sitting on the seats of wagons or carts or sitting even the best-gaited mule pure torture, and such activities or even damp weather would cause her right hip to swell and to ache intolerably, so she knew that her days as a camp whore were numbered. She spent her last few months in her initial profession servicing the winter siege lines around beleaguered Balzburk and, when at last a general attack proved successful and the camps were almost deserted, she and a pack of carefully chosen noncombatant ruffians murdered the guards at the pavilion of the siege commander and made off with the army's pay chest and everything else valuable-looking and portable.

In the course of the long flight from Balzburk in the western mountains, across the widths of both the Kingdom of Pitzburk and the Kingdom of Harzburk, to the port city of New Filburk, on the seacoast, almost all of the ruffians had met with "accidents" and a large part of the loot had been frittered away. Even so, after she had paid for the murders of the last two of her original companions, Djoy still had enough gold to establish and set herself up as madam of a fine bordello, wherein she prospered for a number of years.

But then came the night when, in a drunken rage, she stabbed one of her silent partners—several dozen times. He was not the first man or woman she had slain in New Filburk, but he was not just some nobody of a seaman or whore who could be dumped into a convenient cesspit or weighted and dropped into the harbor. She packed a small trunk with the contents of her strongbox, her jewel chest and her victim's well-stuffed purse, a few items of clothing and a few personal possessions.

She bought passage on the first ship she found and, thus, came ashore in Esmithpolis, where she scouted about, greased the proper hands with gold and set herself up in another bordello. After twelve years of her experienced, ruthless operatio, Djoy Skriffen was more than prosperous and had run to fat, being almost as broad as a huckster's table, though there still were hard muscles, a harder heart and a cold, calculating mind lodged within the mounds of jiggling adipose tissue.

Neeka was not the first kidnapped girl she had bought, but most of her whores were in her house on a voluntary basis, originally at least, though they all soon found to their sorrow that getting in was much easier than was getting out—alive, at least. Djoy handled some of the inevitable discipline problems herself; most she left in the hands of her four resident goons, all former Freefighters and sadistic murderers, all with prices on their heads in the Middle Kingdoms. Recalcitrant "recruits" were given to the foursome for a day and night, sometimes for a weekend; few visible marks were ever left on their flesh, but subsequently a girl so treated would accept, would perform, any act a customer demanded, rather than chance being again turned over to Stoo, Neel, Djimi and Iktis.

On her way down to the lowest cellar to inspect the girl offered for sale by three city guardsmen, a servant reminded his mistress of the unfortunate incident of the previous night—a valued and regular customer had been bitten by a rat.

"Send a boy to the fortress," she snapped. "Tell them to send me a hungry fencat—maybe two, since we have no idea how many rats we have."

As Neeka's consciousness slowly returned, she thought at first that she was back in that horrible, freezing cell in the fortress wall, for she had been stripped of every shred of her clothing and she lay on a narrow cot set against a stone wall. Then, as things became a bit clearer, she could see differences. This cell was wider and she was lying on a true bed, not in a trough of straw. Two walls were of stone, but the other two, including that in which the door was set, were fabricated of wide, age-darkened boards; the board walls reached to within a couple of feet of the timber ceiling, fourteen feet up, from which hung a large brass oil lamp. The cell was comfortable—cool, but not cold. Aside from the bunk, there was a covered slop bucket, a box of hay balls, a stone jug and a clay cup.

She heard voices from somewhere beyond the door, but could not understand what they were saying. The language sounded much like Confederation Mehrikan, but also differed in many ways. Her first attempt to sit up resulted in a sick dizziness. But her mouth felt dry as sand and she was just mustering herself for another effort at reaching the water jug when the door was flung open, then shut and bolted behind a guardsman.

She was taken quickly, brutally. Then, while her ravisher lay still atop her, he said, "Likely you don't know me, bitch, but you will, oh, how you will. I'm Loo Fahlkop and it 'uz my own firs' cousin, Garee, was striped and sent off to fight in the friggin' mountins 'cause of you. Damn barbarian run a spear right through his dang belly 'cause of you.

"Well, I done fixted you good, now, bitch. You ain' no off'ser's piece no more. I done sol' your ass to ol' Djoy Skriffen, and ever payday I means to come back here and screw you silly. Now, turn your ass ovuh, I ain' done yet. I'm gon' plow your othuh hole."

He rolled off to stand beside the cot, one hand on her shoulder and the other on her hip, leering cruelly. Suddenly, Neeka spun on her buttocks, flexing her legs, then driving both her heels into the man's lower belly with all her force. The guardsman was slammed into the board wall so hard that there were crashes and thuds from the other side. Neeka sprang to her feet and leaped for the door—only to find it secured, immovable.

Neeka spun about. The man was staggering toward her, face red, eyes shining hate, lips twisted into a snarl. But her lover had taught her well. She ducked beneath the extended arms, arose on the outside. Grasping his hairy wrist, she slammed the heel of her other hand into the back of his elbow, *hard*. The guardsman screamed once and staggered backward. Neeka got one leg behind him and pushed. Good arm flailing wildly, he fell back onto the cot, half of him still on the floor.

The guardsman's canvas breeches had become but two separated legs, the center seam having parted. With all her weight behind it, Neeka slammed her small heel down on her rapist's genitals, then began working on his face with the nails of one hand while fending off his good arm with the other. She was still at it when his screams brought in three more people.

She was dragged off her erstwhile attacker and held as easily as if she had been a child by an immensely fat, immensely strong woman, who all the while laughed uproariously and made cutting jests at the expense of the crippled, battered guardsman. His face streaming blood, the half-nude man had to be literally carried out of the cell, groaning and sobbing.

When the men had gone, the big woman released Neeka and pushed her down to a seat on the edge of the cot. Wiping at her eyes with the backs of her big, blubbery hands, she chuckled a bit more, then addressed the girl in tolerable if thickly accented Ehleeneekos.

"What's your name, girl?"

"Neeka. Neeka Mahreemahdees. Is what that . . . that man-thing said true? Has he sold me to some brothel?"

The fat woman showed yellowed teeth in a broad grin.

"Not just some brothel, Neeka, the very best brothel this side of Kehnooryos Atheenahs. My brothel, mine, Djoy Skriffen's."

Neeka felt lost, then, helplessly sinking, but she spoke strongly. "Then you'd better get whatever you paid him back before he leaves . . . because I warn you, I'll *kill* the next man to lay hands on me!"

The fat woman chortled again. "I believe you would, Neeka, if what you done to ol' Loo is a example. 'Course, we have ways to gentle frac'shus fillies, in this house. But I like you, girl, you got spirit, more'n any other Ehleen girl I ever seed. You'n me'll talk some more in a day or two, whin it's safe to bring you upstairs. I think we can strike us a bargain."

Some hours later, she was brought a tray of food—freshbaked bread, roast pork, cabbage boiled with onions and caraway, a pint of wine—by an attractive, red-haired girl who looked to be some years older than Neeka. That same girl returned later for the tray and dishes, but also brought a low stool on which she perched.

"You're a *kath-ahrohs*, aren't you?" she asked.

"Yes," Neeka replied, "I'm pure Ehleen. Why?"

The ghost of a smile flickered briefly over the redhead's full lips. "I never heard tell of a Ehleen woman could mess up a grown man as bad as you did that guard bastid. He couldn' even walk when they took him away from here. They had to lug him in a cart. An' they think you done blinded one of his eyes, too. Lady Djoy like to died a-laughin' at him. She 'lowed what-all you done to him and her gettin' a chancet to see it was worth what she paid for you, by itself."

As her visitor was garrulous, Neeka just let her talk on, glad for the harmless company and anxious to learn all she could that she might plot her escape.

Hohp Leebos claimed to be twenty-two, but looked a bit older. She was three-quarters Ehleen. Both her parents were long dead and her husband, a fisherman, had been lost at sea only a few months after their marriage, leaving her almost destitute. Finally, near starvation and having exhausted the charity her late husband's former mates could afford, she had taken to the streets, whoring in the dockside taverns, as had Neeka, briefly. One night, having narrowly escaped being taken by the infamously brutal city guards, she had asked the advice of a friendly tavernkeeper, and so had made her way to Djoy Skriffen's house.

Honest, kind and merry in her quiet way, Hohp Leebos was now possessed of a large clientele of regular, faithful customers and was one of the very few of her whores whom Djoy Skriffen trusted to leave the house unescorted by one of her goons, or to serve food to secret purchases such as Neeka. And Neeka soon found out why.

Hohp shook her dark-red head and said, "Aw naw, Neeka, I couldn' do nothing like that. Lady Djoy, she'd jest skin me alive and, for all we's friends her and me, likely she'd hand me to them house guards of hern, an' I sure don' think I could tek that; them fo' treats women like animals."

Leaning forward, she patted Neeka's hand. "Listen, honey, Lady Djoy's gonna bring you up in a coupla days, soon's the fella you's the mistress of gits outa Esmithpolisport. Things 'll be a whole lot better, then, you'll see. 'Cause Lady Djoy, she really likes you, honey, likes your spunk an' likes the way you tore inta thet bastid guardsman. You jest do whatall she tells you to an' you gonna make out just fine. Most the customers is good men and with Lady Djoy bein' your friend an' all, like she's mine, you won' have to lay with any lessin' you likes 'em, an' too, Stoo an' the rest will halfway kill any bastid what tries to mark you up."

Neeka reiterated with cold intensity, "Hohp, I shall kill the next man who lays hands to me. Believe that, for I mean every word of it."

Hohp shook her head again. "Aw naw, honey, like I done tol' you, mosta the men is real fine fellas, Lady Djoy, she don' let no town trash or dock scum in here. O'course," she puckered her lips as if to spit, "them friggin' guardsmen is another breed of cat, they is."

Then her face brightened. "Come to speak of cats, honey, did you ever see a feucal kill a ol' wharfrat? I tell you, that's a pure pleasure to watch. Them cats moves like pure lightnin'. I 'uz watchin' one of them what come down from the fortress chase this here rat out'n the house an' kill im in the back courtyard whilst I 'uz a-waitin' for cook to make your tray up.

"Well," Hohp stood up and lifted the tray, "I better be a-gittin' back. We'll talk some more after you had your nex' meal, honey."

It had been long since she had mindspoken one of the tencats, and Neeka carefully framed her mental projection. Almost immediately, dear Ratbane was there.

"What are you doing in this unhealthful place, friend Neeka?"

"Oh, Ratbane, please, you must go back to the fortress and tell Djordj what has befallen me. Three guardsmen kidnapped me and have sold me to the evil woman who owns this house."

"The male two-leg called Djordj is no longer in Esmithpolisport. He and his man rode north as we fencats were coming here," replied the animal sadly, for she had been very fond of the young captain. "And the new chief of the fortress cannot mindspeak."

Neeka thought hard and frantically. "Then . . . then, Ratbane, do you know Master Lokos Prahseenos? I have signed a contract of apprentice-indenture with him. Surely he would deliver me from this place?"

"Friend-of-fencats Lokos?" beamed Ratbane. "His is the most powerful mindspeak in all of the *Thoheekahtohn* of Esmith. Yes, I shall go and find him."

Neeka caught Ratbane's instructions to the younger cat to continue exploring the house until she returned. Then the fencat's mind was gone, and Neeka could but lie and worry and wait.

Hohp Leebos brought her next meal—several small rolls, half a baked guinea hen swimming in a rich sauce, peas stewed with garlic and young carrots, a dish of pickled vegetables, a steaming pudding of breadcrumbs and dried fruits with spices and honey, a full half-*leetrah* of really good wine—the heavy tray was fitted with a baked-clay cover and Hohp indicated that the food was to last her needs until midmorning when the kitchen came to life. Despite her earlier promise, she did not linger this time; as soon as she had unfolded the stubby legs of the tray and disjointed the fowl with the knife from her girdle, she departed.

Aside from greetings and goodbyes, her only comments were, "Soon's you git upstairs, you'll be able to carve your own vittles, honey. Lady Djoy, she ain' the leas' bit a-feared you'll kill yours'f, thet bein' why we don' give othuh new gals enythin' sharp," the redhead chuckled. "Aw, naw, honey, she r'spects you; she's a-feared you might use it to carve up me 'r somebody 'n' try to git away."

Though she was not really hungry, Neeka forced herself to eat part of the well-prepared and tasty repast. It was a way to pass the time without worrying herself sick over whether or not Ratbane had been able to find and summon help. The wine was a fine vintage, and she was sorely tempted to seek the temporary solace of drunkenness, but she forced herself to dilute it with a large proportion of water from the jug.

She had barely finished and recovered the tray when she had a second visitor, Djoy Skriffen. Under one fat arm, the huge woman carried a bundle and, in the other hand, a silver decanter and a brace of tiny goblets. Behind the brothel keeper strode the most thoroughly evil-looking man Neeka had ever seen.

The male was tall, but small-boned and very slender, and the wide, padded, carven and inlaid chair he bore so effortlessly looked to be as heavy as he was. His beardless face was heavily pocked, crosshatched and misshapen with the puckered traces of old scars, and a pair of beady, ratlike, black eyes were separated by a great, hooked beak of a nose. The nose was dripping, and he wiped it from time to time on the shoulders of his shirt, breathing through open lips and the gaping void where his front teeth once had been.

Djoy set the bundle on the cot and the decanter on the stool and, after indicating where she wanted the chair, sank into it gratefully. The chair creaked alarmingly under her weight, but held. Noting that Neeka was trying vainly to cover her naked body from the gaze of the man, the big woman chuckled.

"Neeka, don't you worry about Iktis, here. That damn Loo Fahlkop come in here drunk last year and knocked out Iktis' last two front teeth. He was happier than I was when you tore into that bastid this morning. And sincet we got word you killed him, well, you can figger Iktis's your friend for life. Much as he likes hurting women, I doubt he'd do nothing to you, even if I told him to."

While talking, Djoy had unstoppered the decanter and filled the goblets, now she handed one to Neeka, tossed down her own and quickly refilled it.

"He . . . that guardsman is *dead?*" Neeka felt stunned, weak with the knowledge she had killed, though she endeavored not to show her real feelings, sensing that an appearance of tough callousness was all that would impress these evil people and retain their grudging respect for her.

Djoy chuckled again, echoed by the lounging Iktis. "Aye, he's dead, and good riddance, say I. Stoo brought word down from the fortress, about an hour ago. While that Zahtohgahn, Master Hahmeel, was getting the bastid's elbow back in the socket—you gonna have to show me how you done that, sometime, Neeka—Loo started puking up blood and in five minutes, he was dead. The fortress surgeon cut him open and said somma his innards was just split opened.

"This here little Ehleen cunt fixted Loo Fahlkop good, didn't she, Iktis?" Djoy poked at the thin man with an elbow.

Iktis' smile broadened enough to show that his jaw teeth were still in place. "Yeth, my lady. I but with I had been down here to thee it." Despite the lisping impediment of missing teeth, the slender man's Ehleeneekos was pure and unaccented.

"You take your post, Iktis," said Djoy. "I'll be out in a while, but I wants to talk to Neeka a little bit more."

With a nod, the man spun on his heel and departed, moving lightly and almost soundlessly.

Djoy waved a fat, beringed hand at the bundle. "They's some clothes and things there for you, Neeka. Nothing you could use for a weapon, of course." She grinned yellowly. "The Blue Lady knows, you're dangerous enough without one. I never done all this for no new girl afore this, but you is special. You got guts and you knows how to handle yourself, too. And on top of that, you a Ehleen.

"Neeka, I was borned a Kahlinzburker and I been a-whoring the mosta my life, all over the Middle Kingdoms with the Freefighters, and in my first house in New Filburk, and then here. I done never had me no trouble learning new languages, they comes natcherl to me, like. Like you can tell, I learned Ehleeneekos right off the bat and I talks it good."

Neeka had seldom heard the tongue of the Southern Ehleenee so misspoken, thickly-accented and generally butchered, but she wisely kept her thoughts to herself, simply smiling noncommittally.

Djoy poured herself another measure of the fiery brandy and went on. "But, Neeka, these here Ehleenee is a stiffnecked bunch of bastids. I gets along just fine with sailors and soldiers and Confederation folks, but mosta these here Ehleenee treats you like pure dirt lessen you is a Ehleen your own self, and I thinks some of these here rich Ehleenee what lives in Esmithpolisport would make me damn fine customers, if I just had a real Ehleen to deal with them.

"Now, yeah, I got me some Ehleen girls upstairs but none of the whining bitches what I can trust or would trust any further'n I can th'ow a warhorse. Ain't none of them got the frigging sand to even spit, much less maim a man or kill him, like you done. I had plans when I got Hohp, but she's too damn easygoing, she trusts dang near ever'body. But with you working the Ehleen trade, Neeka, I think I could really make something down here.

"And not just whorehouses, neither. I got gold, Neeka, lots and lots of gold, but the dang Ehleenee won't take none of it, for all they always crying, I hear tell, for folks to invest in all the big, money-making schemes they all got going. Now, you're a young girl and just as pretty as you can be. Anybody what sees you or hears you talk wouldn't have them no doubts but you're one of them *kath-ahrohs* Ehleenee. I thinks you just what I been a-looking and a-hoping for, for years."

Djoy heaved her vast bulk onto her big feet and the chair squealed its gratitude. "I'm leaving the resta the brandy here. Help yourself. You may need it to get some sleep, 'cause it gets kinda noisy upstairs some nights. But you can sleep tight and not worry 'bout no mens a-pestering you. This here's a corner of the winecellar and it's always a man a-guarding the door down from the main cellar. Iktis'll be there tonight, and he's the fastest, bestest man with a shortsword or a hanger I ever seed, and I seed a heap of fighters in my time.

"You think on whatall I told you, Neeka. You do right by me and you can be a rich woman afore long. You need anything tonight, you yell for Iktis."

Then she turned about and waddled out the door, closing it behind her but, Neeka quickly noticed, not bolting it.

Unfolding the bundle, Neeka found two undergowns of soft cotton, an overgown of bright-orange silk, a pair of gilded leather sandals, a hairband of beaten copper set with turquoise, a hairbrush, a horn comb and a handmirror of polished brass, all rolled in a quilted coverlet for the cot. She clothed herself immediately; the garments and sandals fitted as if they had been cut to her very measure.

Seating herself in the wide chair, she poured another thimbleful of the brandy and sipped at it thoughtfully. She had had no more contacts from Ratbane or any other fencat and was beginning to lose hope. Djordj had said that Master Lokos was an old man. Possibly such a man would be loath to take on so wealthy and ruthless a woman as Djoy Skriffen over a girl he had never even seen.

If escape was impossible, she must make do, make the best she could of a bad situation. She reflected that the fat woman's offer was tempting. Neeka was certain that she would be well treated as long as Djoy had a use for her, and as long as she did not openly defy her owner. If the guardsman she had attacked had truly died, in fact, she might be safer here than in Master Lokos' employ, for Djordj had been very harsh to those who had slain any of his men and she had no reason to believe that his successor would be less so.

A bare hint of sound from behind. She turned to see the sinister, ugly Iktis standing in the doorway. Laying a finger across his lips, he mindspoke powerfully.

"Say nothing aloud you don't wish overheard, child. That hole in the stone is not for ventilation. There are few mind-speakers here, and no one knows that I am one, save you. I should be at my post. I come only to reassure you that steps are being taken to free you from this foul place. But Djoy Skriffen is a rich woman, and powerful in some quarters. And, since she obtained you illegally, it is felt that your freedom must be sought through legal channels. Such is the feeling of the Council. It will be a test of the power of our *Klirohnohmeea.*"

Neeka wrinkled her brow in puzzlement. "*Heritage?*" That was the meaning of the word.

Iktis smiled toothlessly. "I forgot, you are from the Northern Ehleenee, child. Your lucky folk have not been ground into the dirt by presumptuous barbarians, as have we. The group that will succor you is properly called the Society for the Preservation of Our Ehleenee Heritage, but that is a mouthful, so most of us just call it Heritage. So you need not entertain any thought of cooperation with Our Lady Monster's devilish schemes."

"But . . ." Neeka beamed. "Did I truly slay that guards-man? If so, I'll surely be arrested, imprisoned if not hanged."

Iktis nodded forcefully. "Aye, he's dead, and he had long earned it, child. But do not fear punishment. At the behest of certain Heritage people, his accomplices in this morning's in-famy are even now being put to the severe question, so the new commander will know that your attack on Loo Fahlkop was nothing less than self-defense. Besides, the judge who will hear the case is on our Council." He grinned again at her stunned look, adding, "We Ehleenee must look out for each other, child."

Accustomed to a soldier's bed and daily routine, Neeka woke before dawn, finished what food remained on the tray and drank some of the wine. Then, having too little water left to make even the skimpiest effort to wash, she dressed. It was well that she did for, almost the moment she had finished, she heard voices, then Iktis was at the door.

Coldly, he snapped, "Come on upstairs with me, girl. Lady Djoy wants you." Silently, he mindspoke, "Our people have come for you, child. Judge Gahbros himself came. *Komees* Pehtros Gahleenahnos of Esmith, the city governor, is with him. And Master Lokos, of course. Djoy Skriffen's fat knees are rattling like dice in a cup, and the whale is white as curds."

Neeka was ushered into a huge and garish parlor. Djoy, disheveled and puffy-eyed, sat in another of those padded, carven, overly wide chairs; the fat woman's hands were tightly clasped in her broad lap, so tightly that the knuckles stood out prominently. And Iktis had been right, she did look pale, pale and ill.

Confronting the madam were three men. The most striking of them was a tall, stately, fine-featured old man, white-haired and richly but conservatively dressed. He was not armed; only a purse and a small, flat wallet rode at his belt, but in one manicured hand he held an ivory *lahbrees* set in a fluted golden shaft—the double axe of his office. His black eyes looked hard and cold and his face was set in grim lines.

The second man was not so richly dressed, though clearly as old as if not older than the jurist. He was almost bald; only a few skimpy strands of white adorned the top of his scarred scalp and but a bare fringe circled round the back of his head from temple to temple. His nose was as large as was Iktis' and, brooding over his thinner face, resembled the beak of a bird of prey. In addition to his purse and wallet, he had a sheaf of papers thrust under his belt.

The third man was much younger, no more than thirty, and was dressed for riding the hunt—suede-topped jackboots, leather breeches, canvas shirt and flat, velvet cap, with heavy hanger, dirk and sling at his belt. There was a dent across his high, scarred forehead—Djordj had had an identical mark and so Neeka knew that, since it was caused by long and regular wearing of a helm, the man must be or have been a soldier.

He turned his sloe-black eyes on her and smiled. "Very observant, little cheese," he mindspoke. "In fact, Djordj Muhkawlee was once an ensign in my company of infantry. It was through me that your apprenticeship-indenture was arranged.

"But enough for now. The judge will ask you questions. Answer them fully and truthfully."

The tall man beckoned her forward and she halted before him, near the arm of Djoy's chair.

"What is your name, my child?" he demanded. "And your age."

"Neeka Mahreemahdees, sir," she said softly. "I am seventeen."

The other old man handed his sheaf of papers to the jurist, who unfolded and briefly scanned them, then he asked, "Did you sign an indenture contract of apprenticeship to Master Lokos Prahseenos of this city?"

"Yes sir."

"Then what are you doing in this pesthole? Why are you not laboring honestly in your employer's shop?" His tone was stern and reproving.

Neeka was stunned. Did the old man think that she was here by choice?

The mindspeak of the hunter reassured her. "The questions are mere form, Neeka. Judge Gahbros knows most of the truth already. But the form of an inquiry must be observed, he feels. To simply march in here with a dozen spearlevymen or mercenaries, as I wanted to do when first I learned of this sorry business, and free you by main force would have been effective and personally satisfying, since I hate this sow and all she represents; but such a course would have been barely legal and detrimental to the aims of our group."

Neeka recounted the tale of her abduction and told of awakening, nude, in a cellar cell, adding that a guardsman had told her that he had sold her to Djoy Skriffen for a whore.

The tall man nodded once, curtly. "Very well. It is my judgment that you, Neeka Mahreemahdees, indentured apprentice of Master Lokos Prahseenos of Esmithpolisport, were delivered against your will and choice to the woman Djoy Skriffen. I hereby order you to return to your lawful employer, to whose service you have admitted contracting yourself."

He turned to the other old man, handed him back the papers, and said, "She is now yours, Master Lokos."

At this, Djoy broke her long silence, speaking out in her fractured Ehleeneekos, "Now just a dang minit, Jedge Gahbros. I'm out a hunderd silver *thrahkmehs* for her, not to mention what them clothes she's wearing costed. It ain' right I be robbed thisaway."

The hunter growled audibly and grasped the hilt of his hanger, but the tall jurist waved him to keep his place.

Glowering at the fat woman, Gahbros snapped, "Mistress, you were well advised to hold your piece. I have a statement here that you *bought a free woman.* That statement is witnessed by the *Komees* Pehtros and by a respected craftsman, Master Lokos. Now, before those witnesses, *you* have just admitted to that crime.

"Mistress, do you know the penalties for buying or selling free men and women within this Confederation? The very minimum sentence you might expect on such charges would be ten years of hard labor—in the mines, perhaps, or building fortresses in the mountains on the frontier—plus forfeiture of all lands and possessions. If you are guilty, as I suspect, of more than one purchase of free women, then the sentence would be death by impalement . . . on a short, thick stake, at that."

Djoy shuddered, her gross rolls of flesh rippling with the involuntary movement. She was unable to wrest her eyes from the piercing black ones of the grave, old judge, but it was not those eyes her mind saw. She had seen impalements before. The long stake—sometimes of a tough hardwood, sometimes of iron, dully pointed, five or six feet long and usually about two inches wide below the point—was a gruesome death, with the point jammed forcefully into the rectum and the body's own weight pulling it down the tapering, blood-slimy shaft until the point burst the screaming victim's heart; sometimes the point missed the heart and the suffering wretch choked to death on the blood gushing up from torn lungs.

The more bloodthirsty Middle Kingdoms burklords occasionally used the long stake to execute rebellious peasants or bandits. But the short stake was reserved for only the most heinous of crimes—high treason or crimes against the Sword Council. Short stakes were invariably of wood and were made to order, no higher than the victim's navel, and the point was rounded and sanded smooth so as to slowly rend and tear rather than quickly pierce guts and organs; from the usual two inches below the tip, short stakes tapered to six inches or more at ground level. Sometimes the victim's wrists were chained to a ring about his neck or waist, his legs wrenched apart and he was jammed down onto the stake. Djoy had seen strong men live for an hour or more in shrieking torment, first on their tiptoes, then on their heels, before agony and loss of blood made them too weak to stand, and even then, immediate death and surcease from pain were not certain, for the falling body might tip backward and the point of the stake tear up through the belly and out below the ribs.

At a brief hearing a few days later, Neeka was officially declared blameless in the death of Guardsman Loo Fahlkop, since the deceased had kidnapped her, robbed her and injured her and was attempting to ravish her when his fatal injuries were sustained. Her Ehleen attorney immediately demanded return of her silver ring, the value of her clothing and the sum of five hundred silver *thrahkmehee* as suffering-price, the last to be collected from the estate of the dead guardsman and from his two living accomplices.

"That will be, counselor, from *two* estates and one living guardsman," remarked Judge Gahbros, dryly. "Guards Corporal Lyl Ahnyel showed the discourtesy of dying while being . . . ahhh, *questioned* about his part in the incident. But this court feels that it is unreasonable to expect that all the worldly possessions of any six guardsmen, much less a mere three, would total a value of five hundred *thrahkmehee*. So let us be realistic and set suffering-price at half that figure, eh?"

Eventually, Neeka received one hundred and eighty-seven *thrahkmehee* and her silver ring.

At her worktable, Neeka chose a stone mortar and began to compound an herbal decoction to relieve the cramps and usual discomforts of Treena Sanderz's moon-sickness. Since she habitually kept her equipment and ingredients in meticulous order, she moved quickly and surely.

"Order," dear Lokos had told her so many times. "Order and neatness are the elements of success in our craft, and they are the salvation of those sufferers for whom we labor."

She recalled how the quick, spry old man would take a pinch of crushed, dried herbs between thumb and forefinger of each hand and extend them for inspection by a new apprentice, prospective client or casual visitor. "Observe, two pinches of herbs. They appear identical, eh? If you steep this pinch in a brandy-cup measure of boiling water until the water colors, then strain it, stir in a dollop of honey and drink it down, it will cure your headache. Yet do the same thing with this other pinch . . . and you'll be dead in an hour!"

"*How?*" She put her weight on the pestle and ground

viciously. "How did I, carefully and so patiently trained by Lokos to heal the sick and ease the sufferings of the hurt, get myself into this nasty business of killing old men with slow poison and young ones with quick poison?"

Her line of thought was interrupted by a forceful knock upon her door. Since her present task was in no way dishonorable to her mind or harmful to anyone, she said loudly, "*Ehrkohmai.*" Then she completed her compounding before she turned.

Expecting her visitor to be the *Thoheekeesa* Mehleena, a servant or, perhaps, Lady Treena in a hurry for her medicine as she was in a hurry for most things, Neeka was taken aback to see the richly robed Zahrtohgahn physician, Master Fahreed, standing just inside the closed door. From his dark fingers dangled a slender golden chain, from which depended a lovely crystal prism. The prism caught the light, threw off shafts of it. Neeka thought it the most beautiful thing she ever had seen . . . and she could not seem to take her eyes from off it.

She did not see any movement of those night-dark fingers, but suddenly the prism was moving, spinning, spinning, faster, faster, and her eyes could only follow the spinning light. And she was so tired, so very tired and sleepy. Her eyelids weighed so heavily, so heavily . . .

Chapter XII

Ahrkeethoheeks Sir Bili Morguhn of Morguhn strode out of the main entry of Morguhn New Hall; his three-quarter plate clashed and clanked as he descended the broad steps to the stone-paved courtyard. Softly nickering a greeting, the black warhorse, Mahvros IV, paced to greet his brother, Bili. After patting the big horse's mailed cheek, the old nobleman buckled his cased axe in its place on the off withers, then came back to the near side and mounted.

To flourishing trumpets, Sir Bili led his two-score Freefighter dragoons down the hill toward the ford and the road to Vawn. At the foot of the hill, two noble officers joined the head of the column and another standard bearer—this one bearing a sky-blue standard on which was embroidered, in white and gold, the White Hawk of Vawn-Sanderz took his place beside him who bore the famous Red Eagle of Morguhn. Behind the Morguhn Freefighters, one hundred Ruby Company lancers joined the column, their long, deep-red pennons fluttering on a stiff breeze, the steel points of the polished ash shafts glittering in the sun.

From atop the gatehouse tower, Djef Morguhn watched the departing column until the dust and the rolling landscape had swallowed them up. Then he turned his attention to the camp at the base of the hill, now a howling chaos as the remainder of the Ruby Company struck tents, loaded wagons, hitched teams and otherwise prepared to set out on the trail leading to Vawn.

"Dammit!" he growled to himself as he turned and started down the steps to the wall walk. "I miss all the fun. Papa goes off to chop Ehleen rebels and I have to stay here and command the hall garrison. What the hell does he think his castellan is for?"

Neeka had never been happier than during the brief—too brief—years of her apprenticeship under Master Lokos. Once arrived at his home/shop and shown the small room wherein lay her trunk, she quickly changed into her own clothing, bundled up the expensive, gaudy outfit in which she had left the bordello and asked leave to return the garments to their rightful owner, but Master Lokos discouraged this, saying that, as Djoy Skriffen was known to be a grudge holder, it were best that Neeka never again place herself anywhere near the evil woman's grasp. He sent a servant boy, instead.

About a week later, ugly Iktis strolled into the shop. Master Lokos greeted the known pimp and professional ruffian coldly for the benefit of the two other apprentices and the non-Ehleen customers. He invented an errand to take Neeka through the back storerooms and into the living quarters; shortly, he and Iktis joined her.

When Iktis was seated and sipping at honeyed wine, the master inquired, "What of the barbarian dunghill, does she know you are here? You take far too many chances, friend Ahkiles. You'd be of no use to us dead, you know."

The pocky man smiled toothlessly. "You're as apprehensive as ever, old man. All my life has been the taking of one risk after another; that's the life of a warrior . . . or a conspirator. But your fears are wasted this time. Herself sent me here."

"Really? Why, pray tell?" snapped Lokos. "Are you to be her scout? Is she planning a second abduction from under my very roof? If so, she'd better have more than four bravos."

Iktis waved a hand placatingly. "No, no, Lokos, nothing like that. Djoy Skriffen is cold, cunning and a plethora of other adjectives as well, most of them highly uncomplimentary, but she's too shrewd to butt against stone walls, she recognizes and accepts this defeat.

"No, I was to buy a quarter-*leetrah* of Blue Water for the bitch's chronic biliousness and then find a chance to tell Neeka that herself holds no ill will against her. Of course, she has no idea how news of the kidnapping really was disseminated. She's come to the conclusion that Fahlkop's accomplices broke under torture."

"And so that precious pair did," Lokos shrugged, "but we already knew most of what they said."

Iktis nodded and went on. "Anyhow, Lady Whale wishes Neeka to know that, whenever she tires of you and this kind of work, she will find a warm welcome at the whorehouse."

Neeka's mother, father and siblings had been swept off in one of the fevers which ravaged most cities every hot summer, and she had been reared by relatives who had lavished precious little love or affection on her and, with daughters of their own to provide for, had married her off to the first man willing to accept a minuscule dowry. In the house of Master Lokos, she had her first taste of true, familial affection, for the master and his plump, jolly wife customarily treated apprentices like the sons and daughters they had never had.

Many craft masters used their apprentices for servants and household drudges, but Lokos was a wealthy man, employed a large retinue of servants and saw to it that every minute his apprentices were not eating, sleeping or devoting to duties in shop, workrooms or garden, they were reading his extensive collection of works on pharmacology, human and animal physiology, differing theories respecting the treatment of wounds, injuries and illnesses, horticulture of herbs and a vast array of other interrelated subjects. Some of the better books had been written by Master Lokos himself.

There were four apprentices, all male, when Neeka first arrived. Kohmos, the eldest, was really a journeyman in all but name as he had less than two months until the end of his contract. Djahn, though but a year older than Neeka, was already into the sixth year of his apprenticeship. Zindaros, at fourteen, and Shaidos, at thirteen, were both still in their first year.

The male apprentices had their quarters in a small attic dormitory, but Neeka's room was close by the master's suite. The only other resident on the same level was a man who filled two highly exacting niches in the household—majordomo and head cook—and who called himself Koominon. Neeka had quickly noted that the master treated this mere upper servant as an equal, as he did the outwardly disreputable pimp, Iktis.

It was not until many months later that she came to know the reasons for these and many other discrepancies in the behavior of Lokos, for the master was wisely very closemouthed with any save sworn members of the Heritage Society—*ee Klirohnohmeea*.

Djordj had advised Neeka not to get involved in Lokos' known radical political activities, but the girl had no choice. Her master, assuming that since the Society had helped her she would welcome a membership, informed her long after the fact that he had sponsored her for and she had finally been accepted in the Society for the Preservation of Our Ehleen Heritage.

"After all, child, you are a *kath-ahrohs*—which may not mean much in Kehnooryos Mahkedohnya where most folk are, but means very much here, where increasingly few are not to some extent mongrelized with the so-called Kindred and other strains of barbarian. Of the over eight thousand souls listed as permanent residents of Esmithpolisport, only some fourscore are *kath-ahrohs*, Neeka. I am not, God help me, nor is my dear wife. Indeed, no one in this house is save only you and Koominon."

"Is Koominon a member?" asked Neeka.

Lokos had smiled and nodded. "Koominon is one of the founders of our chapter in this *thoheeksahtohn,* and a life member of the advising Council. The poor man has suffered more, and even more unjustly, than have you under the barbarians, Neeka. He has been cruelly bereft of hereditary lands and position, family and . . . and more."

Lokos and Koominon led the way to Neeka's first meeting of *ee Klirohnohmeea* through a disreputable district of shanties and hovels to a large building of weathered gray granite. Portions of the walls had evidently been knocked down long ago and had been rebuilt in cheap brick. Entrance was effected through a tiny door set into a pair of larger doors. Within, Lokos lit a small lamp he carried and Neeka saw that the building—whatever the purpose for which it may have been built—was now a warehouse.

The first three columns supporting the high, vaulted, soot-encrusted ceiling were roughly fashioned of brick, but the next two, despite the dim, flaring light of the lamp and layer on layer of dirt, could be seen to be of fine, red-veined marble. And the floor beneath their feet, in those places where shifting of heavy cases had scaped away the filth of ages, was of a delicate gray-green stone.

At her questioning look, Lokos spoke. "When the barbarians conquered this city, over two hundred years ago, this was a palace, the seat of the hereditary lords of the city, lands and port. Lord Graikos Pahpahthohpoolos fought the barbarian hordes street by bloody street after the city walls were breached, and he and his brave men made their last stand here. So fiercely did they fight that the barbarians finally brought up siege engines to knock down the walls. The palace, when at long last conquered, all its defenders massacred, was too damaged for habitation, and it sat vacant, tenanted only by ghosts and vermin, for many years; then, as the usurper Esmiths had improved the harbor and trade increased, rough repairs were effected and this noble edifice was converted to a warehouse."

After that, Neeka was very glad that Lokos walked before her and Koominon behind, for it seemed that each patch of darkness, each shadow cast by the lamp was a skull-faced warrior in antique armor, skeletal hand gripping rusty sword or rotted spearshaft. Under her breath, she breathed half-forgotten prayers to Christ, to His Holy Mother and to every other saint she could remember, temporarily forgetting that identical prayers for deliverance had availed her nothing those endless days and nights in that horrible cell in the fortress walls.

Down a flight of worn, stone steps lay a cellar, also stacked with bales and crates, but then what looked to be but a stretch of blank wall pivoted at the touch of Koominon's hand and swung shut behind them as silently as it had opened. They went a few paces along a narrow corridor, down another, steeper flight of stairs, these set at a right angle to the corridor, then along a wider passage to a bivalve door of verdigris-covered bronze. Koominon drew a dirk from beneath his cloak and tapped sharply with its steel ball-pommel on the green-crusted door in a distinct pattern of raps and pauses.

"Open your mind, child," Lokos mindspoke Neeka. "Lower your shield that they may be sure who and how many we are."

Neeka did so and, shortly, one of the high, broad doors swung back. Lokos led the way into another corridor, this one with a down-sloping floor and a clean tang of the sea about it. The ramp curved gradually to the left and, at the foot of it, was another bivalve bronze door. Both halves of the door swung open before them, flooding the sloping corridor with warmth and light from the torches, lamps and braziers within a large, oval chamber.

Out from a knot of soberly garbed men and a few women strode *Komees* Petros. Taking both of Neeka's small, cold hands in his large, warm ones, he bent stiffly from the waist and kissed the right one, but retained his hold when he stepped back, straightening.

"Neeka, until we investigated, none of us were aware that you were of noble birth, that your late father was an *ahstoonohmos*." He half turned to the group and added, "We have no such title here, not any longer, but we did in ancient times; *ahstoonohmos* is a hereditary office and its holder is the deputy to the lord of a city or a district, being roughly the equivalent of our *vahrohneeskos,* though an *ahstoonoh-mos* is salaried and does not actually hold land, as does a *vahrohneeskos.* This poor child's entire family died in an epidemic of summer fever. Her care and her dead father's office were both then assumed by his younger brother, her uncle; he gave her in marriage to a lowborn curdog of a priest, who then sold her to a ship captain and put about the word that she had deserted him."

The nobleman went on, giving a brief account of Neeka's nearly two years in Esmithpolisport. He was an accomplished raconteur. Consequently, there were few dry eyes amongst the throng when he was done.

Koominon had disappeared during the monologue. When he reappeared, he was cloaked in the vestments of a priest of the Old Ehleen Rite and all those present repaired to a canvas-enclosed section of the room for the religious service which always opened a full meeting of the membership. Then, while some members were preparing precooked food and others were laying boards on trestles and bringing chairs and stools from the enclosed area, a woman and three men—*Komees* Pehtros, among them—took Neeka aside and began teaching her the complicated hand grasps and signals, the childish-sounding passwords and the significance of the oaths she soon must swear.

The oaths were sworn before dinner. They were designed to be solemn and awe-inspiring to those who were deeply religious, but the nobility of the north could take religion or leave it alone, generally the latter, and Neeka's firsthand knowledge of the frankly mercenary philosophies of the Church and churchmen, gained from her brief marriage, had rendered her deeply irreligious. So, though she behaved as she assumed she was expected to behave, she actually found the oath-taking ceremony as childishly silly as the secret signs and words.

At dinner she was seated beside the woman who had earlier shared in her instruction, Lady Rohza Ahnthro-poheethees, widow of a former shipping magnate, scioness of a house of the petty nobility and a distant relative of the one-time ruling house of Karaleenos when still it had been an independent kingdom. As big and as powerful looking as Djoy Skriffen—with broad shoulders, slender hips, flat thighs

and buttocks, very small breasts and a set of craggy features—Rohza affected masculine garb, right down to jackboots, hanger and dirk. She spoke loudly and often, shouting
down the length of the table in her deep contralto, frequently
slapping her thigh as she guffawed at her own and at others'
witticisms.

There was something about the middle-aged woman that
put Neeka's little white teeth edge to edge; not even the evil
virtually oozing from Djoy Skriffen's very pores had so af-
flicted her. It was not that the brawny Rohza was cool or
unkind to Neeka; indeed, the very reverse was the case—her
attendance was so warm and constant that she seemed to
Neeka more like a courting swain than a dinner companion.
With almost every word she spoke to the girl, the woman's
big hands were placed lingeringly on shoulder or knee, neck
or arm. Such uncomforting familiarity prevented Neeka from
truly enjoying her dinner, and, at future dinners, she saw to it
that she had other dinner companions.

Though she was, of course, not privy to the meetings or
decisions of the Heritage Council, Neeka could see nothing of
a practical, political nature that was accomplished by *ee
Klirohnohmeea.* It seemed little more than one of those secret
fraternal organizations with which noble Ehleen society
abounded in the north, in Kehnooryos Mahkedohnya, save
only for the religious aspect which the northerners lacked and
which, she shrewdly guessed, was a part of this group's
format only because it was forbidden by law.

True, at almost every meeting of the full membership, certain hotheads loudly prated daydreams of armed uprisings
against the hated Confederation, but a dream that sort of talk
assuredly was, for very few of the members had had any sort
of war training, and if the Heritage had any popular support
in Esmithpolisport, Neeka was never able to discern it. A
conversation one day with *Komees* Pehtros confirmed her
suspicions.

"Engaging together in an illegal act tends to bind the membership more tightly together, Neeka. But were it entirely up
to me, I'd do away with anything pertaining to the Old Faith,
for I was a young ensign in the Nineteenth Infantry Regiment during the Great Rebellion and I personally witnessed
the perverse extremes to which religious fanaticism can go.
Faced with such, I can see why High Lord Milo had no
choice but to proscribe the Ehleen Church and all its clergy.
Indeed, child, I would have done the same in his place. Cru-

cifixion, burning, even impalement was really too good for many of the black-robed animals."

"Even Koominon?" asked Neeka.

He shook his head. "Father Ahreestos, who calls himself Koominon, is truly a devout, good and humble man. That he, who never subscribed to the perversities which condemned his faith, was tarred with the same brushstroke is a tragedy. That he insisted on remaining in direst peril here is even more of a tragedy, for he could go far, could contribute much, were he to enship for a place wherein the Faith still is legal— Kehnooryos Mahkedohnya or Greeah Ehlahs. Here, he is living on borrowed time and, soon or late, will suffer a long, agonizing, messy death. And *ee Klirohnohmeea* will be in a large part responsible, for did he not have a congregation, he might depart for more salubrious climes."

"Then . . . then you must tell Master Lokos this," insisted Neeka. "Tell him quickly, for he is Koominon's friend. He will persuade him to leave."

Again the *komees* shook his head. "No, Neeka, Lokos will not. Lokos is a good man, a kind man, and completely lucid in most matters, but in affairs of *ee Klirohnohmeea*, he is a deranged fanatic." Seeing her horrified expression at hearing her master so maligned, he added, "Oh, it's not entirely his fault, Neeka. The tortures and mutilation to which he was subjected for his very small and inconsequential role in the Great Rebellion, and the sufferings and privations of his long imprisonment, addled him a bit, as they would have addled any man."

"Mutilation?" Neeka queried, puzzledly, for Lokos had a normal complement of fingers, toes, and ears; his face was scarred and his scalp, but so were those of most adult males, and she had naturally assumed that those scars and a limp noticeable in damp weather resulted from youthful warring or dueling.

The *komees's* lips firmed into a grim line. "Have you never wondered why a man who loves children and young people as much as Lokos never sired any of his own, Neeka? The reason is that he cannot. After they had flogged him until the white bone shone through the bloody tatters of flesh from his neck to his buttocks, they gelded him. That he survived such treatment at all is a miracle."

Wholly dedicated to never again being dependent upon anyone for her sustenance, Neeka applied every bit of her not inconsiderable intellect and her youthful vigor to her new craft. Within only three years' time, Master Lokos confessed in mingled pride and consternation that she had absorbed as much as or more than any other apprentice had done in twice the time. Thereafter, Neeka did much of the workaday compounding and distilling, leaving the master free to attend customers, instruct other apprentices and do the research and experiments which were his passion.

When she had read every book in his library written in either of the two languages she had mastered—Ehleeneekos and the various regional dialects of Mehrikan—Lokos taught her to read the flowing, cursive script called Ahrapsahbos, in which most modern medical texts were written by the justly famous Zahrtohgahn physicians.

Therefore, Neeka knew immediately just what the prism dangling from those black fingers was and just what it was for. Summoning the last ounce of will, she fought back up, back out of the beautiful, sleepy world into which the scintillating prism and the soft, soothing words of the skilled man had drawn her.

"Sahlahmoo ahlaik," said Neeka, when she was certain she had regained her self-control. *"Ahlahn wah sahlahn."* When he made no reply to the greeting, she added, *"Fehemtinee?"*

Master Fahreed consciously lowered his eyebrows, unconsciously raised in surprise at hearing the Zahrtohgahn language spoken by this strange, sinister woman. Not many unbelievers expended the effort to learn the difficult, guttural tongue, which was why Zahrtohgahn physicians must, in addition to being accomplished mindspeakers, learn so many languages and dialects, since the Great Council of Masters might send a given physician and his apprentice to any one of a far-flung range of posts.

Big, white teeth glittered as he smiled. *"Ywah, fehemt."* Then he switched to fluent Ehleeneekos. "But if we wish to continue to understand each other, it were perhaps better we speak this tongue or Mehrikan, for," he smiled again, "noble as is your effort, your accent is atrocious."

Neeka shrugged and leaned back against the table. "That is not surprising to me, master. I have spoken your language but little, and that was years ago with one who possibly did not speak it well himself; but I have no difficulty in the reading or the writing of it."

She waved at the prism. "A *Mookahdir,* is it not? I have, of course, read the treatises of the Illustrious Master

Wahdjeed al-Ahkisahee on the production and use of the *Mookahdir*, but this is the first one I have ever actually seen. You were attempting to send me a-journeying, were you not? May I ask why?"

Fahreed spoke bluntly, as was his wont. "I am sworn to exert my efforts toward the preservation of health and life. I was but attempting to make your death unnecessary." He sighed. "It is certainly but the Will of Ahlah, that I should fail."

"My death? What do you mean?" Neeka demanded a little louder than she meant to, feeling a cold prickling coursing the length of her spine.

"The rightful lord of this place, Sir Tim, feels you to be responsible for the senseless poisoning of his friend, Rai, the sergeant. He is a man of action, not subtlety, and he would likely have run his broadsword through your body by now, had I not promised to neutralize the threat you present to him and to his lawful accession by other, less sanguineous, means. But now . . ." He sighed once more and drew from within his robes a small dagger with a thin, tapering, four-inch, double-edged blade of light-blue Zahrtohgahn steel.

Neeka saw certain death in the black man's quick, sure movements, and she felt apprehension but, oddly, no fear. She thought briefly of those instruments on the table behind her that might be utilized as a weapon, then mentally dismissed them all, for the physician was a tall man and no doubt strong and agile. The rigorous pre-apprentice training administered in the Emirate of Zahrtohgah eliminated those applicants weak or clumsy of body or slow of wit.

In a friendly, conversational tone, she asked, "I thought you were sworn to preserve life and health, master? How can you justify my murder with that oath?" While speaking, Neeka realized that it was not a sham; she truly did feel a friendliness, almost a kinship, for the knife-armed man before her. That was why she did not scream or mindcall for help, for such would not save her life and might easily cost his as well. With real shock, she admitted to herself that, die or no, she did not want to cost this man his life. She was tired of killing simply to stay alive; a quick, clean death seemed a pleasant prospect to her after these years of being forced to pervert and prostitute her craft and her person in virtual slavery to the cursed *ee Klirohnohmeea*.

Master Fahreed paused in his slow approach and frowned. "I consider this an execution, woman, not a murder, for if you are of the guild I suspect you have violated oaths no less worthy or binding than mine own. Where do you prefer the knife—heart, throat, or brain? Fear not, there will be but a single, brief pain, if you cooperate with me."

Neeka began to fold down the front of her garments. "I did what I did because I then felt I had no choice—if I did not do what they bid me, I feared I would be returned to a certain coastal city for trial and probable execution. During the twelve years I have lived in this hall, I have shielded my own life behind the corpses of no less than five men who never had harmed me in any manner, simply because an evil, depraved lunatic of a woman demanded their deaths. But there will be no more deaths on my conscience, for my life is no longer precious to me."

She had bared her body to the waist, and now she lifted her left breast and leaned back again, steadying herself with an elbow on the worktable. She smiled and said, "You are doing the best and most proper thing, master, and I go willingly. Strike hard and true."

With a nod, the tall black man stepped close, felt until he found a spot that suited him, then placed the point of the knife where his fingers had been and thrust with controlled strength. The thin, needle-pointed blade entered easily, thin lines of blood welling up about the watered steel. Neeka gritted her teeth, forced herself not to flinch and thereby complicate or lengthen the man's job. She closed her eyes, thinking of her tragically wasted life. How different things might have been if only dear old Lokos had lived but one more year.

Chapter XIII

Tim had refused to await the Zahrtohgahn's return. Leaving Ahl, Giliahna, Mairee and the apprentice physician to look out for each other, he had stalked out, snarling, "If the bitch wants blood, I'll give her blood, though she may not like the color of the stuff I shed." He prowled the corridors and rooms of his dead father's hall, looking for prey.

Once divested of his porridge-caked clothing, Father Skahbros had not redressed himself, rather he had wrapped his pudgy body in a bath sheet, gathered up fresh clothing and padded down to the bath chambers in the north wing. And that was where his coldly raging nemesis found him . . . and dealt with him.

Tim paced back down the old, familiar hallway, his left hand on the well-worn basket hilt of his heavy broadsword. Through the pantries, into the winter kitchen. A burly cook—a *kath-ahrohs* by the cast of his dark-olive skin, black eyes and hair—gripping a big, greasy knife made at first to bar the passage of this apparent northern barbarian mercenary in patched boots and stained clothing. That was before he drew close enough to see that the stains were bright-red splashes of fresh blood, and to be chilled to his very marrow by the icy, murderous rage shining from those slitted blue eyes.

When he did not find Sir Geros in his cottage, Tim paused only long enough to tuck an antique but nicely balanced francisca—one of the old warrior's wall decorations—into his belt, then he headed directly across the rear courtyard to the stables. A row of paddocks adjoined the larger boxstalls, and in one of these he could see a pale-gray, black-maned and tailed bulk that could be none save Steelsheen, his own warhorse. Alerted by the familiar sound of Tim's tread, the huge stallion turned from the manger of fragrant cloverhay

107

and moved to the whitewashed bars. When Tim was close enough to recognize by sight, the horse whickered a greeting, stamping and nodding his scarred head in anticipation of a fondling.

As the man hugged and patted the pale cheeks, rubbing up and down the narrow stripe of glossy black hairs that bisected the animal's face, Steelsheen almost purred. But then the stallion scented the fresh, human blood, recalled the clank of Tim's weapons.

"Steelsheen was tired, my brother, but he is well rested now. Will we fight soon?" The horse mindspoke eagerly, unconsciously pawing at the earth of the paddock with one shod hoof.

"*I* may have to fight," replied Tim. "But it will be afoot, my brother. Are there any warhorses in this place beside you and Redhoney?"

Steelsheen snorted derisively. "There is one who thinks it is such, a gelding, one Tahkoos, but it really is only a sexless hunter of furry beasts and little tuskless pigs. At the bite of blade or point, such a creature would likely buck off its rider and run away. A war-trained stallion is pastured nearby, but he is old, his two-leg brother is dead and no one now rides him."

"Yes," replied Tim, "he must be—must have been—my sire's warhorse. Have you or Redhoney had trouble here?"

Steelsheen gave another derisive snort. "Only mares and geldings are within this place and all are frightened of me . . . of Redhoney, too, for all that she is only a mare." He tossed his raven mane. "The two-legs fear us, too, all save the one called Tahmahs. He respects us but no reek of fear is on him."

Tim reflected that he did not blame the other horses and the stablehands one damn bit. A fully trained warhorse was as dangerous as a stud bull, more dangerous, really, because of the added intelligence. No horse of merely average intelligence ever received full war training, which was one reason why they were so expensive and so treasured by their purchasers. Another reason was their unswerving loyalty to the one man they considered a brother—warhorses had been known to stand, riderless, over the body of a dead or wounded rider and fight with teeth and flailing hooves until aid came or they were themselves slain.

"Whatever happens," he admonished the big horse, "you

and Redhoney are to allow no man to mount you save me or my brother, Geros. Understood?"

"But what of our brother, Rai?" queried the gray.

"Our brother, Rai, is gone to Wind," answered Tim, soberly. "Tell Redhoney that I already have taken a partial vengeance for his killing, and I shortly will take the rest."

Tim found Master Tahmahs in a tackroom-cum-office. Only his silver-shot black hair stamped the horse master as having any trace of Ehleen blood. Otherwise, he might have been a clansman fresh from the Sea of Grass, with his wiry, slender build, fair skin and bright-blue eyes. He was industriously softening a new bridle when Tim entered. He glanced up, saw the visitor and the blood-splashed clothing and smiled, his eyes crinkling at the corners.

"It's started then, my lord Tim? Good! How many dead so far?"

"Two," answered Tim shortly. "My sergeant, murdered by arrow poison and that thrice-damned outlaw priest the bitch was harboring—though he may not be dead yet. I doubt that he is; belly wounds don't kill quickly."

The horsemaster nodded. "But there're no wounds so agonizing. Yet I've heard no screams from the gelded bastard."

Tim laughed coldly. "Nor will you, not from him. I sliced out most of his treasonous tongue."

Tahmahs chuckled. "That will put a burr under her saddle for sure, my lord. I think she dotes on that priest damned near as much as on her tongue-sister or on that sad excuse of a man, Myron. But what will my lord have of me?"

"Please pardon my asking, but ten years is a long time away. Are you trained to arms, Master Tahmahs?"

Tahmahs grinned. "Twenty years a Confederation dragoon, my lord."

"Then I need you here at the hall," said Tim. "Is there a good rider among your men, one you can trust in all things?"

Tahmahs replied, "My youngest son, Divros. He is not yet fourteen or he would, like his brothers, be gone up to Goohm to enlist, but he is as big as me and near as strong and a better rider than I ever was."

"Call him here," snapped Tim, impatient to find Geros and start the action.

When the strapping boy stood before him, the young captain asked, "Divros, is your loyalty to me or to my father's widow?"

Tahmahs snorted. "No need to question that, my lord Tim. Four years ago that precious pair, Lord Myron and his bumboy, found Divros alone and tried to strip and bugger him by force. Of course my lad fought, but what could a nine-year-old do against two lads near as big as I am? It was a near thing and they'd have had their unnatural way with him, had not your brother, Behrl, happened along and beaten Myron bloody and sobbing. So, you need have no doubts as to where the loyalties of me and mine lie."

"Very well, Divros, which is the fastest, strongest horse in the stables?" demanded Tim.

The boy did not hesitate. "Lord Myron's roan hunter, Tahkoos, my lord."

"Have you ever ridden him, Divros?"

The boy smiled. "Oh, yes, my lord. He says he likes me better than Lord Myron."

Tim nodded again. "Good. Saddle him and ride to Morguhn Hall, or until you find my half brother, *Ahrkeethoheeks* Bili of Morguhn. Here," with effort, he wrenched the ruby ring from his finger, "hang this on a thong about your neck, under your shirt; show it only to Bili, as proof that you come from me.

"Tell the *ahrkeethoheeks* that matters here have progressed faster than we had thought or planned for. Tell him to send my company to me at the gallop. Tell him to alert the High Lords that far more than had been suspected is afoot here in Vawn. Tell him that real rebellion is probable unless we strike quickly and drastically. Warn him to not, under any circumstances, impart aught of this to Prince Zenos. Can you remember it all, boy?"

When the lad could repeat the various parts of the message to his satisfaction, Tim sent him off to saddle the gelding and turned back to Tahmahs.

"Do you have any weapons in the stables?"

Tahmahs nodded soberly. "Yes, my lord, Sir Geros secreted a nice little store in my keeping."

"Then arm your son with at least a dirk and a spear; bow and saber, too, if he knows how to use them. No sense in burdening him and his mount with armor or target though. His job is to get to Lord Bili, not to stand and fight.

"Immediately Divros is on the road, turn all the other horses into the pasture. Not mine, though—I don't want him fighting with your king stallion. You might put Redhoney, the mare, in with Steelsheen. They won't harm each other, and as she has just lost her brother, she might be comforted by being nearer to a familiar horse.

"When you're done with that, round up Sergeant Mahrtuhn and his dragoons. They, you and any of your men you feel are loyal to me are to take as many weapons as you can carry, all the food you can find and at least one skin of water per man and come to the *thoheeks'* suite. If anyone—anyone! —gets in your way, you have my leave to cut him down. Understood, Master Tahmahs?"

Tim and Geros found just what the young captain had suspected in the cellar armory—the racks and chests and cupboards were all nearly empty of weapons and armor.

"But, my l . . . but, Tim, there be no place in this hall that such quantities of arms could have been hidden without me knowing of it from the few loyal ones, and that quickly."

"Just so," agreed Tim. Then he asked, "How long since you've been in any of the hall villages?"

"A month, at least, Tim, maybe two. It's Tonos, the major-domo's, part to deal with the villagers, him and the head cook, Myron's bumboy, Gaios."

"I caught that castrated goat of an Ehleen priest in the bath chamber and hung him up on a beam with his wrists lashed behind him while we . . . ahh, conversed. He told me some very interesting things. One of them is that for the last half-year, Mehleena's agents have been hiring bandits and gutter-scrapings from all over the Principate of Karaleenos, bringing them into this duchy surreptitiously and billeting them in the hall villages, at least a hundred of them that the priest knew of."

Geros looked stunned. "But why, Tim? She had no idea you were still alive until you rode in this morning."

Tim chuckled. "She knows the Sanderz Kindred have precious little liking for her and even less for Myron. Had I not come back, if they had chosen one of their own number to be chief of Sanderz, she was going to turn her pack loose against all the Sanderz Kindred, noble or not, and depend upon her cousin, Prince Zenos, to save her hide with Brother Bili and the High Lords by claiming that the Kindred had been in armed revolt against their rightful lord. She might have gotten away with her infamy, but . . ." He shrugged meaningfully.

"So, you can bet your boots that all the arms, save only those you squirreled away and the pitiful remnants in this room, are now on the backs or in the hands of her private army of rebel ruffians, down in the hall villages. Which fact, incidentally, answers any doubts you might have entertained about where Tonos' loyalty lies. He's Mehleena's and no mistake!"

Sir Geros's brow wrinkled. "But . . . but what if you had not come back and if the Kindred had chosen Myron to be chief?"

"Yes, I posed that question, too. The good priest required a bit more persuasion before he'd give me an answer, but after I'd dislocated one of his shoulders, he became much more talkative. If Myron had been elected and confirmed, Mehleena and her banditti would bide their time. It seems that there is a widespread conspiracy afoot in Karaleenos, Geros. The priest was certain that some very high personages—possibly even Zenos himself—are involved. When this pack had gained enough strength, they were to rise up in every duchy, county, baronetcy, city, town and village, slaughter the Kindred and declare an independent Kingdom of Karaleenos."

"Madness!" declared Sir Geros, vehemently. "Utter insanity! In a frontier duchy, say, such a scheme might even work out . . . for a little while. But here, in the very heart of the Confederation, it's doomed from the start. Kehnooryos Ehlahs abuts the whole northern border of Karaleenos and the Ahrmehnee *Stahn* the whole western. To the south, lie the Associated Duchies, and to the east is the sea, commanded by the Confederation Fleet. So who, what idiot, could think such a plan would last any longer than it took word to reach Kehnooryos Atheenahs?"

Tim shrugged. "Present company excepted, of course, what Ehleen ever thought with his head rather than his emotions? Well, there's damn-all here for us. They left only junk. Get back to your house and arm yourself. I'll be in the *thoheeks'* suite with the others."

"But, Tim, would it not be better for us to make our stand down here in the magazines? We'd have no shortage of either water or food here."

The young captain growled, "No, by Sun and Wind, I'll not be driven into a hole in the ground! This is *my* hall, Geros, and by my steel, I'll hold it. Father had the central portion built for just such a contingency as this. With the doors to the wings locked and barred, it can be held by a small force against anyone not willing to burn down the whole place . . . and, grasping as the bitch is, I don't think Mehleena would see the hall in ashes, even if it meant my death."

The horror-laden screams of a maid brought Majordomo Tonos and a hastily sent servant brought the Lady Mehleena to the bath chamber.

The soft, white, womanish body of the priest hung by its bloody, swollen wrists from the central beam. The shoulders had become disjointed and the flesh about them was hideously discolored. A wide pool of blood was beneath the dangling feet, with more dripping from the toes. The hilt of a boot dagger stood out from the lower belly, just a few inches above the stump of the castrate's penis. The mouth continued to dribble blood down the chin and onto the chest, and to give vent to a low, continuous whining, gurgling moan. The empty eyesockets had almost ceased to bleed.

When, at last, Mehleena had stopped her screaming, raving tantrum, Tonos approached her. "Mistress? My lady . . . ? May I kill Father Skahbros? It were the kindest thing anyone now can do for him. He is in great pain and dying . . . but he could live longer without a mercy-thrust."

Her fat face twisted with rage. "You softheaded fool! We don't have time for him now. To hell with him! Send a galloper down to the villages and call out the Crusaders or all will be lost for us here." With that, she slammed the door to the bath chamber and stamped off up the hallway.

When the thin blade was into Neeka's chest a little past half its length, Master Fahreed sliced from side to side, to damage the woman's heart fully and so speed her death. Then he wiped the blade on her shift and stepped back. He did not mean to leave until she had ceased to breathe.

Neeka had just started her last year of the indenture when Master Lokos' merry, plump wife, Yris, died of a fever then raging through Esmithpolisport. Hardly was she decently interred than the master himself was borne home dead from a meeting of the Heritage Council, whereat he had suddenly clutched at his chest and collapsed, expiring before he could be carried to a physician.

Koominon had the corpse borne to what had been Lokos' bedchamber, locked himself in with it and hastily performed in private those last rites that were forbidden in public, while

Neeka summoned the servants to wash and dress their master's body. It seemed to Neeka that fully half the inhabitants of Esmithpolisport attended the public eulogy to Master Lokos Prahseenos; even the *thoheeks*, Dahnuhld Esmith of Esmith—who hated the salt sea and almost never came to the port which produced so much of his revenue—sat with the other notables and speakers on the podium and said a few, halting words in praise of Lokos, whom he had never met personally. At least three-quarters of the attendees joined the procession that bore the cypresswood casket to the necropolis and saw it placed between those of his two wives in the splendid mausoleum of pale-green Theesispolis limestone, with its entrance flanked by two fluted columns of white, purple-veined marble from the Associated Duchies, far to the south and west.

So far as Judge Gahbros, the executor of Lokos' sizable estate, or anyone else knew, the late master had no living relative, so inquiries for the closest relatives of his two dead wives were sent far and wide. In the meanwhile, Koominon kept the house as orderly as ever he had for Lokos and Neeka managed the shop with all that that entailed and continued the training of the apprentices. At length, two months after Lokos' demise, Judge Gahbros came calling just after the dinner hour one evening.

Once he was seated and had sipped at the wine, he said, mock-chidingly, "Koominon, I told you to come to me for any funds needed to maintain poor Lokos' establishments, yet you have not come in two moons' time."

Koominon smiled. "There has been no need to do so, Lord Gahbros. Our little Mistress Neeka has done so well at the shop that not only have the profits been sufficient to pay all the household expenses and salaries, but to pay as well the full expenses of the shop and to put by a few *thrahkmehee* beside."

Neeka blushed furiously and both the men laughed. The judge reached across and patted her small hand. "Child, do not be embarrassed at honest and well-earned praise. All the business and professional community is full of your praises these days. You are proving a true credit to Master Lokos' memory. If the man who is journeying here from Linstahkpolis has a grain of sense, he'll keep you on as his manager and trainer until you've put by enough to buy his shop or to set up your own."

Koominon asked, "Then you've located an heir, my lord?"

The jurist nodded. "The only son of Yris' elder sister. A merchant, he is, one Pawl Froh, now resident in Linstahkpolis."

Koominon sighed. "A Kindred barbarian?"

"Yes," agreed Gahbros. "Half, anyway. His sire was a mercenary badly wounded in the Great Rebellion, who settled down with his loot in the Confederation, rather than returning to the Middle Kingdoms. He had three sons by Yris' sister, the other two went a-warring and are now dead. This man is in his late twenties and is, I understand, a middling successful dealer in hides, horns and tallow, raw wool, horsehair, bristles and suchlike."

Koominon shook his head slowly. "Hides? Bristles? What could such a man know of the craft of an apothecary?"

"Precisely," smiled the Judge. "He'll be needing a good manager to run the business . . . and who better than Neeka, eh?"

But Koominon was clearly unconvinced. He looked deeply disturbed.

Three weeks later, Pawl Froh appeared, and when Judge Gahbros brought the heir to the establishment that had been Master Lokos', he looked as grim and worried as Koominon. It was easy to see why this third son of the retired Freefighter had not gone a-warring with his two elder brothers—no army or condotta would accept a hunchbacked cripple.

When the judge introduced Froh to Neeka, she tried hard to conceal her immediate dislike of the sharp-faced, shaggy-haired little man, with his scummy-toothed leer and his way of looking at her that made her skin crawl.

Froh's normal speaking voice was a whining rasp, and he never ceased to rub together his grubby, ink-blotched hands. He seemed a little awed by the tall, dignified jurist and so waited until he had finished glorifying Neeka's management of what was the most prosperous small shop in all Esmithpolisport.

With a wave at the apprentices, he whined, "What fer do you need *four* shop boys? I only got the two, and my place's a whole lot bigger nor thisun."

Before Neeka could frame an answer, the judge said, "They are not shop boys, Master Froh, they are apprentice apothecaries. Master Lokos turned out at least half the best apothecaries in the Principalities of the Three Karaleenosee, and Mistress Neeka is finishing these boys for him."

Froh loudly sniffed his dripping nose, then wiped the back of one hand across it. "They be mighty damn well fed for mere apprentices; heh, ol' Lokos, he musta been gittin' inta his secon' chil'hood. But I'll see to the stoppin' of thet, and damn fast, too."

The judge frowned. "Master Froh, you should know that this duchy has laws dictating the decent and humane treatment of apprentices and resident journeymen, such as Mistress Neeka, here. I have the honor to be the senior jurist for Esmithpolisport and I see to it that abuses of the apprentice laws are handled most harshly."

"Oh, your worship, please don't misunderstand this humble businessman," whined Froh, bobbing up and down in little, short bows and wringing his dirty hands. "We have such laws on the books in Linstahkpolis, too, and ain't no man but would say Pawl Froh heeds to the very letter of 'em."

Neeka felt a cold chill of apprehension. Master Lokos had never fretted that craft masters of other trades laughed at him, he had treated his apprentices like his own sons and daughters, rather than doing for them only that which the law commanded.

While one of the boys raced back to the residence to fetch Koominon into the shop and while the heir nosed about the storerooms and workrooms, the judge drew Neeka aside and spoke in low tones. "Child, this creature is not what any of us expected. He is crude, vulgar, avaricious, a miser and, I doubt me not, more than a little dishonest; in the three hours we have been together, I have not heard him say a single good thing about anyone, living or dead.

"He seems to have the distorted opinion that 'apprentice' is but a synonym for 'slave.' Such is not the case, of course. As apprentices, you and the boys have all the rights and protections of any other subcitizen of the Confederation. He, Froh, is a subcitizen, himself; he showed me a copy of a letter proclaiming him a citizen of the Baronetcy of Awstburk, whence came his late father. He chortled and crowed that such subterfuge prevented the *Thoheeks* of Linstahk levying taxes on anything besides his profits.

"He is not a good man, Neeka. I'm telling you now, and I'll be telling Koominon later, should he offer abuse to anyone in this shop or the house, I am to be immediately notified. He may feel himself secure in this windfall, but he is not. Mistress Yris had other sisters and they, too, had children and I shall remain in charge of poor Lokos's estate until . . ."

He broke off, perforce, as Pawl Froh limped back into the main room of the shop, bringing back with him his perpetual sniffle and a reek of unwashed flesh that overpowered even the clean scents of the herbs and spices.

The riding mules were the first to be sold, then the two little asses Master Lokos had used to bear the panniers of herbs and roots from his fields beyond the city and from his frequent expeditions in search of those plants which could not be cultivated and needs must be gathered from streams and forests.

"Master Froh," she asked, "without an ass, how can I and the apprentices bring back the herbs we need from the woodlands and our fields?"

He looked up from the tally sheets, whining annoyedly, "Their backs look strong enough to bear a few pounds of roots a few miles."

"But when we harvest the fields next year—" Neeka began, only to be rudely cut off.

"Don' chew worry none 'bout thet, sweetiepie, ain't no more fiel's. I done sold 'em. Got me a dang good figger for 'em, too."

When he had sold the feed and hay and had discharged the groom for whom there was no longer any use, Froh had the quarters of the apprentices transferred to the draughty stable loft, but all the beds and other furniture was ordered left behind. Then he commenced letting the beds by the week to sailors and wagoners, who often caroused far into the night, robbing the servants on the floor below and adjoining neighbors, alike, of sleep. But Froh seemed not to care, so long as silver and gold coins continued to amass in the iron chest he kept chained to his bedroom wall.

Then, unexpectedly, Judge Gahbros was called to Danyuhlzpolis to sit on a special, three-judge panel convened by *Ahrkeethoheeks* Hari Danyuhlz III of Danyuhlz to hear an important case. Twenty-four hours after the jurist's departure, Froh sold the indenture contracts of the two newest apprentices to a Middle Kingdoms merchant bound back to Harzburk.

Again, Neeka confronted her new master. This time, she was coldly furious, frantic for the safety of the little boys she had come to love like younger brothers. "Surely you must know, Master Froh, that the moment that merchant's wagon crosses from the Principate of Kuhmbuhluhn into the Kingdom of Harzburk, those children will cease being contracted apprentices and become true slaves for the rest of their lives! How? How in God's name could you do such a thing? It . . . it's inhuman!"

He did not even look up from his tally sheets. "I be master here, missy, don' you go a-lectrin' to me, heanh? I made me a fine profit off'n them two contrac's, and there's two less moufs to be fed to boot. Whatall thet fine, upstandin' merchant does oncet he's out'n this dang Confedrashun's 'tween him and his burklord. But us burkers is honest folks. We ain't all borned liars and rebels like you friggin' Ehleenee is. Now, gitchore purty ass out'n here and let me be!"

After Tilda, one of the servant girls, was raped in her bed by a drunken sailor who had wandered down from above, all the servants demanded that Master Froh afford them protection from the depredations and petty thefts of his roomers. Froh's "answer" was to fire them, en masse. Then he moved more roomers into the vacated chambers of what had been the servants' quarters. He would have fired Koominon, as well, save that that worthy produced a properly drawn and witnessed contract guaranteeing him employment as majordomo and chef by Master Lokos or his assigns for a period of thirty years, and there still were more than eight years to go.

Thereafter, Neeka seldom saw the remaining two apprentices, as Froh saw to it that the boys stayed busy doing the work of the fired servants. Consequently, Neeka's workload in shop and workrooms trebled and, shortly, she began to feel and show the strain. She had to exercise more and more self-control to keep from snapping at customers. It became harder and harder to force her dead-tired body to do the compounding and distilling the proper, time- and energy-consuming way and not allow herself to succumb to the temptation of dangerous shortcuts and half measures.

Which was probably why she forgot to throw the big iron bolt on her chamber door that one night. She fought her way up from the depths of a sound sleep, trying to recall what noise had awakened her. There was only the merest ghost of a shuffling, scraping sound in her room, though on the two floors above, the usual carousing was still in progress.

Then she became aware of the smell, that sickening stink of a filthy human body. Then Froh sniffled. A cold hand touched her face and, before she could even gasp, clamped down over her mouth. The coverlet was suddenly ripped from off her, then his dirty, misshapen body was pinning her down, his foul breath nauseating her.

Chapter XIV

While his other hand and one bony knee were occupied at the task of trying to force her thighs apart, Neeka raked the nails of her left hand across his face. At the same moment her right hand grabbed his scrotum, squeezing and twisting at the sac, while kneading the testes agonizingly.

With a whining howl that quickly became a scream, Froh let go her mouth and sent both hands to the crotch she was punishing so savagely. Quickly, she smashed the heel of her left hand into his dripping nose. The cartilage snapped loose from the bone with an audible crack, and his blood spurted down on her face and body. As she fought from under the sobbing, bleeding man, she saw Koominon standing in her doorway, a lamp in his hand.

"Holy saints preserve us," the undercover cleric gulped. "What wickedness have you done?"

"The pig would have taken me, half-asleep, by force, Koominon," panted Neeka.

"But . . . but he is master here, child! All in this place are his to do with as he wishes."

Neeka felt as if a war club had come crashing down upon her head. "But, Koominon, didn't Judge Gahbros speak to you about our rights? He said he would."

Koominon shook his head. "Judge Gahbros is a full week's journey west of here. He cannot help you, now."

Neeka thought quickly. "Then, Koominon, you must go at once to the city governor's palace. *Komees* Pehtros will see that justice is done."

Koominon looked down. "Can't you send one of the apprentices?"

"Damn it, Koominon, of course not!" snapped Neeka. "You know the guards would never pay any attention to a stripling."

"Then . . . then one of the barbarians upstairs?"

But Koominon finally dressed and left. Going across to his room, Neeka armed herself with one of the prized knives he kept there since so much had been stolen from the kitchen by Froh's roomers. Then she dressed and kept watch over Froh's moaning, groaning, bleeding carcass until the majordomo returned.

Komees Pehtros strode into Neeka's room with fire in his eyes, two scale-shirted Freefighters behind him, along with another man, another noble, by his dress.

Froh had apparently recovered more than he had been willing to let the grim-faced, knife-armed Neeka know, for he suddenly sat up on the bloody bed. One hand clutched his aching scrotum, the other pointed a shaking finger at Neeka. "Arrest her!" he whined. "She . . . she attacked me fer no dang reason. She'da kilt me, likely, iffen you hadn' come up here."

But he wilted into silence under the cold glare of *Komees* Pehtros, who regarded the naked, gory hunchback as if he were some particularly loathsome form of vermin. The noble turned to Neeka. "What happened, child? If it was what I think, we'll find this . . . this creature a safe lodging in the palace dungeons until Gahbros gets back."

At an unusually loud burst of noise from above, Pehtros turned to one of his Freefighters. "Sergeant, go back out to the street and get a squad, then roust those scoundrels up there out. Use whatever force you feel you need. Crack heads or spill guts, I don't care, but get them out!"

"Now jest a dung minit," Froh recovered from his intimidation at the thought of possibly lost profits. "You ain't got chew no right to put my guests out inna street. This here's my house and them mens has paid for—"

"Shut your mouth!" snarled Pehtros. Turning to the other Freefighter, he said, "Go stand by Master Froh, corporal. If he opens his damned mouth without my leave once more, put your fist in it!" The big armored man grinned, nodded and, for Froh's benefit, loudly cracked a big fist into the palm of the other hand. Froh appeared suitably impressed by the demonstration.

When he had heard Neeka out, the *komees* turned to Koominon. "How much of this infamy did you see or hear?"

Refusing to meet either his questioner's eyes or Neeka's, the "chef" replied, "Why . . . why none of it, my lord. I was unaware aught had transpired until . . . until Neeka came knocking on my door."

"The fat bastard is lying!" Neeka mindspoke to Pehtros. "Why, I don't know. But he was there, standing in my doorway with a lamp, during that last part at least."

The *komees* pointedly turned his back on Koominon. To the Freefighter, he said, "Take that piece of dung down to his bedchamber and see that he clothes himself. We'll be taking him back with us. He's under arrest."

"No!" whined Froh. "No, it won' thet way atall. She come an' got me, brung me in here, she did. Then . . . then, when I wouldn' pay her all what she ast fer, she hurt me, she hurt me bad. You cain' put me in jail on jest the word of a dang ole whore. An' everbody in this whole dang town knows my crazy ole uncle got her outen a friggin' whorehouse. An'—"

He was interrupted by the Freefighter's craggy knuckles. The buffet knocked his twisted body completely off the bed, to roll across the chamber into a corner, where he lay moaning. Lay, at least, until he was grasped ungently by his scrawny neck and dragged out of Neeka's room by the clanking soldier.

The moment captor and captive entered the master's suite, Pehtros grabbed Koominon and jerked him into the smaller room, slamming the door behind. When he had shoved the priest-cook to a seat on the mussed, blood-smeared bed, he but furious whisper. "Now, father, will you speak the truth or two, that these may know it's safe to talk."

With a small smile, the tall, heavily muscled, black-haired man's thick fingers sketched certain signs in the air before him, signs known only to sworn members of *ee Klirohnohmeea*.

Pehtros then turned upon Koominon, speaking in a low but furious whisper. "Now, father, will you speak the truth or not?"

Koominon looked up, met those hard black eyes briefly, then returned his gaze to the floor as he said, "But . . . but I have told the truth, my lord *komees*. Would you then question the word of a humble priest of Holy Mother the Church? No true son of our Faith would do so."

Pehtros snorted and the one called Pahvlos chuckled. "Save your verbal goosedung for those simpleminded souls it impresses, humble priest. The tale you told me on our way here matches that just told by Neeka. Why are you trying to change your story? Are you in fear of that stunted little barbarian apelet? Speak, damn you!"

Koominon squirmed and shuffled his feet. Finally, he said, "Lord *komees,* you all know who I am, what I really am, and how much in danger I am as a consequence."

"What the hell," snapped Pehtros, "has all that got to do with this matter? If you don't publicly tell the truth in this matter, Neeka could be sentenced to a flogging. Is that what you want to see, humble priest?"

Koominon cleared his throat and looked up finally, speaking in a strong whisper. "All must sometimes make painful sacrifices for our Faith. My background will not tolerate too close a scrutiny, and you know it, my lord. It might well mean my death to appear as a witness in a court. If I aver that I saw and heard nothing, I will not be summoned.

"I regret that Neeka must suffer, but she should have considered my precarious state in this house, this city, this accursed Confederation, before she so rashly injured her lawful master. 'Render unto temporal rulers that which is their own.'"

Him called Pahvlos looked as if he needed to spit. "What an utter shit you are, priest. If you are so fearful for your life, if you so fear martyrdom, you should take passage on the next ship for the north. The more contact I have with your kind, the more I find myself in total agreement with the High Lord."

Pehtros said, disgustedly, "For a bent copper, I'd drag you up to the fortress and turn you in myself were not so many others involved. But the full membership of *ee Klirohnohmeea* will know of this by tomorrow night, rest assured of that, humble priest."

Koominon's whisper became pleading. "But I must do it this way, cannot you see, my lord? I . . . I have a duty to my flock."

"Of whom Neeka is one," snapped Pehtros. "What of your duty to her?"

"But . . . there are all the others who need my spiritual guidance, don't you see, my lord. Besides, you're taking the barbarian, Froh, to jail."

"Where I am not at all certain I can legally keep him until Gahbros gets back from Danyulzpolis." Pehtros rasped a thumbnail against one stubbled cheek, then turned to Neeka. "Well, my dear, now you know just how much support you can expect from this pious coward, and just how much he can be trusted in future. As for Master Froh, hmmm. I have the right to jail anyone responsible for creating a public nuisance for up to three days and nights without trial or bail. And that racket that was going on abovestairs when I arrived constituted a public nuisance if ever I heard one; I've heard Ahrmehnee wardances that were quieter. Then, too, he resisted arrest, which is why my guard hit him, of course. So there's another two days and nights. After that, we'll just have to see. Pray as you've never prayed before that Gahbros gets back before those five days are up."

The next day, the Heritage Council notified Koominon that he was thenceforth barred from any full or partial meeting of *ee Klirohnohmeea*. Sometime that night, he left the house that had once been Master Lokos'. No one ever saw him again in Esmithpolisport.

At the end of a week, Judge Gahbros still had not returned and the city governor felt compelled to free Pawl Froh, but he himself accompanied the released prisoner back to his inherited property. In front of Neeka and the two apprentice boys—those three being the only other souls now resident in the once busy, bustling, cheerful and happy house—he said, "Master Froh, if you know anything of me by now, it is that I do not often threaten and never idly. But I hereby warn you, I shall be having this house and your operations closely observed. If any harm befalls any of these three, if any of them suddenly disappears, I shall see you brought to full account.

"Hire on some good servants. Working mistress Neeka and these boys sick will be considered harm. So will starving them and poisoning them with that rotten swill we found in your larders. These boys are now back in this house and they will stay here; in that damned stable loft, they'd have been dead of lung fever before spring. You'll be in need of a new cook, too; the good Koominon decamped—after breaking open your strongbox. I've no way of knowing how much he took, but it would appear several bags are gone."

At this revelation, Master Froh suddenly began to weep noisily, like a whipped child, and, heedless of *Komees* Pehtros' shouts, scuttled rapidly up the stairs toward his rooms and his ravaged strongbox.

Pehtros shook his head. "Not only his body is deformed, Neeka, his mind is too. I think he's quite mad, and I racked my brains to try to think of a legal means of keeping him in my dungeon where he belongs. But the law is written for all, even such as him. Be very wary of him, all of you. Should he become violent, let me know at once. God keep you all. Now I must go."

Not wishing to chance a return to the dungeons of the city governor, Master Froh grudgingly obeyed the *komees'* dictates, rehiring Ahrohnos, who had been Koominon's assistant cook, and two elderly women recommended by that worthy. The two boys had been moved into vacant rooms on the one-time servants' floor and Ahrohnos appropriated Koominon's small suite. The apprentice dormitory remained vacant, for Froh had been sternly warned that any repetition of the night-long brawls would see him heavily fined, something which he feared much more than being jailed. When Neeka announced that she would stay in the room that had always been hers, Pehtros sent workmen who fitted the door with a self-locking mechanism, as well as with iron brackets for an oaken bar. Paying them out of the strongbox Koominon had so thoughtfully broken open seemed to make the *komees* inordinately happy.

But Neeka was no longer worried about nighttime forays by Froh, for Ahrohnos, who recalled the unfair circumstances of his firing, bore no scintilla of liking or respect for his employer and was not at all averse to adding to Pawl Froh's evening meals certain tasteless herbs given him by Neeka. The heir blamed his constant evening sleepiness on shamefully overheated rooms, but even so he made no move to install another lock to replace the one broken off the charcoal shed at Pehtros' order.

For a brief two weeks, it seemed to Neeka almost as if dear Master Lokos was still alive and simply gone from the city on a trip, but it was too good to last. One afternoon, Ahrohnos hurried into the shop and drew Neeka aside. The slender man's face was drawn with worry, and his voice was tight and harsh.

"Mistress Neeka, Lord Pehtros was attacked as he passed through the central marketplace this noon. The men who attacked him and his guards were all slain, but he was gravely injured. Some say he's near death, some say already dead. Mistress Neeka, I *saw* the corpses of the men who struck him down. All of them were men who roomed in the apprentice dormitory . . . and at least two of them were closeted with Master Froh yesterday afternoon."

Komees Pehtros died that night, and most citizens of Esmithpolisport mourned his tragic passing, for he had been an efficient, honest and fair city governor, with many friends and few enemies. Sizable rewards, to be paid jointly by fort commander Major Pahvlos and *Thoheeks* Esmith, were shouted through every street and alley by brazen-throated town criers all through the following day. On the morning of the second day after the murder, Ahrohnos hurried into the shop, red-faced and sweating heavily, despite the bitter chill.

"Mistress Neeka," he puffed, his little round belly jiggling to his labored breathing, "Master Froh is making ready to leave the city. Should I go to the fort and tell what I saw on the day before they killed poor *Komees* Pehtros? Should I, Mistress Neeka?"

"How do you know Froh is leaving the city, Ahrohnos? Maybe he's just going out to sell more of Master Lokos' estate," said Neeka.

"Mistress Neeka, he had me and the boys carry three travel trunks down from his suite. His iron box is open and empty, and it took all three of us to carry that last trunk downstairs, and it the smallest one, at that. He sent one of the boys to find a carter, too," replied the chef. "Oh, Mistress Neeka, I just know he means to leave on the noon coach. Should I go to the fort? Please tell me."

Neeka thought hard. Of course Ahrohnos should tell his tale to the authorities. Froh should not be allowed to get away with a conspiracy to murder, nor should he be allowed to quit the city with the specie into which he had converted so much of Master Lokos' estate. On the other hand, she had no wish to be left alone with the hunchback. She had hurt him, humiliated him and been responsible for his incarceration, and she had no doubt that the vindictive little barbarian swine would at least try to accomplish some sort of revenge upon her before he left Esmithpolisport.

"Do you have a weapon, Ahrohnos?"

From within the tops of his calf-length boots, the chef withdrew a pair of short, edgeless stilettos, five inches of blued blade and guardless bone hilts. Wordlessly, he laid them on the counter, his bushy brows raised in silent question.

Neeka nodded, picked up one of the needle-pointed instruments, hefted it, then thrust it deep into the large, gleaming bun of blue-black hair at her nape. Reaching into a secret place beneath the counter, she laid a couple of silver *thrahkmeh* pieces before Ahrohnos.

"For the gate guard," she told the man. "There'll be no

waiting for you to see Major Pahvlos if you spread a little silver amongst the guards. Hurry, Ahrohnos!"

Master Fahreed nodded to himself. The bleeding from the heart thrust under Neeka's left breast had slowed to a trickle of pale pink—blood mixed with clear serum. Stepping back over to his victim, his sensitive fingers found the throat pulse. They found it easily, for it was *strong*.

"*C'est impossible!*" In his shock and wonderment, he reverted to the language to which he had been born on an island far to the south in the hot seas beyond the Witch Kingdom.

Crouching, the physician placed an ear to Neeka's breast for a moment, then straightened, stood and stepped back with a muttered "*Merde!*"

The woman's heart, which he had so carefully damaged, supposedly shredded, with his skill and the little knife, was beating as rhythmically and as powerfully as before ever the blade had tasted of her blood. Crouching down again, he gently lifted the left breast.

An icy-cold prickling suffused his entire body and the small room seemed to be spinning about him. The narrow wound had now ceased to bleed entirely, *and it was closing, healing,* even as he watched!

Ahrohnos had not been gone ten minutes when Master Froh shuffled into the shop from the rear. As the cook had said, the cripple was dressed for travel—thigh-high boots, linsey-woolsey trousers and shirt, a wool scarf wrapped around his scrawny neck, a fur-lined leather cap; over the shirt, Neeka noticed that he had donned one of the several old brigandines that Master Lokos had customarily loaned to the hired bravos who accompanied him on long journeys. The armored garment might even have been a fair fit, save that Froh's hump caused the back of it to ride far up.

Behind the shuffling little man came two bigger, normal men. Neeka recognized one of them, and her heart sank. She knew what the abominable creature was going to say even before he showed his rotting teeth in a leering grin.

"Betchew thought as how you's gonna git away with breakin my nose and damn near pullin my balls off and gettin me thowed inna friggin jail, dintchew, you Ehleen bitch? I thought on havin you kilt, too, but then I figgered thet wouldn' make no sense when I might be abul to turn me a hones' profit. Well, these here mens jus' branged me half the money and, when we all gits to the whorehouse, Mistress Djoy, she'll gimme the rest. And I might even spend some of it to buy me a piece off'n you, 'fore I leaves this dunghill town."

Stoo Shif, the pimp bravo Neeka had recognized, grinned too. "Don't give us no trouble, Neeka, honey. If you do, I'll feel obliged to knock you in the head, and Lady Djoy, she's real anxious to talk private with you, soon's you git there." He came around the counter and reached out for her body with both hands and, when she flinched away from him, he said in a placating tone, "Now, honey, just hold on, I ain't trying to cop no feel off you, I just wanta be sure you ain't got a knife or nothing." He chuckled and added, "Howsomever, as I recalekt, you don't need you no knife to kill a man."

He hooked a thumb at the other bravo. "This here's Alik Dahl. He's a ole Freefighter, like me, but he ain't been with Lady Djoy but 'bout a year. He was hired on after a damn drunk sailor kilt ole Djimi one night."

Neeka went quietly. After the cautious Stoo had meticulously examined the garment for hidden weapons, he helped her to don her cloak, then he and his partner followed Neeka and the grinning, chortling hunchback out of the shop and down the street toward the dockside section in which was located Djoy Skriffen's bordello.

Neeka made no attempt to leave a message for Ahrohnos. For one thing, the cook's reading ability was minimal; for another, he was not a member of *ee Klirohnohmeea* and would have had no idea how to help or whom to approach for advice. On the other hand, Iktis was a member—a high-ranking member, at that—of the Heritage, and he would certainly be at the brothel, for Dejoy Skriffen never allowed more than two of her four goons to be absent at any one time.

Even so, Neeka's mind was awhirl with thoughts of vengeance upon the evilly grinning Froh. From his comment about his thought of having her killed *too*, she was now dead-certain that he had been responsible for the fatal attack on *Komees* Pehtros. Ahrohnos had gone to tell his tale at the fort, but it was just possible that the wily thief and murderer, Pawl Froh, rich with the proceeds of Master Lokos' estate, might be able to elude justice—slip secretly out of the Duchy of Esmith or even take ship and leave the Confederation entirely.

As the party left the better sections of Esmithpolis, the streets became narrower. Finally, almost within sight of the bordello, a street was completely blocked by an enormous wain with a broken axle, two huge oxen and a half-dozen shouting, gesticulating men. Stoo insisted they backtrack a few yards and enter a parallel alleyway down the length of which they could see the windowless facade of Mistress Djoy's place of business.

When Neeka and Froh, in the lead, were but five yards from the mouth of the alley, a cur dog ran past them and began to snarl and snap at the two bravos, behind. When the men stopped, cursing and kicking at the animal, Neeka saw her chance. Swiftly, her right hand went to her nape and drew the small stiletto from her hair. She allowed Froh to advance a step ahead, then jerked aside his cloak and drove the sliver of steel with all her force between his belt and the lower edge of the brigandine, deep into his left kidney.

Hissing, close to his ear, "This is for *Komees* Pehtros, you barbarian ape!" she withdrew the stiletto and stabbed again, and once more, nearly deafened all the while by her victim's shrill, falsetto shrieks of agony.

Then a big, powerful hand clamped onto her wrist. Letting go of the bloody, imbedded weapon, Neeka got her slender body beneath the arm and exerted the leverage Djordj had taught her so long ago. The new bravo, Alik, whooped in surprise as his feet left the ground, screamed briefly in his flight. Then his breath left him as his body slammed down upon the greasy cobbles of the alley, the ringing clash of his scaleshirt drowning out the snapping of his neck.

Stoo Shif did not make the same error of judgment. He wrapped both brawny arms about Neeka, effectively securing her own arms, hugging her body close against his own and lifting her feet clear of the pavement. Snorting with laughter, the man proceeded rapidly down the alleyway, ignoring both the still-screaming Froh where he stood slumped against a wall and the unmoving corpse of Alik.

Chapter XV

Drawn by the screams, Djoy Skriffen, trailed by Iktis, had come out of her front door and descended the steps to street level just in time to watch Stoo Shif trot out of the alley with the kicking, struggling Neeka hugged tight to his chest.

Grinning like an opossum, he spoke when still several paces distant. "Lady Djoy, she ain't changed one damn bit, I tell you. I searched her and me and Alik watched her ever step of the way, and somehow or t'other she still had her a knife or got one. Give it to that humpbackted asshole three, four times, right under the loose ribs in the bastid's back."

"He the one what's a-screamin'?" demanded the madam.

Almost choking on his laughter, the bravo just nodded, then gasped, "And the bugtit'll be howling like a fucking wolf till he finely does die. It's damn near as long and hard a death as a frigging stab below the belt. Atop of that, I think she kilt ole Alik, too. I warned him to stay clear of her, I did."

"What happened to him?" Djoy Skriffen asked, conversationally. "Did Neeka attack him?"

The bravo shook his head. "Naw, Lady Djoy, we 'uz two, three steps back of her and the gimpy humpback, and like I say she'd put paid to him 'fore we hardly knowed whatall'd happund. Well, ole Alik just run up and grabbed her knife arm and then I cain't really say just whatall she did, it all was so fast. Next thing I knowed, Alik was flying down the fucking alley and a-yowling and all and then he hit so hard I ache to think about it, I do. I think his neck is broke, Lady Djoy, mebbe his frigging back, too. But I warned him she 'uz a killer."

Djoy Skriffen smiled. "Don't fret about it, Stoo. You know and I know that Alik must've been out for a piss when they passed out brains. I told you all Neeka was valuable to this business, well worth the price that ugly little cripple demanded. For all Iktis and Neel thought it was a mistake to bring her back here, I knowed I was right. Soon's she cools down a mite, she'll likely see things that way, too."

Iktis had spoken not a word, aloud, nor had Neeka. Their communications had been silent. To her appeal for help, he had answered, "Even with poor Pehtros dead and Judge Gahbros still away, you'll be free soon enough. There are more ways in and out of this house than Lady Sow ever imagined. Now stop struggling. Stoo Shif's sex drives are warped, perverted—a resisting woman arouses his lusts."

But it was too late. Iktis could see that it was even if Neeka could not. A pulse had commenced to throb visibly in Stoo's temple, his eyelids were twitching and he repeatedly extended his tongue to wet his lips. Iktis knew the signs, and knew all too well what they portended.

When Stoo again spoke, his voice was thick with desire. "Lady Djoy . . . ? Please, ma'am, give her to me, to us, for a little while. Me and Iktis and Neel will cool her down quick enough, and I promise you we won't mark her up none, or not bad, enyhow."

"Well . . ." Djoy scratched her head. "Well, Stoo, maybe a little gentling will put her in a better mood to talk to me. Maybe she'll see, then, jest how much I'm off'ring her."

Unnoticed by either Djoy or the preoccupied Stoo, Iktis sauntered a few steps forward. He mindspoke to Neeka. "Child, the bitch has just consigned you to several hours of torture and rape and humiliation. I'll not allow it to happen, but you must do just what I say. When you see my left hand come to rest on the hilt of my hanger, duck your head as far down and forward as you can. I'm going to slit Stoo's throat. The moment his arms relax, throw yourself to the ground; the old bitch has a throwing knife up each sleeve, and she's deadly with them at short range, so this will be a chancy thing."

Horrified by the pulse of the hard maleness she could feel against her leg through Stoo's clothing and her own, Neeka, beamed her assent. Even so, she instinctively flinched when Iktis, leering, reached out to fondle her breasts. Chuckling evilly, Iktis stepped back and, with a natural, casual appearance, his left hand came to rest on the hilt of the weapon slung from the left side of his body.

Neeka ducked her head, felt her hair ruffled by the wind of the blade's passage, then her head and neck and shoulders were suddenly drenched in a shower of hot liquid. Behind her, her captor was making horrible gurgling noises. Then he loosed his hold upon her and she threw herself forward and down onto the pavement. Lady Djoy shouted something, but her shout was cut off in the middle of a word by a meaty *thunnk* and her next sound was a gurgling gasp.

Up at the head of the alley, there were yells and the thump-thump-clankety-rattle of men, armored men, running. Pawl Froh's ceaseless screams of agony finally had brought a patrol of guardsmen. Similar sounds caromed off the window-less walls of the street, as well, indicating that a patrol was proceeding from a second direction.

Iktis grasped Neeka's arm and pulled her to her feet. She gasped and almost retched at what she saw. Stoo Shif had sunk to his knees, his arms hung limply by his sides; bright blood and bubbly pink froth gushed regularly from the deep wound just beneath his stubbled chin. His eyes followed Iktis with a pleading, questioning look and his lips shaped words, but his severed windpipe could provide no air to give those words life.

Djoy Skrifnuh sat on the pavement, leaning against the house wall, the thick plaster of cosmetics and the thin trickle of blood from the corner of her mouth standing out in garish contrast to the grayish pallor of her skin. The skirt of her red silk gown had ridden up to bare her fat, splayed legs almost to the crotch. Her big, square, beringed hands lay palm up beside her massive hips; near the right one lay a flat, hiltless iron knife, its point smeared thickly with a viscous venom. Her little piggy eyes, though glazing, were fixed upon the hilt of the hanger standing up from a thick roll of fat, just below her well-padded ribs and centered between the mountainous breasts.

Iktis pulled Neeka by main force along with him. "Snap out of it, girl! It will be far better for us both not to be on the street when those armored barbarians get here. True, we could flee toward the docks, but we'd be seen by these, certainly, and possibly run into another patrol down there, as well. But just let me get into the cellars and they'll never find us."

Leaving Neeka on the stairs for a moment, he turned back to Djoy. Planting a foot to steady her, he drew the hanger out, drawcutting downward, his face twisted with the disgust and rage which had so long seethed within him.

Inside the foyer, Iktis slammed the heavy, iron-banded oak

door and dropped the three hinged bars in place, after shooting home the thick iron bolts. "Lucky for us," he mindspoke, "that these ancient buildings are constructed like little fortresses. It'll take those guards a considerable time to knock down this door, and there're no windows on the front or the sides, so neither Neel nor Hohp Leebos will have any idea what happened out there. Come on, the quicker we get downstairs, the better."

But it was not to be so easily accomplished. Neeka had but barely gotten out of sight under the front stairs when Hohp appeared at the head of them, her hair disheveled and her eyes heavy and swollen with sleep. But those eyes popped open wide when she saw Iktis, who had caught the fringes of the initial spray of Stoo's blood, had had more rub off on him as he manhandled Neeka into the house and was gripping the gory hanger just pulled out of his former employer.

"Neel!" The tall redhead screamed in alarm. Then, "What happened, Iktis? Whatall's going on out there?"

"Go to the head of the cellar stairs, child," Iktis quickly mindspoke. "Shut the door behind you and stay there until I join you."

Neel had come up behind Hohp, stark naked, but with a lead-filled leather cosh in one hand and a wide-bladed dirk in the other. "What'n shit's goin' awn, Iktis? Soun's like they skinnin' some bastid out there." He referred to Pawl Froh's screams, hoarser now, but still audible even through the stone walls and thick door.

"Guardthmen and tholdierth!" lisped Iktis, excitedly. "They theemed to think we all had thomething to do with the murder of *Komeeth* Pehtroth. They've already cut down Thtoo and Alik and that hunchback. Before Lady Djoy fell, the thaid to bar the front door and get everybody out through the thtable tunnel. If the can talk or buy her way out of it, the'll join uth at her warehouth. Hohp, you get the girlth up and drethed and out. Neel, you get the thtrongbokth out of Lady Djoy'th bedroom. I'm going down and thlit that new-bought girl'th gullet, then I'll meet you there."

There might have been questions, save that fists and sword pommels had already begun to hammer at the barred and bolted door, and, rising above the tumult, an authoritative voice could be heard shouting for a timber suitable for use as a battering ram. Hohp whirled about and began to open doors and scream orders to the sleepy whores.

After hurriedly wiping his blood-dripping blade on the rich

samite draping the entrace to the front parlor, Iktis sheathed
it and raced down the hall to the cellar door. He and Neeka
descended the broad steps, their way lit by another of those
large, chain-hung brass lamps that Neeka remembered had lit
the cellar room to which she had been confined during her
brief stay here, years back. All the rank of doors facing them
at the foot of the steps were identical—thick, iron-studded
and ironbound, and each wide enough to allow, when
opened, the passage of a rolling wine tun or a barrel of
pickled turnips or cabbage.

Without hesitation, Iktis strode to the third door from the
right and inserted an iron key into the big padlock, then
waved Neeka through the opened door. Immediately, Neeka
became aware that they were not alone down here, for she
could hear the whimpering sobs of a woman somewhere
ahead. The passage, for all its darkness, seemed vaguely
familiar, and, when they emerged into the stone-paved room
full of huge, age-darkened wine casks, kegs and shelves of
jugs and bottles, she knew where she was. Iktis had lingered
to secure the door behind them; now he strode past her to the
high, open-topped cell built into the corner, jerked back the
bar and flung wide the door.

At the first sound of the bolt, the occupant of the cell began to scream. Iktis stood for a moment, then turned and
beckoned to Neeka. "I'd thought to take her out of here with
us, but she's hysterical, and with cause. Stoo and Neel and
Alik were at her early this morning so I haven't the heart to
hit her." He mindspoke. "She's an Ahrmehnee girl, but she
speaks both Ehleeneekos and Mehrikan, as well. See if you
can calm her down while I open the passage."

The naked girl who had flattened herself against the stone
wall in the farthest corner of the cell was as tall as Neeka,
though she seemed barely pubescent. Both her long-lashed
eyes were blackened and her face was swollen and discolored,
while her olive-skinned body was one mass of welts, bruises,
abrasions and scratches from neck to knees. Neeka felt ill;
this poor child could have been her, but for brave Iktis.

She tried in vain to establish mindspeak communication
with the girl. If the Ahrmehnee was a mindspeaker, she was
too upset to use the talent; nonetheless, Neeka continued to
beam a meaningless but soothing reassurance which did have
its effect. By the time Iktis beamed that the passage was
clear, the girl, trembling like a foundering horse, sat beside

Neeka on the narrow bed, enfolded in her arms and sobbing on her breast.

There was nothing whatsoever in the cell, save its furnishings and a pair of felt boots, so Neeka wrapped her own blood-sticky cloak around the girl's abused body, gently laid her back on the bed, then tried the boots on her. They fitted perfectly. Supporting the stumbling girl, she led her out of the cell to where Iktis had removed the center of what had looked to be a solid brick hearth to disclose a trapdoor of rust-pitted iron.

The Ahrmehnee had come that far quietly enough, but when her eyes lit upon Iktis, she began to whimper again and weakly resist Neeka's efforts to lead her forward. The closer Neeka's efforts brought her to the impatiently waiting bravo, the louder became her wordless cries and the more violent her struggles. Finally, Iktis shook his head.

Silently, he beamed, "There's no hope for it, child. Turn her around, I don't want to hit her face."

Neeka obeyed him, watching over her shoulder, but saw only a blur of movement of his hand and arm. She felt the shock of the blow through the girl's body, heard Iktis's low grunt, then was forced to release her hold lest the cloaked body pull her down too.

The pock-faced little man shook his head once more. "I'd like to leave her here, but those damned lustful guardsmen would likely take her for a whore and gang-rape her. Besides, she's seen that trapdoor, and the fewer folk know of these ways, the better."

Above their heads, the hanging lamps swayed and the flames danced to the regular, heavy thumps of a timber being hard-swung against the street door of the bordello. There were no other sounds; apparently the occupants had all made good their escape.

Each carrying a smoky torch, Iktis burdened as well with the unconscious girl, he and Neeka shivered in the chill of the dank, slippery passage. "Aye, it's cold and damp enough at any season. Still I'd rather be here in fall or winter, for there're no snakes now."

"What is this tunnel?" queried Neeka silently to save breath. "A smugglers' way?"

"Yes, smugglers and such often make use of some of them, child," he answered, "but they didn't build them. Parts of these ways, the round, dirt-floored parts, are so ancient that no one knows just who did build them. They were here when the first Ehleenee came and raised the city that stood before Esmithpolisport and were discovered by the men excavating foundations for the city walls and for houses. In those days, many tons of iron, brass, copper and lead were brought up from them, but there's little of it left now. Only a few of those curious round iron trapdoors remain unscavenged."

They splashed through puddles, waded through sucking mud, traversed firm, water-soaked sand and slipped on stones slick with the ooze of centuries. When Neeka remarked upon the dearth of rats or mice in such a natural habitat, Iktis mindspoke, "When my grandfather was a lad, these ways swarmed with vermin, but then the fencats were brought up from the swamps around the Great Inland Sea far southwest of here in the Associated Duchies; these days, it's hard to find a rat in Esmithpolisport, under or over the ground, save for the trickle that come off ships."

They had walked for miles, it seemed to Neeka, though with the numerous turns it would have been difficult for her to estimate just how much real distance they had put between them and their point of entry into the maze. Both torches were now guttering, and, at a word from Iktis, Neeka used hers to light another pair from the half-dozen spares he had had her bring along.

"Iktis," asked Neeka, "for all her size, that girl is barely out of childhood, so why were Stoo and those others allowed to so abuse her? Wasn't ravishment enough?"

"She's not been ravished, Neeka—tortured, degraded, humiliated, terrified, yes, but not ravished. The old bitch paid a whopping price for her because she is a virgin, and avaricious as Djoy Skriffen was, you may be damned certain that she'd not have allowed the girl to be deflowered by a mere bodyguard. She was bought for an aging degenerate whose lusts can only be stirred by immature females. But neither he nor Djoy had figured on the strength of the girl, who not only successfully resisted his attempted rape of her but kneed him in the balls to boot. She was back down in that cell to be played with until her spirit was broken."

Twice they had to backtrack from tunnels blocked by cave-ins. At the second such, Iktis cursed sulfurously, damning all smugglers, the late madam, the Heritage and persons of whom Neeka had never heard for failing to keep the tunnels in repair or at least apprising him of the locations and extents of disrepair. Then he sighed. "I'd hoped to lead you into the secret subcellar wherein the Heritage meets, but these were the last two tunnels to it; the others are long years flooded.

"The ancient, round tunnel we crossed back there passed beneath the palace of the city governor, but with poor Pehtros dead, that's not the place I'd wish to come up, thank you. All the ways that lead to the fortress have been deliberately flooded or otherwise blocked over the years. Since I slew both Djoy Skriffen and Stoo Shif—that screaming hunchback saw it all and you can bet he told of it to the guards—the patrols are certainly out for me, and you too, likely. Djoy was no great loss to Esmithpolisport, mind you, but she was the uncrowned queen of the city's criminal element, and, if we are unlucky enough to be arrested, you may be sure that we'll never live long enough to come to trial."

"Then what can we do, Iktis? Where can we go?" asked Neeka.

"If only Lord Gahbros were in the city . . ." mused Iktis. "There is a way that comes under his mansion, but his wife, worse luck, is a barbarian, a Daiviz of Morguhn; she's not a member of *ee Klirohnohmeea,* and there's no telling which way she'd jump if a couple of fugitive murderers and a kidnapped girl suddenly came trooping out of her cellars.

"There is one more possible hidey-hole, of which I can think," the sharp-faced man went on. "I know that you and this girl would be safe there, but I . . . well, the Lady Rohza dislikes men in general almost as much as she hates the barbarians. It's a long way, too, outside the city, which will mean taking to the lowest ways, under the walls . . . and praying that there's been no collapse of them in the years since I've been that way."

He resumed his burden of the limp girl, crossing himself awkwardly. "Pray, too, that this poor child remains in swoon a bit longer, for we must retrace our way directly under the bordello, and they are certain to have left guards there."

If prayers are truly effective, theirs were answered, for it was not until they were well upon the downward-slanting way that led under the inland walls that the Ahrmehnee began to moan and weakly squirm on Iktis' shoulder. Iktis stopped and set the girl upright against the stone wall of the tunnel and Neeka tore the hem from one of her undershifts, wet it in a nearby puddle and gently bathed the child's battered face, both she and Iktis beaming silent soothing assurance, just as they would have to a hurt, frightened animal.

This time, the sight of Iktis brought no screams from the

Ahrmehnee, though still she trembled and eyed him warily. She said something that Neeka could not understand, then began to speak in Mehrikan.

"Where have you taken me now? What are you going to do to me?" In the light of the torches, tears glittered on her long, sooty lashes and down her bruised cheeks.

"We have taken you away from that place, child," said Neeka. "We will try to find a way to return you to your home."

"She . . . that huge, terrible old woman said that . . . that the only way I ever would leave that . . . that house of horror was . . . was *dead*," gulped the girl.

"Djoy Skriffen is, herself, now dead," said Neeka. "This brave man, Iktis, killed her. I saw him do it, child. He also killed one of those men who abused you . . . and I killed another." Neeka had felt remorse at the death of Loo Fahlkop and was a little shocked to discover that she could feel no such emotion upon the reflection that she had slain two men this day. Her uncle, who had been a warrior and duelist of note in his youth, had often said that the first kill was the most difficult, both at the time of killing and immediately after, but that all subsequent kills were increasingly easy. Neeka thought that now she could understand.

After a few more minutes, the Ahrmehnee girl, Shireen Mahsohnyuhn, was able to walk with minimal assistance from Neeka, so the three proceeded faster than before. The way went downward, downward, ever downward, then began to slant into a very gradual ascent. They were lighting the last brace of torches when Iktis announced that they were nearing their goal.

"The city of which these ancient, subterranean ways were a part must have been a monster among cities—larger than Kehnooryos Atheenahs, Harzburk and Pitzburk combined—for the ways extend more than a mile inland and, it is said, once ran almost as far seaward. We now are over a half-mile outside the walls and might be safe aboveground, but they might also have mounted patrols out—I would, were I Pahvlos—so I think we'll go on underground."

In places they were compelled to bend low, almost to crawl, due to the accumulations of tree roots growing down through the rough, porous stone of the tunnel's arched ceiling. But at last they came upon an ancient, badly rusted ladder leading up to another of those curious round iron hatches. Handing his torch to Shireen, Iktis climbed up and attempted to dislodge the cover. The two young women could hear his gasps and grunts of exertion, the cracking of his straining sinews, and finally the iron disc shifted with a grating sound that echoed down the long, dark tunnel.

They emerged into a stock cellar even larger than Djoy Skriffen's. Against one wall were ranged massive stationary wine casks larger in diameter than the tunnel below, their staves and bandings darkened with age. Elsewhere were stacked hogsheads and barrels of pickled vegetables and pickled or salted meats, stone crocks of salt or honey, stone jugs of brandy and cordials, kegs of oil and, near the stairs leading to the upper cellar, several ironbound caskets secured with huge padlocks.

It was evident that an earnest attempt had been made to conceal the round iron disc leading to the ways below, and the great difficulty in lifting it was explained by the three inches of packed earth which it had been covered with. Iktis kicked as much dirt as he could back over it, then manhandled a great tun of pickled turnips onto it.

Weaving and bobbing to avoid the apples and pears hung from the ceiling on strings, Iktis, Neeka and Shireen mounted the stairs and entered a lamp-lit upper cellar. With all its compartments included, it was larger than the one below though not so high-ceilinged. On either side of the staircase huge bins of white and sweet potatoes, and elsewhere were bins of turnips, horseradish root, onions, squashes, pumpkins and the like. Garlands of dried fruits and great bunches of garlic hung from the ceiling. Barrels of flour and meal were stacked in the center of the floor.

From behind this stack of barrels came a short, stout man, tally slate and chalk in hand. At sight of the three interlopers—all three filthy with soil and soot, their clothing damp and disheveled, the two women carrying guttering torches and the man grasping a bared hanger, its pierced brass guard crusted over with dried blood—he squeaked, dropped his slate and sprang for the stairs to the ground level—but Iktis made it there before him.

Leaning his head to one side and regarding the pudgy man closely for a brief moment, Iktis sketched a sign in the air between them with his empty right hand. Neeka recognized the sign, and so too did the strange man. His relaxation was visible and a tentative smile creased his round face as he answered the sign with another. Stepping closer, he and Iktis exchanged a complicated hand grip, then he turned and walked back to pick up his slate and chalk while Iktis sheathed his hanger.

When Lady Rohza Ahnthroheheethees had heard out the stories of all three of her surprise "guests," she frowned and rapped her short, square-cut nails on the table for a moment before she spoke. "Well, the hue and cry is up for you and Neeka, friend Iktis. Both the hunchbacked barbarian and the old whorekeeper were still alive when the city guard reached them, and they named you two as their murderers and the killers of the other two men.

"The killing of that hunchback is of little real importance since he was being sought anyway for suspected complicity in the assassination of Pehtros. But the deaths of the Skriffen bitch and her two pimps is another kettle of fish. She had recently bribed full citizenship for herself and them out of a crooked city clerk and an even crookeder undermagistrate, none of which would ever have happened had Gahbros not been off at the bidding of that asshole of a barbarian, Hari of Danyuhlz. So now you are wanted for the slaying of two citizens and Neeka for slaying one, which means that, if caught, you'll be tried by the *thoheeks* himself, unless Gahbros comes back sooner than anyone expects. And considering the fact that our barbarian lord was a silent partner in the operation of that brothel, I'd not wager a pinch of turkey dung on your chances of staying alive."

The pock-faced man shrugged. "Well, it is perhaps time that I moved on anyway, Rohza. Perhaps I'll drift up to Goohm and try a hitch in the Ehleen dragoons."

Lady Rohza pulled at her full lower lip for a moment, then nodded briskly. "Stay here for a few days. I'll secure clothing and boots in your size and see about providing you with a trained warhorse. You'll have enough gold to see you to Goohm and enough left over to outfit you as befits your inherent station—good-grade armor, hallmarked sword and so forth. I'm sure that *ee Klirohnohmeea* will reimburse me."

Iktis nodded. "And if the Heritage doesn't, you know I will. But what of Neeka and Shireen?"

The big noblewoman scratched her mannishly coiffured head. "The Ahrmehnee girl is no problem at all. Apparently no one living is aware she was even in the city. She can stay here until I have word of a westbound Ahrmehnee party—these Ahrmehnee are all thick as thieves and even if they are not of her tribe they'll surely see her safely home.

"But as regards Neeka, it is not certain that even Gahbros

could offer her protection from the *thoheeks,* so I'll write a letter to an old friend who is now an intimate of Prince Zenos. Sweet little Neeka will be safe with me until my letter is answered."

Iktis rode out in the mist and drizzle of a cold, gray dawn seven days later, looking not a bit like the foppish bravo who had for so long befriended Neeka. The garishly hilted hanger—chosen weapon of bravos and city ruffians—was gone from his side to be replaced by a heavy saber, old but well-kept. His trousers and overshirt were of plain, practical linen canvas, his thigh-high boots and leather cloak were oiled and wax-impregnated to shed water. The hanger, the stones prized out and the gilt silver wire of the hilt replaced with brass, hung sheathed on one side of his pommel, balanced on the other side by a light axe. Saddlebags and a bedroll encased in oilskin were lashed behind the high-cantled warkak, along with water bottle, food wallet and a plain, open-faced helm. On the road, mounted on his war-trained piebald mare, he would look like simply another independent Freefighter riding from one contract to the next.

Neeka could not repress a shiver of dread and apprehension as she saw the strong and efficient, but quiet and unassuming man put booted foot to stirrup, swing aboard the mettlesome mare and ride out of the courtyard of Lady Rohza's hall.

However, by the time Shireen Mahsohnyuhn departed through that same gate with a party of westbound Ahrmehnee merchants of the Frainyuhn and Grohseegyuhn tribes, both dread and apprehension had been replaced with dull resignation tempered with self-loathing—even as she feigned passion in Lady Rohza's bed and embrace, she loathed herself for placing more value upon her life than upon this utter degradation of her body and soul, loathed herself even more than she loathed the ugly, perverted, grunting creature who tried so desperately to deny her own femaleness.

And that was why she leaped so eagerly at the opportunity to go west when it was offered. She had been unaware until she actually reached Vawn Hall that the Lady Mehleena practiced the same hideous perversions as had the Lady Rohza. But over the long years, as Mehleena drifted further and further into religious fanaticism, poured more and more of herself into planning and preparing for a true, armed, violent—and predoomed to failure—rebellion, she had eschewed sex of any variety; moreover, as she became aware of Neeka's undeniable talents and her ability to kill or cure without a subject's knowledge, the fat woman began to respect her tame witch to the point of fear.

When Tim finally returned to the *thoheeks'* suite, he carried with him a keg of brandy and a bundle of old polearms which had hung on the walls of the entry foyer for nearly thirty years. The suite, spacious as it was, looked crowded already, what with a half-dozen middle-aged Freefighters and as many Ahrmehnee grooms under Master Tahmahs; Brother Ahl and Mairee and her father, Sir Geros; a burly man with a thrusting sword and a Confederation-pattern dirk belted about his beginning of a paunch and beside him a younger man of similar build and identical armament. But what riveted Tim's attention when once he had dumped his burdens and looked about were the physician, Master Fahreed . . . and the person who stood beside him.

Chapter XVI

The majordomo, Tonos, chose the three fastest runners from among the young men of the hall and sent each off to one of the three hall villages; it was all he could do, as only the two northern warhorses were left in the stables and he knew better than to attempt to mount either of the stamping, head-tossing, eye-rolling beasts. Then he and his picked band of menservants armed and set themselves to the pleasurable job of butchering all other servants—male and female—not definitely known to be loyal to the lady and the True Faith.

He decided to start in the kitchens with that arrogant bastard of a meat cook, Hahros, and his adopted son/apprentice, Tchahrlee, the both of them loudly self-avowed pagans. But such was not to be.

The kitchen, when they reached it, contained no living men. The pantries had been partially looted and Mitzos, the storeskeeper and a good Christian man, lay face down in his own blood with his head stove in. In the bakery, only two or three foot-trampled loaves were left of the day's baking and the baker, Kristohfohros, was huddled before his ovens with an iron spit run clear through his chest from front to back.

But the most horrible sight was come upon in the caldron room. The legs and hips of a man hung limply over the rim of a huge soup caldron, flesh and clothing smoldering in the heat creeping up the sides of the vessel from the coals beneath. When they at last got the body out of the soup, they discovered it to be Leeros, the pastry cook. There was no wound in his flesh, so they could only assume that he had been forcibly drowned in the boiling broth.

From his fruitless search for horses, Tonos already knew the stables to be empty of Tahmahs and his godless crew as well as of any save the two warhorses. Therefore, he and his murderers carefully surrounded and ever so carefully crept closer to the house of Sir Geros, their reverent bloodlust well-tempered by the knowledge that this quarry was a warrior of storied skills and valor and likely to be armed, as well. But when finally they kicked open the door and burst into the neat rooms, only an old, white-muzzled boarhound lay regarding them with rheumy eyes, his tail slowly thumping a welcome. Raging with frustration, Tonos jammed the broad, knife-edged blade of his wolf spear into the body of the aged, inoffensive dog again and again and again. Then he turned and stomped out of the tidy house.

In the rear courtyard, the pack claimed their first human victims—old Gaib, the hall farrier, and Hail, his strapping but seriously retarded son. Caught in the open, unarmed save for the drawknife he had been sharpening, Gaib was easily struck down, yet he rose again, his lifeblood gushing out, when he saw the mob stalking his childlike son. Lifting the heavy honestone, wooden cradle and all, he hurled it with such force as to smash the ribs and spine of one of the men. Then, hurling his rapidly dying body onto the back of another, Gaib bore him to the ground and had pulled the drawknife almost through the neck before the stabbing spears and hacking swords finished him.

Tonos ruthlessly thrust his spearblade—bloody with the gore of the father—deep into the belly of the towheaded son, then stood laughing as the boy stumbled about, screaming piteously, until he tripped on his own guts and fell sprawling into the gory mud. When one of the white-faced men stepped forward, his sword raised for a mercy stroke, Tonos pushed him back.

"No! Let the heathen halfwit die as did Father Skahbros . . . slowly."

Then they went on in search of more prey.

Mahrkos Kahnstahnteenos sat up and yawned widely, scratching at his hairy chest and reflecting that rural life was not so bad after all . . . not when the alternatives included the distinct probability of dancing a *kahlahmahtzeeos* at the end of a rope. City-born and -bred, he had had no slightest intention of leaving the city of his birth, until his mother had caught him having his way with a younger half brother and he had, in a rage, slain both of them. Only a few jumps ahead of the law, he had stolen a mule and ridden west and north to fade from sight in the—to him, huge—metropolis which was the capital of the Principate of Karaleenos.

For five years, he had plied various trades—footpad, sneak thief, pimp, hired bravo—anything requiring muscle and ruthlessness rather than wit. Then, one drunken night, he had thrown a drover into an inn fire after an argument over the favors of a pretty boy. But such things were not unusual happenings in the low places he frequented, and after the drovers had quitted the city, his life might have continued as usual, had he not compounded matters past mending by slaying the innkeeper—a full citizen—as well.

He had been languishing in the city dungeon for long weeks, awaiting trial and the certainty of either a quick hanging or the slower death of a sentence to quarry, mine or road and fortress building, when a burly jailor and two well-armed city guards fetched him from his cell to throw him, still weighted by his heavy fetters and chains, into a bare chamber some four levels up from his place of confinement.

Shortly, three men—gentlemen by their dress, manners and speech—entered by a door in the opposite wall. All three wore steel helmets, with beavers up and visors down so as to completely cover their faces and impart a muffled, booming quality to their voices.

"Fagh!" snorted one of the men. "He stinks! He stinks worse than the others even. Let's get this done with quickly. My stomach can't take much more of the stench."

"Please . . . please, my . . . my lords," stuttered Mahrkos, blubbering. "I . . . I didn't mean to kill 'im! As God's my witness, I dint. I . . . I jest thought . . ."

Another of the helmed men waved a gloved, beringed hand in a curt gesture, saying, "We are not interested in what goes on in your sewer of a mind, you pig. Speak when your betters tell you, not before."

The speaker turned to the third man and said, "The bastard's name is Mahrkos, no one seems to know his family name . . . if he had one . . . and he has not volunteered any. From his accent, I'd imagine he's from farther south, but he's lived here about five years, I'm told. He burned a drover alive and strangled an innkeeper, a citizen."

"He's to hang, then?" asked the third man.

"Oh, no," replied the second, grimly. "Just look at the shoulders on him. The mines need men of such strength, the quarries, too. Why he might even live ten years . . . if he doesn't prove too intractable."

Mahrkos shuddered and whimpered, wetting his filthy rags in his terror. Lost in horrible mental imagery of all he had heard of the mines and quarries, and picturing himself enduring the agonies of the drawn-out and hideous death such a sentence represented, he was deaf to the first questions put to him. It was not until one of the gentlemen put half an inch of swordpoint into his arm that he again became aware of just where he was.

Carefully wiping the tip of his ornate, bejeweled smallsword on a corner of his voluminous cloak, the second man said, "Answer the questions, you whoreson, or you'll suffer for it! Are you of Ehleen stock or barbarian? Do you reverence God or something else? If we could free you from prison, would you go where you were told, do as you were told, kill whomever you were ordered to kill, so long as you were well paid?"

And so, within a few weeks, Mahrkos had found himself among some eightscore other hard cases, gathered from all over the principate and beyond, living in tents pitched in the forest of some duchy south of the capital. For two hellish months, they had undergone intensive military training at the callused hands of grizzled veteran soldiers and a few nobles, these always masked or helmed.

Mahrkos had always thought of himself as tough, dangerous and cruel . . . but that had been before he learned the true meanings of those three words in that woodland camp. Not all of the men who started finished. In the beginning, some ran away from the harsh discipline and unaccustomed labor under pitiless taskmasters. Those who were run down and killed were the lucky ones; the others were—in the full and horrified sight of their erstwhile fellows—slowly whipped to death, impaled or crucified on a beam lashed to a tree near the camp latrine. Tormented by hunger and thirst and pain, pecked at by crows, they sometimes took three days to die; but still they hung there and it was only when the stench became too bad that the cadremen hacked through the ropes and, after sinking hooks into the rotting cadaver, had the corpse's former comrades drag the carcass off and dump it in a pit. No one ever got away clean, and, after a few examples, no one tried.

At the end of two months, the survivors of the original number were divided into three groups of between forty and fifty men each, then Mahrkos and two other bully types were placed in charge of the contingents. Slowly, a few men at the time, traveling in various ways and under various guises, the hundred and fifty bravos were funneled westward, laying over for long or short periods in many out-of-the-way places, often in woodland tent camps, sometimes in tiny villages, sometimes in towns or just outside them.

It had taken them the best part of three months to circuitously cover the distance to the far western Duchy of Vawn in the foothills of the Misty Mountains. There, the hundred and fifty had been reunited one last time, for two nights and a day in another wood, but this time without tents. Then two of the helmed nobles had come riding in, trailed by three men who rode barefaced. None of the bravos had seen any of the three before, but they did not need to know them to know immediately just what they were, not after two months of hell.

The voice booming from within the metallic confines of the helm sounded almost inhuman. "Allright, you gutterswept scum, gather closely about. These men," he languidly waved at the three, hard-faced men sitting their mounts beside him, "are Deemos, Plehkos, and Ahreestos. They will henceforth be your commanders and will own the powers of life and death over you. They will march you to the villages in which you will be quartered until the weapons skills you have been more or less taught are needed.

"Arms will be provided you eventually. Until they are, you will drill and practice with wooden substitutes. You *will* drill and practice, you swine, practice and drill, for you may think you are warriors now but you are not. A bare tenth your numbers of first-class soldiers would go through you like a dose of salts, would make blood pudding of the lot of you. It takes years to make soldiers out of first-grade material, which you poor shits certainly are not. But we have invested money and effort on you, nonetheless, and we will see to it that you give us at least a bare minimum return on our investment.

"Insubordination of any sort will be considered mutiny and will be dealt with harshly and fatally. These three captains will choose four sergeants and one senior sergeant to assist them. Orders from these sergeants will, in the absence of the captain, be considered as binding as if they came from the officer.

"Understand, please, if dimwits like you can understand, you are here without legal leave in a basically hostile duchy. It will be as good as your life to go wandering about the countryside, not to mention the danger your capture by the local barbarians would cast all the rest into.

"Do as you're told, stay where you're told, hone your arms

skills and you'll have food, lodging and your pay . . . with the probability of a bit of loot in time. Disobey in any manner and you'll be killed. Filth of your like are easily replaced; the gutters and jails are full of such."

Thanks to his abilities with cudgel and staff, as well as to his bullying assertiveness, Mahrkos was chosen by Captain Deemos to be his senior sergeant. After the village headman and a few other natural leaders had been killed or terrorized, Deemos, Mahrkos and their forty-one men had experienced no trouble in taking over the village.

After another gaping yawn, Sergeant Mahrkos threw off the blanket and looked about for his shirt and breeches. Arising, he hopefully shook the wine jug, then raised it to his fleshy lips and thirstily guzzled the last few ounces before starting to dress. He had just buckled the swordbelt about his waist when he chanced to notice the red-brown blotch on the mattress and the trail of crusty splotches leading from the bed to the door.

Chuckling to himself, he thought of the red-haired boy, the freckled youth he had dragged—bawling and sniveling and begging to be let go—from his lean-to hovel last night. He thought, deliciously, of that smooth, hairless body writhing and struggling futilely, of the way the little darling had screamed when Mahrkos entered him, took him. He was still musing and rubbing himself when Deemos, in three-quarter plate, sword and dirk at his sides, an axe in his hand and his helm under one arm, stamped in.

"You wallowing swine, aren't you dressed yet? Get into your cuirass and rouse the men. The summons just reached me. We're to march on the hall immediately. Damn your lights, you lowborn cur, *move!*"

Vahrohneeskos Tahm Adaimyuhn rode in high spirits at the head of his party of young Ahrmehnee and Kindred retainers. They had left the little town nestled at the foot of Lion Mountain well before dawn and set a slow pace, easy on horses and men alike. Shortly after dawn had first reddened the sky, they had been met and joined by Tahm's cousins, Kahrl and Bahb Sanderz, and their party. Bahb, a couple of years older than Kahrl, his brother, had been designated to stand for his father, *Vahrohnos* Tchahrlz Sanderz, too old and infirm to make the journey to Sanderz Hall. Nor were the three gentry the only relatives among the two entourages, so the two columns were soon one intermingled cavalcade.

Though both the Sanderz men were somewhat older than the swarthy, black-haired Tahm, the nineteen-year-old had their full respect and occasional deference. Right often, their glances strayed to the Ahrmehnee necklace of silver links and semiprecious stones, each stone representing a warrior's head taken by Tahm in personal combat. Since his fourteenth year, the big-boned, brown-eyed young man had taken part in many of the frequent raids made by his sire's tribe upon the mountain folk always encroaching upon the Ahrmehnee holds.

Three hours after sunrise, the combined parties stopped to rest the horses and munch journey food on the banks of an icy brook. Almost all the men were young and they chatted, gambled, wrestled and footraced; they threw knives and light axes and darts at marks on trees or devised difficult moving targets at which bowmen could try their skill. Finally, they saddled the horses and rode on to the beat of a small brass hand drum, the damned-soul wail of an Ahrmehnee flute and bursts of song.

Less than five miles from their objective, a faster-moving column caught up to them. *Komees* Dik Sanderz was fully armed, as were they all, but his old, lined face was grim and his men rode in tight column, with targets unslung and weapons ready.

"Greet the Sun, uncle," grinned Tahm. "Why so grave? Whose funeral are you riding to?"

"Yours, mine and all the rest of our kin and Kindred, belike," growled the aged fighter—who had been a grown man when the Clan Sanderz had fought its way east from the Sea of Grass and helped to hack out a duchy in Vawn. "Form your men up on ranks, young kinsmen, for we may well have to fight our way to the hall . . . and fight again when we got there.

"The elderly prairiecat who lives at my hall, old Steelclaws, was farspoken by Ahl Sanderz. Tim Sanderz is alive and has returned to Vawn. He's at the hall now, preparing to defend it against some rabble the bitch, Mehleena, has sneaked into the duchy and armed. It smacks to me of the Great Rebellion reborn!"

With *Komees* Dik commanding the main body, Tahm Adalmyuhn took the strong vanguard, maintaining a quarter-mile of distance between the two groups, riding as warily as ever he had in his five years of raiding. When they came to the outskirts of a village—one of the three hall villages, as

Tahm recalled—he had it carefully scouted out before he led his men down the dusty street between the silent houses.

The only things in sight that moved were a few chickens, a pig rooting in a garbage heap and a couple of shaggy dogs. A quick search of the cottages, hovels and outbuildings showed signs of a hasty departure—hearthfires were still alight. Pots bubbled and chores were left half-done. But the only sign of humans was in the form of a red-haired boy-child lying dead in a lean-to shelter, the grayish little body evidencing the unmistakable marks of shameful abuse.

Tahm sent a rider back to *Komees* Dik, then had his patrol remount and ride on, drawing his flankers in tighter since the broad, cultivated fields to either side left insufficient cover to hide ambushers, and if any force should come out of the distant woods, the open stretches they would be forced to cover would allow for more than adequate warning. The road, moreover, showed the recent progress of a sizable body of men, moving in close order, four, maybe five horses, the rest on foot. Tahm estimated their numbers at some four tens, horse and foot, together.

Grudging the loss—for he led only fifteen men—he sent another galloper back to the main body to tell of his discovery and urge that the column close the distance rapidly, for a bare mile ahead the road entered a twisting, turning, forest-flanked way.

Mahrkos squirmed, raised himself off the sharp, bony ridge of the plow mule's spine, but could find no comfortable way of sitting the beast. Cursing under his breath, he simultaneously envied Deemos his saddle and wondered for the umpteenth time why he and the other sergeants must ride the bags of bones and could not trudge in comfort along with the men. After the ride between the mile or more of fields, under the blazing, baking sun, the coolness of the trees around and about was pleasant. So too was splashing through several tiny streams, still bitingly cold from the mountains that gave them birth.

After marching in that pace that Deemos called quickstep for half a mile, the men were set to a jogging run for the same distance, before, panting and huffing, they were allowed to slow back to the march. Mahrkos held his bruised rump and crotch up from his jolting, bony seat as long as his thigh muscles would allow, then sank back, groaning.

Beyond a tall, broad cairn of moss-grown rocks, Deemos

abruptly halted and Mahrkos all but rode into the horse's shiny rump before he could make the mule stop. In the roadway before them, three noblemen sat their warhorses, blocking the narrow track, which here wound between gradual, grassy slopes grown with brush and small trees.

One of the three armored men kneed his mount a few paces forward and exposed his face—eyes, skin tone and an errant lock of black hair spoke of the *kath-ahrohs* or pure-blood Ehleen.

"You come from the Lady Mehleena, my lord?" asked Deemos.

The strange noble nodded, his right hand resting easily on his thigh, nowhere near the haft of the light axe lying across his saddlebow.

Deemos advanced a few feet closer, opened the front of his helm and asked, "You are of the Brotherhood, then, my lord?"

Again, the stranger simply nodded silently.

"My lord must give me a sign," said Deemos, tracing some complicated pattern in the air before him with the forefinger of his right hand.

"Aye, I'll give you a sign," agreed the stranger in flawless, cultured Ehleeneekos, smiling. Still smiling, he raised his hand and, with a flick of his gauntleted wrist, sent something shiny spinning through the air between him and Captain Deemos.

The officer grunted, then his horse screamed and reared and, in the split second before Deemos' body tumbled from the animal's back and the deadly sleet of arrows began to fall, Mahrkos saw the polished bone hilt of a knife jutting out from Deemos' left eyesocket.

Komees Dik rode slowly along the gentle slope, viewing the road, now littered with bodies and weapons and liberally besplattered with blood. Across the road, *Vahrohneeskos* Tahm came out of the forest and trotted down the hill, three fresh-severed heads dangling by their hair from his big right hand. He and all his Ahrmehnee relatives who had ridden out in pursuit of the few survivors of the road slaughter were smiling and happy, even those who did not carry heads.

"Did any of the bastards get away?" demanded the old man.

Tahm shrugged. "Maybe one, certainly no more than two.

One of those was mule-mounted, but he was wounded severely, I trow. He'll not ride far."

The old *komees* nodded brusquely. "That was good work, Tahm. A brilliant plan, brilliantly executed. But there're more of these late bastards' kind about, or so Ahl bespoke old Steelclaws, so let's collect such of these weapons and armor as we can use and get back on the road to the hall."

Chapter XVII

As soon as the first company of Brotherhood Crusaders, that from the nearer south village, reached the hall, Mehleena ordered their captain, one Ahreestos, to batter down the thick, barred doors sealing the central portion of the hall off from the north wing. But all the while his men were laboriously lugging a long, foot-square oaken timber up the stairs, she screamed and screeched at them lest they damage the fine, carven paneling, wall hangings or carpets.

Once at the top of the stairs and ready to advance on the doors, the lady insisted that they first lay the makeshift ram aside for the space of time it took them and a few servants to strip the hallway of carpets, hangings and fine furniture. Only then would she allow them to get on with the business of forcing the door, which upon examination Ahreestos deduced was not going to be either quick or easy.

Nonetheless, he set his score of men to swinging the heavy length of well-cured oak against the spot where the two valves of the ironbound doors verged and on the level at which he reckoned the central bar was set. But before the men could establish a telling rhythm of strokes, the door of one of the suites between Ahreestos and the stairs opened, unnoticed.

Unnoticed, that is, until, to the twanging of bowstrings, two of his men screamed and fell. Key men, they were, and arrowed on the backstroke, their loss so unbalanced the rest as to cause them to lose grip on the timber—which, lacking proper handholds or shoulder ropes, was difficult to handle at best. The falling timber smashed one man's kneecap and crushed another's foot.

Nor had the two middle-aged archers been idle during it all. They had dropped another brace of Ahreestos' shrinking command, faced about once to send a scratch force of servants retreating back down the stairs, leaving one dead and one wounded, then turned back to pierce through two more of the ram wielders, before reentering the door from which they had originally come.

Ahreestos sent one of his sergeants down to fetch the rest of his force, then led the thirteen living and unwounded bravos against the door through which the archers had disappeared. Save at its far end, the hallway was not of sufficient width to allow use of the timber, so they were compelled to axe down the suite door, ignoring the livid lady, who winced each time a blade bit into the carved and decorated fruitwood panels.

But when the splintered door finally crashed open, the small entry foyer lay empty and they were confronted by another, even more ornate door through which they must hack. The first two bravos who crowded through the wreck of this second door apparently triggered some cunning device of boards and slender cords, for a bucket full of glowing coals was suddenly tipped and dumped to rain down upon them. And it was as well that the larger room stood empty, for the lady shrieked and cursed them all and would allow no more pursuit of the archers until the last of the coals had been scooped up and the blazing carpet brought under control.

Ahreestos now had ten men left of his score—during the demolition of the second door, one of the men had been working his axeblade loose from the wood when, in the cramped little room, a comrade's stroke had gone astray and taken off most of his right hand—and these ten were tired, shaken, demoralized men. A couple crossed themselves, eyes rolling in superstitious horror, when a thorough search of the suite produced no archers nor any means by which they could have departed.

At that juncture, Lord Myron joined them with two retainers, all three fully armed. When Ahreestos had rendered his report, the hulking noble snorted derisively.

"Then either your scum didn't search very well or they and you have hog turds in place of brains!" Then, striding impatiently over to what appeared but another expanse of paneled wall and had rung as solid under Ahreestos' knuckles as had the areas flanking it, the arrogant lordling had fingered a carven rosette and, with a muted click, a five-foot-square section had sprung open a couple of inches.

Stepping back, the sneering young lord bobbed a mocking

bow and waved a steel-encased arm toward the panel with silent contempt.

Ahreestos was reduced to physically shoving the sergeant and two others through the panel into the narrow tunnel beyond. Trembling like foundered horses, they mumbled prayers, gripping and regripping their weapons in sweat-slick hands. Ahreestos himself felt as nervous as a virgin bride when he ducked his head and entered into the dry darkness, his sword held at low guard before him. At his command, the sergeant halted his men until a brace of lamps could be lit and passed in to them.

The progress was slow and halting, for there were more movable panels along the way and Ahreestos could not feel safe unless the suites beyond each and every one of them was well searched before they crept onward up the tunnel.

And all the way, the lady's strident voice rang and echoed from behind, bidding them have care with the lamps lest they set fire to the hall, bidding them on pain of direst consequences to leave no soot marks on walls or ceiling, bidding them exercise strictest caution that their weapons and equipment not chip stone or scar wood. Ahreestos soon became unclear in his own mind whether the true enemy lay ahead or behind and was thinking how much pleasure it would give him to still the fat, yapping bitch with a dirk in the gullet.

At the right-angle turn where the tunnel from the central section of the hall intersected that which ran the length of the south wing, there were three stone steps up to a yard-square landing, then three more to the level of the slightly higher main building. Just as the sergeant ascended to this landing, a warrior in an almost complete suit of plate descended from the blackness to cut the noncom down with a single, powerful stroke of a basket-hilted broadsword.

The second man had sheathed his sword to better manage the heavy, clumsy brass lamp, and he was given no time to draw it. The third man, pressed irresistibly on by the pressure of Ahreestos and those behind the captain, squealed like a pig at slaughtering time and never even tried to raise his sword to parry the blow that struck between the lower rim of his old-fashioned helm and his scale shirt and cleanly severed his dirty neck. The spouting, gory geysers took Ahreestos full in the face, through the bars of his visor.

Hampered by the twitching, jerking bodies beneath his feet and half-blinded by the stinging, salt blood, the veteran soldier still managed to turn two or three jarring, bone-numbing blows of that dripping, deadly sword with adroit handling of his own. Then his inferior steel snapped and he had a brief moment to stare in stunned wonderment at the scant foot of blade left below his hilt, before all the stars of heaven exploded in his head and he suddenly dropped into a bottomless pit of black nothingness.

By planting himself firmly and loudly shouting that the captain was down, the next man managed to prevent himself being pushed within range of that armored apparition and its death-dealing yard of steel. As fast as they might, but still far too slowly for the foremost men, the long line backed down the tunnel, the last one dragging the inert form of Captain Ahreestos.

In the *thoheeks'* suite, Tim laid his blood-streaked sword aside and lifted off the helm after Giliahna's deft, sure fingers had unbuckled it. Accepting a damp cloth, he rubbed his sweaty face and hairless scalp, then gratefully drained off the big tankard of beer proffered by Sir Geros.

At length, he said in a matter-of-fact tone, "They're in retreat now, back up the passage, but young Tcharlee is out there watching lest they return. I downed four of the bastards. Three were clean kills, but the last man was in three-quarter plate and knew a bit more than the basic rudiments of swordplay. At best, I only wounded him, possibly just stunned him. Most of them are no soldiers, just an armed rabble. Is there any more of that beer, Sir Geros?"

By the time they got Captain Ahreestos back into the suite where the lady and her folk waited and got his helmet off, he was beginning to regain consciousness. He felt kitten-weak, shaky and with trickles of his own blood from nose, ears and mouth corners freshening the partly clotted gore that had sprayed through the front of his helm from the spurting arteries of the decapitated man.

"Captain Ahreestos! God curse you, you craven cur dog, answer me!" The lady bent as far forward as her girth would permit and slapped the man's ashen cheeks smartly, heedless that the stones and settings of her many rings tore his flesh. But her shouts and buffets elicited only a wordless mumbling, and, when she grabbed a handful of his sweaty, black hair and raised his streaked face, his bloodshot eyes rolled, unfocused, and a fresh rivulet of blood coursed from one ear.

She had the unfortunate captain raised to his feet, but, immediately the two bravos released their holds upon him, he collapsed bonelessly and fell to the floor in a great crash and clashing of his armor.

Without turning, Mehleena snapped her pudgy fingers. "Ohrahgos, Broonos, drag this piece of useless filth out into the corridor where his bleeding can't damage anything. Lootzeea, fetch water and cloths that I may wash his dirtiness from my hands. Tonos, get the blood cleaned off this carpet. Quickly, before it dries."

While a serving girl carefully washed Mehleena's extended hands, she ordered Ahreestos' last living sergeant forward, snapping, "All right, you lowborn ape, what happened up there? There can be no more than a score or less including women, in that main section. So how is it that thirty big, brave men, who've lived high on my bounty for months, come scuttling back into this suite with their tails beween their legs? You are all armed and armored at my expense and I was assured that all of you knew how to fight."

"L . . . lady," the fidgeting sergeant, one Limos, stuttered, "the passage in there . . . it's so narrow thet cain't but one man at the time go 'long it an' it's no room to use a axe nor sword properlike. But them what kilt poor Ehmnos an' them other boys was in full plate armor an' more'n a foot higher'n us an' in a higher'n wider place an' thet give 'em more room to fight right. It ain't no room to carry targets in there, lady, so mens what hain't in full plate or dang close to it won't live no longern it takes t' . . ."

"Never mind your stupid opinion, you stinking gutter-snipe!" she snapped impatiently, then turned to her sons and the other two plate-armored men. "Myron, you and Xeelos take fifteen of these brave patriots, go downstairs, back into the rear half of this wing, then come up the rear stairs and enter the tunnel from some point beyond the T. May God damn Hwahltuh Sanderz for so ridiculously compartmenting the various sections of this hall; were it built along sane, logical Ehleen lines, this task of ours would be far easier to accomplish.

"Speeros"—this, to her second-eldest son, at fifteen as tall as his elder brother, but though big-boned not yet filled out—"you and Mailos will lead the rest of this craven pack back from this suite whenever Myron and Xeelos are in position. Your arrival and theirs should be simultaneous, if possible."

"But, mother," Myron replied hurriedly, "should we not wait until . . . until the other two companies arrive from the villages? The heathen cannot get out of the hall. All the exits are either blocked or guarded, and only two horses are left in the hall stables. If we had more men we . . . we could attack this way and batter the doors at the same time."

Mehleena's layers of fat rippled as she shrugged. "What do we need more careless, dirty men in my hall for? They'd track dust and damage furniture. No, the place for the rest of them, when at last they straggle in, is upon the walls; don't forget, the rest of your pagan kin could ride up at any time.

"Now draw your sword, Myron, take these men down and around and show us all what you're made of." She patted the swell of his breastplate, on which was painted a black-rimmed white circle with, at the center, the cross—ancient symbol of their ancient religion—rendered in reddish violet.

"Strike for the True God and the True Faith, Myron, my son. Strike for me, for your sisters and brothers in Christ and for the rebirth of the ancient glories of our blessed race. And if you fall, know that your sufferings will be but brief and that through the rest of eternity you will dwell with our Holy Savior in Paradise."

"But . . . but, Mother," quavered Myron, his voice breaking, his face as pale as that of wounded Captain Ahreestos, now lying unattended in the hallway. "I . . . I'm to be . . . to be the *chief*. The chief must not . . . must never be placed in danger. Speeros will be *tahneestos*, it is *his* place to lead in war, not mine . . . never *mine*! Please, Mother . . . what if they . . . they *kill* me?" Myron's full lips trembled on the last words and a tear crept downward on either side of his aquiline nose. All at once, the big man seemed to shrink upon himself and he whimpered in almost a whisper, "Mother . . . please, Mother . . . please don't make me go."

Mehleena shuddered and her eyes looked fit to burst from their sockets. Throwing back her head she emitted a scream of pure rage that could be heard even in the sealed-off and besieged central portion of the hall. Raising her thick, jiggling-fleshed arms high above her head, she shook both small fists at the ceiling and shouted.

"Why, God, why? Why did You in Your infinite wisdom see fit to immure my man's soul in this hateful woman's body? Despite Your lifelong sentence of torment, have I not always striven to serve You well? Why then was it needful to further torment me by giving me for a son this pitiful coward? Why, oh, God I have served and honored my life long? Why? *Why?* Why? *Why?*"

Recognizing the too familiar signs, most of the servants rapidly and silently quit the chamber, the suite and close proximity to their infuriated mistress. Tonos and a few of the more courageous and/or agile servitors lingered in the foyer, but even they made certain of a clear line of retreat. Speeros, Xeelos and Mailos were among this smaller group.

To their sorrow, the score and a half of bravos clustered close about had never seen Mehleena Sanderz in one of her murderous tantrums and were completely unprepared when she suddenly whirled, wrenched an iron-shafted horseman's axe from a nearby bravo and commenced to lay about her, concentrating upon the steel-clad body of Myron, her sobbing, shaking son, but careless of who or what the blade or shaft or knife-edged terminal spike encountered in its travels.

All the while, the blubbery woman screamed and ranted and raved. Half her utterances were incomprehensible, the other half damned first Myron, then every man in the suite, then every man in the hall, then every man in the duchy and, at last, every man on earth.

One of the bravos was down with his brains gushed out on the precious carpet and two others were badly hurt before the remainder of the thirty became one kicking, clawing, shouting mass as each strove to be first through the door. Myron, though his fine plates were battered somewhat and his chin had been cut by the tip of the terminal spike, was so far lost in his blue funk that he still stood unmoving. And his immobility saved him, for the ravening beast now possessing his mother was drawn to moving prey—the broil of panicky, struggling bravos—and she spun and waddled closer, still gripping the bloody axe in both hands.

Gone too far from sanity for words, only hisses, spittle and snarls of bestial fury came from between her skinned-back lips and bared, gnashing teeth. She beat on helmeted heads, stove in ribs and shattered shoulders through scale shirts and mail, hacked deeply and sanguineously into unprotected legs and arms and the occasional neck.

At length, one bravo—his lifelong respect for and fear of the nobility submerged in the agony of a deep thigh wound, terror for his threatened life and cornered-rat ferocity—turned about, drew his antique Ehleen shortsword and drove its leaf-shaped blade into Mehleena's flopping left breast to the very crossguard, even as the last swing of her axe smashed the spine of the man behind.

Chapter XVIII

At the same moment Mehleena was decimating her own ragtag little army, Uhlos, the wine steward, now commanding the walls, was notified by a tower sentinel of a cloud of dust rapidly approaching from the direction of the west hall village. Jumping to the sadly erroneous conclusion that said dust cloud heralded the arrival of the expected company of Captain Deemos, Uhlos set his few men to the laborious tasks of lowering the drawbridge spanning the twenty-foot width of the deep ditch fronting the hall, raising the oak-and-iron grille that served to protect the outer gate from rams, then unbarring and swinging wide both the outer and inner gates.

These lowerings and raisings and openings took much time and effort for the undermanned, inexperienced contingent to accomplish, and by the time Uhlos became aware of his fatal error, it would have been too late to even attempt to reclose the approaches to the hall. Far too late even had not he and the few survivors of his force been cowering in the low, central tower, while the rest of the unarmored men lay still or feebly twitching on the wall walk, with bright-feathered arrows jutting from various portions of their anatomies.

While their retainers went about retrieving their arrows and such weapons as were on or about the fallen, then shoving dead and dying alike through the crenels to thump onto the bottom of the boulder-strewn ditch forty feet down, the nobles got quick and complete answers to all their questions from the pale and trembling wine steward, Uhlos.

When they had returned to the main courtyard below, Tahm Adaimyuhn stepped to his horse long enough to unstrap a case containing his silver-mounted throwingstick and six Ahrmehnee darts—short, heavy and infamous. He tightened the carrystrap over his armor and baldric so that they jutted in easy reach over his left shoulder.

160

As he returned to his three peers, *Komees* Dik was saying, "Well, to put it all in a walnutshell, Tim and the loyal folk hold the central portion of the hall, that bastard didn't know how many levels and neither do we; the Ehleen bitch and her whelps, most of the servants and one company of those ruffian-soldiers hold the rest of the hall; but we hold the walls and this courtyard and those murdering rebel dogs don't know that fact yet.

"So there's one company in the hall, one feeding the crows back up the road yonder and one unaccounted for. Now it's a pretty fair bet that the other company won't have engines or rams, but let's play it safe and raise that bridge. If we do that and place guards on the posterns, the dung-spawned rebels will be rats in a pit and we, my lads, will be the terriers. Too bad none of us is much good at farspeak, for I know good old Sir Geros will regret missing the fun."

Leaving a dozen men to man the walls and guard the small rear gates, the four gentlemen clanked into the south wing at the head of thirty-two fighters. The intaking was ferocious, brutal and quickly done. No quarter was expected or proffered, but at *Komees* Dik's express command, Speeros Sanderz and his two maternal cousins, Xeelos and Mailos, were taken alive—battered but alive. So, too, were the younger, prettier Ehleen serving women—at no one's command, rather by an unvoiced but general agreement. Mehleena's younger children were in the north wing and were not found until long after the heat of blood lust had cooled.

It was near sunset before the company marched in from the eastern village. Captain Plehkos spurred ahead of his men and reined up at the edge of the ditch, demanding that the bridge be lowered. In the dusk, he failed to recognize the stiff, grayish, naked corpses of Mehleena and Captain Ahreestos, dangling by their ankles above the gate. His armor saved him from the arrows, but his horse lacked any such protection. Captain Plehkos executed a retrograde movement at a limping run, commandeered the mule from a sergeant, then led his forty-eight bravos far enough down the hill to be well out of bow range.

Komees Dik, *Vahrohneeskos* Tahm and the others were all for mounting and sallying out to finish the job of rebel eradication, but Tim—who had assumed overall command with natural ease and without argument—shook his head.

"No, Kinsmen, you have had your fun. There are those coming who have not, so leave yon bandits to them." Then he added, on a serious note, "If you want an occupation for your men, set them to finding that whoreson Myron. We found his armor in that room where his bitch-mother was killed, but sword, dirk and the pervert himself are gone, along with his bumboy, the cook, Gaios. You say you had all exits guarded so he must still be in this hall. I charge you, Kindred, find that precious pair. I've a stake prepared that will no doubt tickle his arse to such a degree that the folk off in Morguhnpolis will hear his shrieks of pleasure!"

But when a nightlong search failed to produce even a clue to the missing men, Tim sought out Sir Geros, locating him at last lowering a cloth-wrapped bundle onto a pyre of faggots he had laid between his small house and the outer wall.

There were tears in the baronet's eyes and the traces of more down his stubbled cheeks, as he lifted his head to face Tim. "Poor old Brownie," he said chokedly, his lips drawn in a tight line. "The oldest hound in the duchy. The last gift *Komees* Hari Daiviz of Morguhn presented your late father, near eighteen years agone. He was near blind and his teeth were so worn down that he could not eat meat unless I chewed it for him first, so I kept him here by me where I knew he would sleep warm of cold nights. Those bastards couldn't find me here to kill, so they murdered old Brownie, speared the poor beast where he lay on my hearth."

They sent the faithful old dog to Wind together, Tim chanting what he could recall of the *Lament of Sanderz,* as he would have sung it for the sending to Wind of a human Kinsman.

Later, over brandy in the sitting room of his cottage, Sir Geros remarked, "Tim, I hate to discourage you, but Myron and Gaios might've got away clean . . . or they could still be in the hall."

Tim shook his head, tiredly. "Not in *my* hall, Geros. I'd stake my horse on it! Why, man, we went through that place from top to bottom, then from bottom to top, from the cisterns in the spring cellar to the bat roosts in the attics. And every one of the outbuildings, too, and all the towers, and down the stable well and the privies. We found some remarkable things but not one hair of my perverted half brother and his *pooeesos.*"

Geros sipped at the fiery brandy, then said slowly, "No, Tim, you're wrong, though you have no way of knowing it, not till now, at least.

"Tim, your pa was haunted by the shades of the Vawn

Kindred, and it was for long his constant terror that he would be trapped in his hall, and helplessly murdered as were so many of them by the Ehleen rebels in the Great Rebellion. Therefore, when his old friend and comrade Sir Ehdt Gahthwahlt designed this hall, he prepared two sets of plans. When the building was done, one set was burned. It's the other, incomplete set that's among your pa's papers.

"Tim, there's tunnels and stairways and passages and hidey-holes in this hall even *I* don't know about, and I've been castellan since it was finished. Only your pa knew them all, and there's a good chance Mehleena got some of those secrets out of him from time to time, her and her witch."

Tim pursed his lips. "Friend Geros, I wouldn't throw that old charge of witchcraft about too much from now on, were I you. If Mistress Neeka passes all the tests they'll put her to in Kehnooryos Atheenahs, she'll be declared a High Lady of this Confederation of ours, and it has been my experience that women—all women, high or lowly—have long memories for insults or slights." He chuckled. "Not to mention that most women are far more dangerous than men, because their strength and determination are so often underestimated."

The hapless rebel bravos of Captain Plehkos milled about the base of the hill in uncertainty for an hour too long, only attempting to disperse and scatter when they spotted the vanguard of *Ahrkeethoheeks* Bili of Morguhn's column . . . and by then, of course, it was far too late for any of them. The middle-aged archduke led his dragoons, and Tim—on a hastily saddled Steelsheen and accompanied by his four noble relatives—spurred forth to take command of his own company of lancers. Then the horsemen rode down their two-legged game with the whoops and shouts of the hunt rather than war cries. Tahm took one more head, and only Captain Plehkos, rendered insensible when his wounded mule bucked him off, was taken alive.

The rebel captain would much have preferred a quick death from lance or saber, axe or arrow, for Bili of Morguhn—who had right speedily pressed his rightful claim to Speeros Sanderz, the captain and the majordomo, Tonos, who had been found cowering in an old privy pit during the searching for Myron—made no secret of the great delight he would derive from their interrogation, torture and eventual execution.

Tonos collapsed, befouling himself in an excess of unconcealed terror. The veteran Plehkos' face went white as whey, but he just set his square jaws in silence. Speeros Sanderz, at fifteen, more of a man than his hulking elder brother had ever been, just sneered, then coolly spit at the archduke's feet.

"Threaten and bluster all you like, cousin," he snapped, superciliously. "But we both know, you and I, that you dare not harm or slay me for fear of our prince, my poor mother's cousin. Her murder alone already weighs right heavy on your head!"

Bili grinned like a winter wolf. "Once that was so, young sir, but no more, Sun and Wind be praised. You and your ilk have removed yourselves from any scintilla of protection. You rose in armed and organized rebellion against your rightful overlords, and were Zenos to try to intercede for you in any way, all loyal noblemen would view him tarred with the same brush . . . and you may rest assured that the prince, your cousin, recognizes his jeopardy as clearly as do I.

"As regards your late dam, the valiant Tonos, here, has signed a sworn statement that she went berserk when your dear brother publicly demonstrated that he held his wretched life of more value than his honor. Stout Tonos goes on to say that she then attacked your brother and a whole roomful of men with an axe. Tonos saw no more after that, but your mother was already dead when first the loyal warriors entered that room. As she was run through with an antique slashing sword, I think it safe to assume that one of her own armed jailbirds did it; so she was hoist on her own treasonous hooks, and I only regret that she did not live to be hoist upon a dull stake."

Bili had the three prisoners manacled and weighted with chains and guarded closely by his hand-picked dragoons, lest they find a way to take their own lives.

While Tim and his noble guests dawdled over their post-prandial wines and cordials in the lamplit dining chamber, tall bonfires threw leaping, dancing shadows in both main and rear courtyards, where lancers and dragoons, Ahrmehnee and Kindred milled and laughed and shouted, gorging themselves on coarse bread and dripping chunks carved from the whole oxen slowly revolving on the spits, guzzling tankards of foaming beer, tart cider and watered wine.

The Ahrmehnee loved music and dancing even more than did the Ehleenee, and their musicians never went far without their instruments. Around one of the bright, crackling fires, a circling line of the young warriors of *Vahrohneeskos* Tahm Adaimyuhn of Lion Mountain stamped and leaped in a fast-paced and intricately complicated dance, their deep chorus rising in the refrain of the ancient melody.

"*Nee-nie, nee-nie, nee-nie, nie. HEY!*
"*Heh-lai, heh-lai, heh-lai,*
"*Nee nie-nie!*"

And the chorus and the shrilling flutes, twanging ouds, jangling tambourines and roaring rank of drums were almost enough to drown out the tearing screams of the captured rebel Ehleen serving girls, stripped, staked out and suffering repeated ravishment.

The noblemen and ladies strolled out onto the wide balcony that ran the length of the central portion of the Hall and connected the two wings. From there they watched the Ahrmehnee dancers for a while as Tahm Adaimyuhn recited the history of the songs and the significance of the dances. Then Tim, Bili, Tahm, *Komees* Dik, Sir Geros and the brothers Sanderz, Kahrl and Bahb, descended the stairs to make an appearance among their troops, drain off a tankard or two, nibble a little beef and publicly commend those fighters who had distinguished themselves in some way.

Blind Ahl and Sir Geros' daughter, Mairee, retired to the suite they shared. Mistress Neeka, who looked to be and truly was still moving in a daze, made her way up to her old, familiar rooms, preferring the known comforts to the sumptuous south-wing suite Tim had offered her. Another reason she remained in her cramped north-wing quarters was the proximity to Mehleena's three daughters, whom she had taken it upon herself to console in their grief and fear.

Giliahna and Widahd lingered abovestairs only long enough to collect the necessaries, then trooped off to the semi-detached bath chamber, returning a good hour later. She and her dusky companion shared a minty cordial, then, while Giliahna sipped yet another thimbleful, the slender, graceful Zahrtohgahn girl went into the main room to turn down her mistress' bed and bank the hearthfire.

While sitting and musing, Giliahna chanced to think of a particularly treasured gift of her late husband she wished to show Tim when he presently came up to bed. But a quick fumbling through the trunks in the big closet failed to locate it.

"Widahd," she muttered to herself, "will know where it is."

She opened the door to her bedroom and moved into the

large, dim chamber, shrugging off her quilted robe and dropping it into a chair. But before she could kick off her low felt boots, a big, callused hand clamped over her mouth from behind and the icy needle point of a dirk or dagger was pressed painfully against her soft throat, just below the jaw where the vein throbbed.

Myron Sanderz's deep, hateful voice growled in her ear, "If you scream or try to farspeak, you incestuous bitch, I'll open your throat from ear to ear!"

Giliahna licked her lips and by a great effort of will kept her voice to a normal speaking level, devoid of any emotion or quaver. "What have you done with my friend, with Widahd? If you've slain her or harmed her . . ."

Myron removed the hand from her mouth but not the steel from her throat, took her shoulder and turned Giliahna to the right, so that she could see Widahd across the room near the hearth. The small woman had been gagged but was unbound. The cook, Gaios, had his left arm clamped about her arms and upper body while he menaced her with the broad blade of a Confederation-pattern shortsword.

Abruptly, Myron pushed his captive forward far enough to hurl her nude body down upon the big bed. "Keep your mouth shut and your mind shielded, you sinful, unnatural slut, or Gaios will let the guts out of yon dung-colored pagan bitch!"

Giliahna's initial shock and terror were being speedily replaced by cold rage and disgust—the rage directed toward the filthy, disheveled, stubble-faced and wild-eyed Myron, the disgust toward herself for having allowed this craven, perverted whoreson of a half brother to glimpse even a bare eye-flick of her fear.

She levered herself up on her elbows and smiled at the black-haired man, mockingly. "*You* call *me* unnatural, brother dear? Then what, pray tell, are you? As regards dung, you should certainly know the color of it, since your abiding lust is to wallow in it.

"Were you a natural man of normal lusts and designs, I'd assume you'd come to my suite to ravish me, steal my jewels and gold, then slay me before you sought out Tim and your own death. But I cannot picture you ravishing any female; a young lad, perhaps, but never a girl. As for my treasure, I'll not make you a gift of it. If you want it, look for it. And you will find that Widahd and I will face such death as you and your bumboy mete out to us with more courage than such a known craven as you will ever be able to muster when your time comes!"

Myron had gone livid, his face twisted in wrath. "Kill you, bitch?" he snarled. "No, there be better ways to deal with strumpets like you!"

Before she knew what he was about, Myron was on the bed, kneeling astride her body, his weight and the strength of his legs pinning down her arms. His left hand clamped tightly over her mouth, grasped her jaw and turned her head. Then the sharp dirk opened Giliahna's face to the bone from temple to jawline.

She struggled frantically but futilely, for Myron was nothing if not as strong as the proverbial ox. Finally, she sank her teeth into the palm of his hand. He did not lift the hand. Instead, he poised the point of his bloody blade above her face, grating, "Loosen your damned teeth, or I take out an eye!"

Widahd, like many Zahrtohgahn women, went waking or sleeping with a pair of thin, flat little steel daggers hidden beneath her garments but within easy reach. These purely Zahrtohgahn items were sheathed in tight metal cases, sealed with dense wax, and they required a real effort to uncase or draw. Such precautions were necessary to prevent fatal accidents, for the needle-tipped and razor-edged little weapons' blades were coated their full length and width with a poison that brought slow and agonizing death and for which no antidote was known.

Moving slowly and carefully, Widahd had managed to draw the one on her right side. Ever so gradually, she brought her arm up, up, up, flexing it just enough to give power to her thrust, and cocked her wrist to impart the proper angle. Then, mustering all her strength and her not inconsiderable courage, Widahd drove the full three inches of the blade deep into the muscles of Gaios' swordarm.

The former cook vented a strangled scream. Widahd wrenched herself out of his slackened grasp and made for the bed, not even bothering to pull off the gag so intent was she on the deliverance of her loved mistress from the hulking torturer.

It was a brave effort, but it was doomed at its inception. Forgetting his wound, which though stinging ferociously was not bleeding very much, Gaios brought up his sword and stamped forward. With a meaty *tchunnk*, the broad, heavy blade descended to strike the valiant brown-skinned girl at the angle of her slender neck and her right shoulder, cleaving through flesh and bone to the sternum. The very force of the blow drove Widahd to her knees, and her shriek of mortal agony was muffled in the gag.

Setting a foot against the girl's back, Gaios jerked his shortsword free, propelling Widahd's body face down on the thick carpets, which quickly became soaked with more blood than one would have thought so small a body could contain. A glance showed Gaios that his master, Myron, had taken no notice of the brief, bloody affair, being completely absorbed in the disfigurement of his own victim. Grinning, the former cook dropped his clotted sword, rolled Widahd onto her back, hurriedly shredded off the front of her skirt and set about raping the dying young woman, heedless of the spurting gushes of blood that soon soaked his shirtfront.

Myron took his time on Giliahna's right cheek, deliberately prolonging the agony. Tears poured from the suffering woman's blue eyes to water the blood on her cruelly slashed face, but she had set her teeth and her will and no slightest sound came out to meet the barrier of that thick, dirty hand mashing down on her lips.

All the while he carefully marred Giliahna's beauty, Myron hissed his plans for her and for Tim in a half-whisper. "The way you barbarians searched this hall was comical. Gaios and I could have departed anytime we wished, and we can still, unseen and unsuspected. I only remained to deal with our barbaric brother, Tim, and with you.

"I know that he will come here, soon or late, intent upon doing more of his sinful incest with you. He certainly will be alone and unsuspecting and, like as not, unarmed, so Gaios and I should have no trouble dealing with him.

"By all that is holy, *I* should be *Thoheeks* and chief of Sanderz-Vawn, but simply because I am a good, Christian man, my patrimony, my very birthright, is denied me. But if *I* cannot be chief, *he* will not sit in my place. As God is my witness, he will not!"

Showing his teeth in a grin of pure, evil malice, he went on, "Your barbarians will not have as new chief any maimed or crippled man, so when once we have immobilized dear Tim, I mean to dig out his right eye. I'd take them both, but I want him to have one so he can forevermore gaze upon what I'll have done to you, sweet sister.

"Then, when I'm done gelding him, I mean to hack off his

right hand and his right foot and char the stumps in yonder fire."

Widahd was not yet dead. She knew what the man was doing to her body, though she could not feel her defilement or much of anything else. But she was come of a warrior race and refused to die leaving her foe a chance of life. If the arm she had stabbed was removed quickly enough, he might just live. What she must deliver before she surrendered to oncoming death was a wound impervious to treatment.

Awkwardly, her numbing left hand sought and found the hilt of her second little dagger, but the cold unfeeling fingers kept slipping off the abbreviated hilt and it seemed for long and long that she would not summon the strength to draw it. Then, at last, it was free, but she found she had used too much of her waning power. She could not stab up.

Haltingly, she worked her small hand and the knife between their two close-pressed bodies. As her ravisher raised himself slightly in preparation for a deeper thrust, she maneuvered the blade to an upward slant so that the straining man impaled himself on it, taking the length of it in his belly, between navel and crotch.

There was nothing strangled about Gaios' second scream. It rang loud and long . . . and it served to alert Tim, just approaching the suite, and Sir Geros, who had bid his young lord goodnight and was about to descend the stairs.

Myron ignored the scream for the very good reason that he knew from the earlier sounds that his cohort was raping the Zahrtohgahn and was wont to make loud noises in transport of pleasure. While a woman's scream within the hall would have been sure to bring unwanted visitors tramping through the corridors and banging on doors and barging into suites, a man's would not, not with wounded men and prisoners under the roof.

He had done at last with Giliahna's right cheek. Turning her ravaged, gory face back, he hissed, "Hold still now. I'm going to carve a *pi* for *Porneea* on your brow, so that all will know you for the arrant whore you are."

Tim and Geros, broadswords bared and ready, kicked open the bedroom door and burst into the room. Myron left off his carving of Giliahna's ruined face and slid himself down her body far enough to get an inch of his blood-slimy dirkblade into her left breast, then he half-turned to face the armed men.

"Take one more step toward me, pagan bastards, and I'll drive this blade into her heart!"

He had taken his hand from her mouth, and his weight now was on her belly rather than her chest and arms. Giliahna swallowed a mouthful of thick, hot blood, then shouted, "No! I am already hurt, terribly hurt. Take the swine alive, for Archduke Bili and my brother. Tell Tim I love him." Then she grasped Myron's knife hand and wrist with both her own hands and forced her body up violently, so that half the length of the wide, thick blade sank into her chest.

Tim was at the foot of the big bed in a single leap and the flat of his sword crashed against Myron's temple, hurling his body to the floor in an unconscious heap. But then the young captain's sword dropped from fingers suddenly gone cold and nerveless, and, as hot tears ran, he could but stare in grief and horror at what had been wrought upon this, the only woman he ever had loved . . . or ever would.

Her face was a mask of blood, with jaw, teeth and white bone winking through the slashed cheeks. Just above the red-pink nipple of her full right breast, the hilt and part of the blade of a heavy war dirk jutted up.

Geros glanced at what lay on the bed, then averted his eyes and stalked quickly to where Gaios had rolled off the body of Widahd and, his trousers still bunched about his knees, was sitting in obvious agony with a handful of cloth from her skirt pressed against his lower belly.

Geros sheathed his sword. "What ails you, bumboy? Bellyache, is it? Mayhap six feet or so of oaken clyster will, if not truly ease you, at least serve as a counterirritant." He chuckled, then added, "That's what you get for eating your own cooking, of course. You should've known better."

Giliahna said weakly, "Tim . . . my love. Please . . . it hurts . . . so much . . . please take . . . it out."

Tim walked on wooden legs up to where he could grasp the hilt of that cruel dirk that had robbed him of so much, of so many happy years. Quickly, he jerked the steel from his sister's chest. He did not bother to try to staunch the bloodflow that followed the blade out, for he had seen many death wounds, and from its location, this could be nothing but such.

But she should have been dead long since. He was too experienced a warrior to deny that incredible, astounding survivals occurred now and then. And with the flare of a spark of hope, some of the leaden enervation left his body and his mind.

"Sir Geros," he snapped. When that man stood close beside him, ho ooid, "There may be a chance to save her. Go fetch Master Fahreed. At once!"

Even as he raced across the deserted balcony toward the north wing where several adjoining suites had been temporarily converted to a hospital and surgery, Geros knew himself bound on a fool's errand. No mortal man or woman could survive a war dirk in the heart. But if fetching the Zahrtohgahn physician would ease young Tim's grieving mind, that is what he would do.

In the hospital, Geros had to pull his rank and almost his sword before Master Fahreed was finally summoned from another room. The tall man's white robe was liberally spotted and smeared with fresh blood. He was scowling and his manner was brusque.

"Say your piece quickly and begone, Sir Geros. I'm in the middle of a chancy bit of emergency surgery on a brave young Ahrmehnee, whose skull was cracked in a drunken brawl. You Kindred are all mad. When all your enemies are slain, you turn on each other like starving wolves."

But Geros could not speak fast enough for the master, who suddenly snapped, "You can mindspeak? Then lower your shield, man, I cannot waste more time."

When he had scanned the contents of Geros' mind, his scowl vanished and his tone softened. He placed a hand on the aging castellan's shoulder and said, softly, "I grieve with you and your poor young lord, friend Geros. It was a terrible act, even for an Ehleen, and I of all men in this hall know that these Ehleenee can be beasts incarnate. But I must agree with your prognosis. A wound inflicted with a weapon like that in that area of the chest is invariably fatal.

"I could do nothing for the woman, even were I to come, and I cannot come, nor can my apprentice, not now. I'm sorry."

The blue-black man turned to go, shaking his shaven head. All at once, he turned back. "Sir Geros, Mistress Neeka, for whatever else she may or may not be, is a skilled and most talented apothecary. She assisted me here during the rush of battle casualties, and I found her performance most impressive. Her suite is just down the hall from here. Why don't you go to her and open your mind as you did to me? If nothing else, she can administer the young man a draft to ease his shock and hurt and grant him restful, healing sleep."

Mechanically, Tim arose from beside Gilliahna. She lay unmoving save for the barely perceptible rise and fall of her chest. Myron seemed to be still unconscious, but taking no chances, Tim retrieved his sword and ran two inches of the blade into his half brother's buttock. When the carcass did not even twitch, Tim was satisfied.

Gaios still sat near the corpse of his victim. Moaning, he rocked from side to side, both hands still pressing the rags to his belly. His eyelids were pressed tightly shut, but tears still managed to ooze from beneath them, joining a copious sweat to impart a glistening sheen to his face, now twisted in agony.

Turning back to the bed and Giliahna, Tim noted that her slashed face and the stab wound in her chest had ceased to bleed. Moaning louder even than Gaios, he tried not to think of the licking flames that so soon must be set about her lovely body, tried not to think of the long and bitter years he still must live without her . . . and he made his decision.

He lifted off his baldric, stripped off tunic and shirt and stretched himself beside his sister, his lover, she who should have been his wife. He kissed her cold lips, then reached out and took from the bedside table Myron's blood-sticky dirk.

Softly, tenderly, he said, "We shall go to Wind together, my love, never again to be parted."

Then Tim Sanderz grasped the wire-wound hilt in both hands and ran the full length of the blade into his own chest, skewering his broken heart.

When Sir Geros and Neeka hurried into the suite, the old soldier reeled against the door frame in shock, but Neeka bustled over to the bed. Ignoring for the moment the man, who had obviously taken his own life since his hands were still gripped about the hilt of the knife, she set about examining the woman.

When Geros had more or less composed himself, he approached. "Dead, is she not? Poor little Giliahna."

The answer he received then was like the crash of a warhammer against his head. "Not dead nor even dying, Sir Geros, she has only swooned."

Hesitantly, Geros laid a trembling hand on Giliahna's flesh. "But . . . she is cold as death . . . and she no longer bleeds . . . ?"

Neeka just sniffed. "You'd be cold to the touch, too, if you'd lain naked in this icy chamber for who knows how long, not to speak of the large amounts of blood she must have lost before the bleeding stopped."

In his own state of shock, Geros at first could not understand. Even so, he proved far easier to convince than either Tim or Giliahna.

Chapter XIX

Ahrkeethoheeks Bili, *Thoheeks* and chief of Morguhn, *Vahrohnos* Deskahti, *Vahrohneeskos* of the Order of the Golden Cat of the Confederation, Knight of the Most Noble Order of the Blue Bear of Harzburk, was nothing if not stubborn and set in his ways. Not even the rising wrath of his supreme overlord, Milo of Morai, High Lord of the Confederation, not even the vicious temper of the High Lady, Aldora Linszee Treeah-Pohtohmahs Pahpahs, could persuade him to leave Morguhn before the harvests were all in, the archducal taxes collected and his personal affairs set in order.

To one of the Undying High Lady Aldora's more violent outbursts, he had replied with a calmness that further infuriated her, "Aldora, I don't want to go north and become Prince of Karaleenos, and you well know it. I only do so out of loyalty to the Confederation and willingness to serve it when and as called upon.

"But if go I must, then I'll do it in my own way and at my own pace. There is much my son, Djef, must know if he is to be a good chief and *thoheeks* of our clan. I must be certain that all sits well in Vawn and that young *Thoheeks* Tahm Adaimyuhn of Sanderz is adjusting well to his new and heavier harness of duty. At the same time, I must attend the thousand and one small but important functions of my present office, entertain my distinguished guests . . . and often waste precious time soothing the temper tantrums of one of them."

The small, olive-skinned woman went livid and speechless with frustration and rage. She snatched her long belt dagger free of its case and made to slash its keen edge at Bili's maddeningly unruffled face. But suddenly she became aware of the huge, slavering hound, stalking in from the next room, stiff-legged, with tail tucked and lips wrinkled up from the

174

bared foam-covered teeth. Whirling, she flexed her knees and held her blade ready for stab or slash.

"Quick, Bili," she said calmly, her temper dissipated in the urgency of the moment, "get a spear. I'll hold him here. He looks to be gone mad."

But he moved not a muscle, he only chuckled and, in less than the blinking of an eye . . . the hound was gone!

Aldora spun about, shouting, "Damn you, Bili Morguhn! Ahrmehnee magic! How *dare* you do that to *me*? Do you forget who I am?" She lunged upward at his body with the long dagger.

Still chuckling, he lightly skipped from the path of the thrust and struck the hand wielding it hard enough that the weapon went clattering into a corner. Then the delicate-looking little woman went for his face with her nails, but he clasped his arms around her, easily immobilizing both arms, while his questing lips found hers, locked upon them and remained for a long, long time, before wandering downward to pay brief court to a flat, tiny ear, and then burying themselves in the hollow of her throat.

Much, much later, as both lay, tired and disheveled, upon a badly rumpled bed, Aldora's fingers traced the scars on his smooth, fair-skinned body, recalling that she had done so thirty-odd years before when this same, marvelous man had been a boy . . . no, never a boy, not him, not Bili! . . .

She sighed and lay back down beside him, snuggling to the hard warmth of his body. "How old are you now, Bili?"

He turned his head to smile down into her upturned, heart-shaped face. "Nearly fifty summers, my love. Why? Does this old man displease you?"

She shivered with thought of the recent pleasure he had given her and briefly raised her mindshield that he might know and be forever answered. "Oh, Bili, Bili, my own Bili," she murmured with intense feeling. "Why could it have not been you, rather than this half brother of yours?

"I had almost forgotten, you know? Had almost ceased to remember just how wonderful, how complete and perfect it has always been with you . . . and only with you."

In another part of the archducal hall, Milo of Morai—once Undying God of the Horseclans, now Undying High Lord of the Confederation, by his own reckoning, at least eight hundred years old—sipped wine and chatted with the three newest-found of his rare, mutant strain.

The tests devised by him and by Aldora and administered

under their constant supervision had shown positive results in all three cases. The ancient High Lord was inordinately pleased and showed it plainly.

"Giliahna, Neeka, you'll both love the new capital, Theesispolis, and especially the palace there. My wife, Mara, designed it and oversaw every step of its construction. And, speaking of Mara, she'll be more than overjoyed to see you. She and Aldora, they . . . well, Aldora is seldom happy or contented for long and she envies Mara so much that about twenty years ago she tried to drown her—that being one of the few ways our kind can be slain. Since then, the two have consistently and most wisely avoided being in the same city at the same time.

"I am, perforce, often in the western mountains on campaign and poor Mara grows lonely with only old Drehkos for company." He took a long draft of the brandy-laced wine and clapped Tim Sanderz on the shoulder.

"As for you, Tim, you're the incarnate answer to centuries of prayers. You enjoy campaigning and warfare. You're good at it. You're a natural leader and, moreover, you're an experienced commander of organized troops, so presumably a good tactician. If you prove out as a strategist, as well, I may finally be able to get a few years of rest.

"With Drehkos to govern the settled lands—something he's quite skilled at—and you to command the armies and the frontier, Mara and I might go away for a while. We might sail out to the Islands or even clear across the Eastern Sea to the lands beyond—Ehspahneeah, Gahleeah or even Pahl'yos Ehlahs—it's been centuries since either of us has seen those lands, or even been much beyond the borders of our own."

Tim's blue eyes were wide with amazement. "But . . . you mean you'd trust *me* with your entire military establishment, my lord Milo?"

"Tim, you'd better start remembering to call me 'Milo' and comport yourself as the equal, the peer, that you all truly are. With luck, we'll have many centuries together, and even a single hundred years is a hellishly long time for one man to defer to another.

"Yes, I'll trust you with the armies . . . when you've proved you can handle them properly, win victories without too high a butcher's bill, think for yourself, yet have the good sense to know when to accept and defer to the advice of your staff. But that will be five or ten years from now, Tim.

"Immediately we all go back to the old capital, Kehnooryos Atheenahs, for the winter, you three will enter the Confederation Mindspeak Academy and we'll then learn just what active and latent talents you each possess. But you'll not only be studied, you'll be taught, as well.

"You'll learn the many different levels of mental communication, and how to speak on two or three at the same time. You'll be taught how to get around or through closed mindshields and, if you own the innate ability, how to do it without the shielded mind even knowing it. You'll be taught to farspeak, and your range—with and without the added power of other minds—will be meticulously measured and recorded.

"You may—one or two of you, anyway—learn to fargather, though I confess we've had precious little success in teaching that highly esoteric skill. Those who have been able to learn already possessed the rudiments. The Academy simply honed an existing edge, as it were."

Neeka shook her head slowly, then asked, "Lord, what is this fargather? I've never heard the term."

After long years with the arrogant, outspoken, bull-headed and often violent Aldora; with his loving but self-assured and frequently argumentative wife, the Undying High Lady Mara, Milo had felt instantly attracted to this quiet, humble and unassuming, basically gentle, raven-haired beauty. Though they two had been sharing a suite and a bed for some weeks, her public manner toward him remained one of humility and deep respect. He was becoming more and more fond of her and was seriously considering marriage to her after a few years, if Mara approved.

"Fargathering, Neeka, is the rare ability to mentally detect danger at distances and through many barriers. It is most applicable to soldiering and warfare and most useful therein. In the century or so of the Academy, the number of actual occurrences, either natural or induced, of real strength in its use has been pitifully small. All of those, saving only one, have been men.

"That single exception was our present host's first wife, Rahksahna Morguhn—Ahrmehnee-born, now deceased. Bili, himself, owns the strongest fargathering talent ever recorded, yet none of his brothers so far tested has the power to any degree, and his three children by Rahksahna lack it entirely. I am now hoping against all the odds that Tim and Gil, as they both had the same mother as Bili, will prove latent fargatherers."

Milo drained off the other half of his goblet, then refilled it, continuing to talk while reaming his pipe and packing it with tobacco.

"You'll learn to mindspeak with animals, not just horses and cats, but all manner of beasts. You'll learn to see with others' eyes, hear with their ears, smell with their noses, taste with their tongues and feel with their skins."

His eyes caught Neeka's and she lowered her gaze, flushing darkly, a small smile tugging at her lips. In their nights together, he had already commenced her education in those particular and erotically pleasurable directions.

"Finally, when you've absorbed all the Academy has to offer you, you'll start learning languages and dialects. All of you know Mehrikan—Neeka knows one dialect, Gil two, and Tim five, but there are more than a dozen all told in the Confederation alone. You all can read and write and speak Southern Ehleeneekos, and Neeka knows the Northern dialect, but you'll all have to learn the Island dialect, which differs markedly from mainland Ehleeneekos.

"Tim and Gil speak a passable Ahrmehnee, already, and Neeka can quickly master it, no doubt, but you'll all have to learn to read and write it, and that will take time, since they use an alphabet entirely different from Mehrikan and only distantly related to Ehleeneekos.

"Neeka reads and writes Zahrtohgahn, but she can't speak it. Tim speaks Kweebehkeekos and Nyahgrahee, which are almost the same language, and a bastard pidgin-Zahrtohgahn. The only language that at least one of you doesn't have is English."

All three looked puzzled at the unfamiliar word. Before any could frame the question, Milo explained.

"English was the language that was spoken and written by the people who dwelt on this continent almost a thousand years ago. The gullible and the superstitious of our time call those long-dead people gods, but they were not, any more than am I or are you. The Witch Kingdom, so called, deep in the southern swamps, is the only place that English still exists as a spoken language, though all the many Mehrikan dialects are its direct descendants.

"If, after you've mastered all the more needful languages, you want to learn to speak English properly, fine, I'll be happy to teach you . . . and I'm the only man outside the Witch Kingdom who can. But you must all learn to at least read English. Now and then, one or two or more of the ancient books turn up somewhere or other, my agents obtain them by hook or by crook and they are rushed to Theesispolis to be carefully preserved in the great library there, along with the volumes of my personal journal, which is also in English.

"These books contain, ofttimes, knowledge which has, does and will prove invaluable to us and our people over the centuries. So we must all have the ability to partake of it."

All three nodded assent. Then Neeka's brow wrinkled and she shyly asked, "But why learn all these other languages, my lord, when we can all mindspeak?"

Milo had arisen and was standing with his pipestem in his mouth, its filled bowl inverted over a candle flame, while he sucked mightily and little spurts of wispy smoke jetted from his mouth.

Tim answered the question. "Because, Neeka, outside the Confederation, mindspeak ability is far less common than it is in our lands."

Milo resumed his seat, he and his now well-lit pipe emitting clouds of fragrant, blue-gray smoke. He nodded. "Tim is right. But even in the Confederation, only a little more than half the people have real, everyday-usable mindspeak even though the percentage has been climbing every year for the last two hundred or more.

"When I led the first ten thousand or so of the Kindred from the Sea of Grass and into Kehnooryos Ehlahs a bit more than two centuries ago, mindspeak—since it had long been a survival trait in the hard and too often short life of the clanspeople on the prairies and high plains, as it was the means of communicating with their horses and the allied prairiecats—was present to some degree in between seventy and eighty percent of them.

"But in the Southern Ehleenee, whom we conquered piecemeal, only one or two percent were accomplished mindspeakers, and even those with latent powers only brought the figure to something less than ten out of every hundred. There were two reasons for this: Since their culture differed so drastically from that of the Horseclans, they had no real, pressing need for the ability and so had never nurtured and developed it; and since their antique religion considered any unusual mental abilities to be an indication of witchcraft—for which 'sin' the penalties were harsh, hideous, agonizing and fatal—those who did possess mindspeak seldom used it.

"As the Kindred and Ehleenee intermarried and interbred, the talent began to crop up with more frequency, especially among the nobility. Then, after I broke the power of the Ehleen Church a century and a half back; after I stripped their clergy of many of their ancient rights and privileges, revoked their tax-exempt status retroactively and seized much of their property for back taxes along with tons of gold and silver; after I disbanded and either killed or imprisoned their secret packs of night-riding terrorists; after I released the common Ehleenee from the Church's emotional stranglehold and turned them against the clergy by exposing those clergymen for what they truly were—smugglers, brothel owners, receivers of stolen goods, extortionists, rapists and murderers, and most telling, slavers of the worst sort, who maintained a fleet of merchant ships to transport the children the priests demanded of their parishioners for 'holy orders' across the sea to be sold at auction; after all this had been done and most of the Ehleenee were truly free in both mind and body, the percentage of mindspeakers really began to climb.

"But what I consider—as will you—progress is seldom comprehensible to those whose lives span only fifty or sixty years and often less. Nonetheless, the population of the Confederation now includes almost sixty percent mindspeakers, and that is a hopeful sign that, someday, all our people will share the same gift."

In the late evening of yet another day, Milo sat with his pipe and a small goblet of fiery cordial, his nude, freshly bathed body wrapped against the chill of the night in a chamber cloak of silk and fur. His long, almost hairless, bare legs were extended before a fragrant fire of oak and applewood.

Across the width of their chamber, warmed by a nearby brazier, sat Neeka. The woman occupied a low, padded stool, faced a mirror lit by flanking lamps, and was raptly concentrating on the meticulous brushing of her buttock-length black hair. Her own goblet of cordial sat on her dressing table, barely sipped, and the small, richly jeweled pipe she was trying to learn to smoke had been set aside to smolder out.

Between them, a big bed, its cherrywood headboard carved with the arms of Clan Morguhn, awaited them. Milo was eagerly anticipating the warmth of feather mattress and quilted coverings, but Neeka, it soon became apparent, was thinking of other things.

"Milo," she asked, still brushing, "people have to have something to believe in. It was wrong for you to destroy the Church, and that destruction can only breed more and more rebellions over the years. Someday, the Ehleenee may even unite and—"

Milo chuckled and interrupted her. "Ehleenee unite? Never! Necka, they couldn't even unite to face the threat of my armies conquering them, so factionalized and backstabbing were they . . . and they've not changed one whit over the years.

"My few thousand Horseclansmen and Freefighters could never have defeated any really united Ehleen kingdom, especially if that kingdom had had the minimal support of the others, but none of them was ever completely united or even minimally supported. No sooner did I invade Kehnooryos Ehlahs from the west than that unhappy realm was invaded from south by other Ehleenee—the Karaleenoee, to be exact—from the north by Middle Kingdom types and threatened from the sea by the Ehleen pirates, plus being faced with one large and numerous smaller internal rebellions.

"When I invaded Karaleenos, it was the same story. Karaleenoee nobles who had bones to pick with Zenos and his successors either openly allied with me or weakened his armies by refusing to contribute troops and supplies or actually rising and laying waste to his rear areas.

"The last King of the Southwestern Ehleenee, Zastros, might easily have crushed the combined armies I had raised to oppose his advance north had not certain of his chief *thoheeksee* decided they'd had enough of him and his Witch Kingdom queen, slain her, turned him over to me and disbanded the army.

"Even the people of whom you were born, the Northern Ehleenee, regularly have a civil war once or twice each century. The only Ehleenee who ever enjoyed any kind of stability for any length of time were the Islanders, those who used to be pirates. And the last king of the pirates, Alexandros, used to say that that was only because every pirate understood that total unity alone prevented the utter extirpation of them all.

"No, little Neeka, I don't doubt that there'll be brief, bitter risings from time to time, but we actually have more of them amongst the recently conquered mountainfolk than amongst the Ehleenee. However, very few of them require intervention by Confederation troops, most being put down on the spot by locals."

"But still, Milo," Neeka went on relentlessly, "if you'd allow those who wish to to follow the Ehleen Church openly, one bone of great contention would be removed and most of the present secret societies which often breed these rebellions would no longer have much cause for existing."

Milo shook his head. "Neeka, all you say may well be correct, but such a reestablished Church would require close supervision, lest it become as rotten, corrupt and powerful as its predecessor. I simply have never had the time or energy to spare for such a task . . . or the inclination, to be honest. I've lived for a millennium, and in all that time, in all the many cultures in which I've resided, through which I've moved, my experiences with organized religions have never been good, so my opinion of them is abysmal.

"But, if long life has taught me nothing else, my dear, it is that flexibility is a true asset, so I'll promise you this: When, in twenty or so years, you've learned all that you must, if you still want to see an Ehleen Church reestablished and *you* are willing to supervise that Church and keep its clergy at least law-abiding if not really honest—no one could keep either a politician or a priest honest anymore than they could render chicken dung into gold filigree—I shall then allow such reestablishment to take place."

Tossing off his cordial, he laid his pipe on the hearth and stood up. "Now let's get to bed, woman. We ride north tomorrow, and the dawn will come soon enough. Besides, you have at least five hundred years to brush your hair."

Epilogue

Dr. Sternheimer painfully flexed his arthritic joints enough to take his place at the conference table. All chitchat among the men and women already at that table had ceased immediately he entered the room at a shuffling hobble. Despite the pain of his swollen, inflamed joints, he was smiling broadly. But his smile did nothing to ease the nervous tension which crackled like electricity in the cool, humidified atmosphere of the locked, soundproofed room.

This body, the Council of Directors, might rule the Center in theory and in name, but in actual fact there was only a single individual who had guided it—through fortune and misfortune, through victories and defeats, through good years and lean—almost from its very inception nearly a thousand years in the past. That man was David Sternheimer, D.M.S., D.S., Ph.D.

He cleared his throat, but still spoke huskily. "Doctors, for centuries we have been seeking a way to displace the mutants whose advent foiled our reconquest of the areas that were once known as Georgia, North and South Carolina, Virginia and Maryland. We attempted many fine, well-laid-out plans, only to find that some were not laid out well enough.

"But in all these efforts, we were treating the symptoms—as it were—rather than attacking the disease, proper. Because of the very real and very dangerous mental abilities of the mutants in general and of their leader, Milo Moray, in particular, we feared to put a body occupied by one of us into really close proximity to the mutants.

"However, a little more than ten years ago, a new and radical plan was broached to me. I first weighed all aspects of it with my usual thoroughness, then began its implementation. In order to do this, I was forced to sacrifice something which I—which we and the Center—have been seeking since first we became aware that such existed; I refer, of course, to a live mutant. Our agents in the north had access to a young female mutant, but I ordered that that person be prepared for a mission, rather than be brought here for experiments."

"Now, dammitall, David," snapped a black-haired, blue-eyed young man, who looked about twenty years old, "you exceeded the authority we—this Council—granted you! It is of vast importance that we learn just what processes make a mutant. For only when we share their strengths and know their weaknesses can we stand up to these people with even a bare chance of defeating them and reuniting our nation. And if we don't have a mutant or two to take apart, how can we hope to understand them?

"I, for one, will here state that I'm damned tired of transferring my mind to a younger body every two- or three-score years. If we could have bodies that never aged, that were next to impossible to kill, as the mutants have, think of what we could accomplish.

"I say that we void this current scheme, reclaim the mutant and bring it here."

All looked to Sternheimer, but he just shrugged. "Dr Seigel, even if I agreed with you, and I do not, reclamation of that particular mutant will be impossible for some years to come. It is now accepted by the chief mutant and en route to the capital of that so-called Confederation. Not even it knows that it is anything more than what it seems, so mental prying will not betray it. Only an intricate series of tones will awaken the memories deeply buried in its subconscious . . . and only I own the instrument capable of producing that series of tones.

"You will get your experimental mutant in time, Lewis, never fear. Maybe you'll even get more than one. And that damned Milo Moray will get his comeuppance, too! He's been happily torturing and butchering our colleagues and agents for far too long with virtual impunity. But now, *now*, I've implanted a humanoid time bomb in his very bosom. And when I feel the time is right . . ."

THE END